YOURS SINCE YESTERDAY

JENNIFER BERNARD

PROLOGUE

Fifteen years ago

EVEN THOUGH THEY'D been talking nonstop since they'd beached their kayaks, as soon as Padric and Zoe stepped into the ancient hush of Lost Souls Wilderness, they went quiet. They'd fought so hard for this chance—a hiking trip across Misty Bay...together...alone—that it seemed almost overwhelmingly exciting now that their trip had begun.

With each step, Zoe's feet sank deeper into the thick moss of the path that led to Overlook Ridge. Up there, that was where they wanted to go, to where they could see all of Misty Bay, the vast ice fields of Lost Souls Wilderness, and even to the Gulf of Alaska. They'd been talking about it all summer, every time Padric stopped in for pizza on his way back from a fishing trip. He worked on his father's fishing boat, while she worked at her family's pizza shop. Neither one had much free time in the summer, but every time they saw each other, it felt like nothing had changed.

Best friends. With maybe something more hovering at the edge of possibility? Something almost too perfect to dream about?

Behind her, Padric made an eerie cawing sound that got her jumping. "Don't do that!" she scolded him.

"I'm trying to warn the forest spirits that we're coming."

"The forest spirits?" She scoffed at his imagination. Of the two of them, he was the dreamy one drawn to the weird and the unusual. He blamed it on his Gaelic ancestry. She was more practical and good with her hands. "If they're spirits, wouldn't they already know?"

"If they know, isn't it better to get on their good side?"

She laughed. "So that's what that sound was all about? Getting on their good side?"

"It must have worked because no one's pelting us with spruce cones."

Just then, something dropped right onto the top of Zoe's head.

She shrieked and jumped about a foot in the air. When she landed, her foot twisted under her.

"Ow!" Hopping on one foot, she grabbed for Padric's hand. He helped her to a boulder that lay along the path—gray granite sparkling with embedded bits of quartz. She propped herself against it. Even though not much sunlight filtered through the tall canopy of the forest, the rock felt warm against her backside.

"Are you okay?" Padric knelt next to her in the moss. He picked up her leg and propped it on his strong thigh. A hidden shiver swept through her. So many girls at school had crushes on Padric, even though he was on the shy side. But he was picky about who he befriended, and for some reason, as soon as Zoe's family had moved to Lost Harbor, he'd chosen her.

"I just twisted it a little." She bit her lower lip to hold back the tears. Of all the stupid things to do only five minutes into their trip. "Maybe if I just let it rest for a minute?"

He nodded. "I'm gonna take your shoe off so I can see if it's swollen."

She gestured for him to go ahead. He rolled up the hem of her baggy pants—she was in the phase of hiding her body, embarrassed by all the new curves. Her skin shone white against the emerald green of the summer forest. He unlaced her canvas sneaker and ever so gently pulled apart the two sides.

When he rolled down her sock, she shivered again. His touch was so impossibly gentle. His hands were strong and tough from working on his dad's boat, but somehow he managed not to hurt her at all as he probed her ankle.

"It's a little swollen." His voice sounded funny, tighter than normal.

"Hand me my pack. I have a first-aid kit with one of those ice packs that you crack to make it cold." She was working hard to come off as purely practical. It was hard because the energy shimmering between them made her light-headed.

He opened up her pack and found the first-aid kit her mother had insisted she bring. "Props to your mom. How'd she know we'd need medical help in the first ten minutes?"

"She always thinks the worst is going to happen."

Padric was peering farther into her pack. "Does she think we might get stranded for a year?"

She giggled as she cracked the quick-freeze ice pack. Mom had loaded her pack with last night's spanakopita, an entire bag of cooked sausages, a two-pound hunk of cheese, homemade baklava and a few more goodies. "You know how the Bellini family is about food. There's a reason we own a pizza shop."

"I'm not complaining," he said devoutly as he handed her a piece of baklava. "Here, want a bit to distract you from your pain?"

"Sure." She accepted the baklava while he took the ice pack.

Very carefully, he placed it around her ankle and tugged her sock up to keep it in place. The cold immediately soothed the painful throbbing.

"Excellent work, doctor. I can pay you in dessert," she teased.

Sitting back on his heels, Padric opened his mouth so she could pop the baklava onto his tongue.

They both savored the honey-drenched, flaky phyllo as it melted on their tongues. "That's the most incredible thing I've ever tasted," he moaned. "What *is* that?"

"Just some Bellini family magic."

And for some reason, those words filled her with a sense of power. Often she felt embarrassed by her family—so loud, so food-focused, so dark and curly, so *hairy*. But right now, looking at Padric as he swallowed down her mother's baklava, she felt like a queen.

So she leaned forward and pressed her lips against his.

She tasted honey and the eagerness of a boy. After a moment of surprise, he kissed her back, clumsily, lips bumping against her teeth. It took them a moment, but then they figured out how to fit together, how if they slowed down and opened their mouths just a little bit, lips could pillow against lips and tongue touching tongue could send electric shocks along their skin.

She didn't know how long the kiss lasted. It might have been just a few moments or it could have been much longer. She wasn't paying attention to the passage of time at all. Her entire focus was on the exciting sensations somersaulting through her, and the sense of having stepped through a veil into a new world.

She was kissing Padric Jeffers—her best friend, her favorite person in the world. KISSING HIM. What did it mean? What would happen next?

Her phone rang.

The sound penetrated through the soft forest sounds— mosquito whine, creek murmur, squirrel chirp—like a buzz saw.

It wasn't even really her phone. The only one in the family

who owned a cell phone was her father, but her mother had insisted she bring it in case of emergencies.

She drew away from Padric. They looked at each with wide eyes, as if they'd just witnessed some amazing new discovery that was going to change the world.

Her phone rang again, and this time it was joined by the sound of *his* phone. Padric actually had his own phone, which he'd bought with his fishing money. He used it, among other things, to call her from Dutch Harbor and Bristol Bay when he was fishing.

They both looked at their phones—alien hunks of plastic in this peaceful rain-fed wilderness.

"We're both getting calls at the same time?" Padric said uneasily. "This can't be good."

Zoe felt the same; her throat had gone tight with anxiety. Her father had a heart condition, and she worried about him all the time. "Who's going to answer first?" she asked nervously.

"How about the same time?"

She nodded.

Holding each other's gazes, they opened their flip phones and answered their calls.

Immediately, a loud, angry voice rang out, reaching all the way from Lost Harbor to destroy the moment.

"Get home, now," Zoe's mother was shouting. "Get away from that boy!"

"What? Why? What are you talking about?"

But her mother sounded nearly out of her mind with rage. "You are never going to spend another second with him. Ever!"

"Wha— You mean Padric?" For a wild moment, she wondered if somehow her mother had been able to *see* their kiss. The only reason Zoe was allowed to go hiking with Padric was that everyone knew they were friends, not dating. Their kiss could ruin everything.

"That family's dead to me. All of them. A water taxi's coming to get you. I want you home in an hour. An hour, you hear me?"

"But *why*? What's going on, Mama? Can you at least give me a reason?"

"Ask *your father!*" After sobbing those last words, her mother hung up the phone.

Heart racing as if she'd just downed an entire urn of coffee, she swiveled to look at Padric, whose phone call was the opposite of hers. He listened quietly, eyebrows drawn together, while someone spoke in level tones on the other end of the line. The contrast summed up the difference between their families.

"Okay," he said. Just one word, but it sounded so sad and final. He closed his flip phone and put it into the pocket of his cargo pants, every move slow and deliberate, as if he was trying not to get hurt.

"What's going on? I think my mother just completely lost her mind. She wouldn't even—"

"We have to go." He shoved all her things back into her pack —baklava, first-aid kit. "Can you walk with that ice pack on?"

"Sure. I mean, I think." She stood up, testing her ankle. Not too bad. Not nearly as bad as the fear threading through her heart. "Do you know what's happening? Is someone hurt?"

"No." He swallowed hard. His face was pale. The usual dreaminess had vanished from his blue eyes. His mop of brown hair flopped over his forehead where he'd shoved it out of his face. He looked...shell-shocked. "Not exactly."

"I swear to God, Padric, if you don't start talking—"

"Your father...and...my mother. They were just...caught together. In...at a hotel."

At first she couldn't even grasp his meaning, not even a little bit. What hotel? Lost Harbor didn't have "hotels." The town had lots of bed and breakfasts and a couple of inns, and ground had just been broken on a fancy new hotel at the end of the harbor.

She just kept staring at him blankly as he shouldered his backpack.

"They're having an affair," he said harshly.

He turned and stalked down the trail toward the beach. She knew he wasn't angry at her. He was probably trying to hide his emotion. In his family, emotions weren't indulged the way they were in hers.

"No way." She limped after him, oblivious to the throbbing in her ankle. "That's ridiculous. They're...*old*. My dad's like, over forty. His hair is completely gray and he has a heart problem. The twins were just born! It must be a mistake. Padric, wait."

Finally, he paused and ran back up the path to help her. She saw the fear in his eyes. "I don't know, Zoe. My father sounded like it was real. He says we're moving right away."

"*What?*"

"He wants to get as far away from here as possible. We're moving to Florida."

"Florida?" All of this was too much to take in. The thought of Padric leaving was...surreal. Unbearable. His family roots went back further than most in Lost Harbor. One of the main streets in town was named after his family. Jeffers Drive connected Main Street to Harbor Way. "But you have a street here," she said stupidly.

"The street will probably stay," he said.

"Is this funny?"

"No, it's not fucking funny." He looked at her in despair. "I've never heard my father like that. He was crying. My dad *never* cries, not even the time he got a fish hook right through his cheek."

She knew Billy Jeffers well enough to be stunned at the thought of him shedding tears. "Wow."

They emerged from the forest and reached the pebble beach where they'd left the kayaks. The water taxi was already there, the kayaks already loaded onto it. They both started toward it, but the pilot, Old Crow, held up his hand. "Zoe only. Your father's coming to get you, Padric."

They looked at each, and suddenly all their time was gone. This was it—no more. A force bigger than them had swept through their lives and changed everything.

"Zoe..." he said, then shook his head. "I'll call you."

"Yeah." Her throat was so tight she couldn't say any more, especially not with Old Crow watching. She limped the last few steps down the beach toward the flat-bottomed boat. Old Crow helped her step onboard and closed the hatch behind her. She sat down on the closest bench seat she found and put her backpack on her lap.

Numb, confused, frightened, she watched the beach recede, with Padric standing alone against the backdrop of gray pebbles and soaring spruce. The taste of honey still lingered on her tongue.

Many things changed after that day, among them the fact that she completely lost her taste for baklava. Even the honey-and-walnut aroma of it brought back the shock of that time in the Lost Souls forest. That time when she kissed—and lost—her best friend in the same two-minute span of time.

CHAPTER ONE

Present day

ZOE SHADED her eyes and craned her neck to get a better look at the man steering the small—but obviously expensive—pleasure craft into the harbor. It sure looked like Padric Jeffers, but the chances of it actually being Padric seemed ridiculously small.

In the past fifteen years, shy, creative, crush-worthy Padric Jeffers had grown into jet-setting, famous, still crush-worthy Padric Jeffers, the superstar singer-songwriter. He would be more likely to cruise into the Monte Carlo harbor with a movie star in the passenger seat.

He hadn't been back to Alaska in fifteen years, why would he come back now? It made no sense, and yet the closer the boat came, the more the man at the helm looked like Padric.

Then again, her eyes could be fooling her. She wouldn't be surprised, since it had happened a few times at the pizza shop. So many customers came through over the course of the summer, and inevitably a few blue-eyed, dark-haired men resembled

Padric. Even though he'd barely turned fifteen the last time she saw him, she knew exactly what he looked like.

He was hard to avoid, being a superstar singer-songwriter, after all.

Dimly, she realized that everyone else had left. Lucas Holt, Megan Miller, the rest of the "harbor rats," as the workers who populated the harbor boardwalk called themselves. They'd all gathered on the float to welcome back Lucas and Megan, who had just gotten engaged. And then she'd caught sight of the mystery boat, and she'd completely forgotten everything except possible-Padric.

No—definite-Padric. He must have felt her staring, because he turned his head and met her gaze. Dreamboat eyes, bluer than ever, captured hers.

The effect was electric. They hadn't looked each other in the eye since that crazy-ass trip across the bay. Just like that, all those emotions came storming back. Confusion, fear, anger—a lightning bolt ripping open her heart.

Astonishingly, Padric didn't look much different from his fifteen-year-old self. He was taller and broader around the shoulders. Under the watch cap he wore, his jaw was firmer, his face more hollowed out, dark with scruff. His hair, longer than before, peeked from under his hat. The dark blue knit cap emphasized the strong bones of his face and the shine of his blue eyes—the eyes that had doomed so many women to hopeless crushes.

A smile began in the corner of his mouth. Eyes plus *smile*— now, that was a lethal combo. No way could she stay here and subject herself to that.

Without responding, she whirled around and headed for the ramp that led to the boardwalk.

She had work to do. A pizza shop to run. She had no business mooning around here in the harbor.

At a run, she took the steep ramp at twice her usual speed.

Good thing they'd just put in new treads with great traction, or she would have twisted her ankle all over again. A seagull abandoned its snack—someone's leftover fries—and flapped away as she charged past. A few tourists gave her curious glances as she landed panting on the boardwalk. She still wore her apron, after all. The damn thing was practically part of her by now.

Ignoring their glances, she took a shortcut between Soul Satisfaction Ice Cream and a new fish and chips stand. The boardwalk extended almost the full curve of the harbor, with just about every inch inhabited by businesses catering to fishermen, tourists, or sports fishermen. It had grown organically over the years, so instead of the buildings being lined up in a logical way, they tended to pop up wherever space became available. Occasionally someone added a planter filled with petunias or an old half-barrel with a hardy tree.

The entire boardwalk had a makeshift quality, from the stilts that held up the cantilevered wooden balconies to the ever-changing shape of the beach on the ocean side of the boardwalk. In the winter, storms and fierce winds battered the harbor and only the very hardiest ventured onto the ocean. Most of the businesses shut down—Last Chance Pizza included—and hoped that everything would survive until spring.

She knew every inch of this boardwalk. Her entire adult life had been spent out here. She'd taken over Last Chance Pizza right after high school and never worked anywhere else. After Padric and his family left, the boardwalk and its constant tides of strangers had provided a haven for her.

And now he was back.

WTF?

Why? For how long? Why hadn't anyone warned her?

For a long time, she'd wondered if everything that happened that day was punishment for them kissing. It had felt so innocent. Just two mouths touching; what was the big deal? But all hell had broken out after that. And even though she knew with her brain that her father and Annie Jeffers had been carrying on an affair for four months—long before the kiss—the timing had really messed her up.

She darted across the road that traveled the length of the harbor, dividing the boardwalk into an ocean and a harbor side. Last Chance Pizza was situated on the ocean side, perched on the boardwalk like an old ship about to set sail. Weathered sage-green paint, white trim and a hand-carved wooden sign hanging from iron chains added to the overall maritime effect. With that prime location, Last Chance offered customers a stunning view of the long sweep of the beach, as well as Misty Bay and, on the other side of the bay, Lost Souls Wilderness.

They often had lines winding down the planks of the board-walk, to the great annoyance of their neighbors, a native arts craft shop and a fish-cleaning station for the charter boats. But right now, only a few people clustered around the front door —thankfully.

Zoe was rattled. Seriously rattled. She'd stopped assuming that she would ever see Padric Jeffers again. And she'd been okay with that.

This—him reappearing so suddenly—this, she was not okay with.

Her twin sisters, Monica and Alexis, started talking as soon as she pushed through the door.

"Where have you been? You said you'd only be gone a second and we have stuff to do. Like, important stuff." Monica untied her apron and tossed it on the dishwashing table. She was the dramatic one of the two, although both had their moments.

"Seriously important stuff that we can't talk about yet," added Alexis as she punched numbers into the cash register to ring someone up. "It's about the beach festival."

The two of them were planning a music festival for Labor

Day weekend. They were calling it "Last Chance to Rock." It was safe to say they'd had no idea how much work it would be.

Zoe hurried to the floury counter where the pizzas were assembled. Several order slips hung from clothespins on a line overhead. "One of you has to stay," she told the twins. "I can't take orders and make pizza."

"But—"

"No sense in arguing about it. It's simple math." She scattered sausage over a pie that Monica had abandoned halfway through. "Alexis, you stay, since we don't have anyone for the counter. Monica, you can handle the incredibly, seriously important thing on your own, right?"

A tragic expression of outrage crossed her sister's face. "It's not as *fun* alone."

"It's good for you to do things separately sometimes."

"Says who?"

"Says your big sister who you should listen to."

Monica rolled her eyes. "Then tell me why it's such a good thing."

"Because everyone has to learn how to be alone at some point." That sounded so dire and lonely that even she winced. "You know what I mean."

"Zoe, if I ever want lessons in how to be alone, I know where to turn." Monica's sassy tone made Zoe itch to fling shredded cheese at her. Instead, she added it to the pizza. After sliding a paddle under the pie, she thrust it into the wood-fired brick oven that her parents had trucked all the way from Rhode Island.

"One of you stays," she said firmly. Don't take the bait, that was the trick with the twins. If you got down to their level, all kinds of drama would ensue.

The door opened—the cowbell jangled—and Yanni, one of the fishing old-timers, came in. "Looks like we got a celebrity in the harbor," he announced as he slid onto one of the stools at the counter.

Most tourists took their pizzas to the glassed-in deck, where they could enjoy the views at tables draped with cheerful anchor-print tablecloths. The locals, on the other hand, had no need for more scenery and preferred the counter, where they could gossip as they waited for their pizza.

Zoe's body went tense. On autopilot, she continued to build the backlog of pizzas that Monica hadn't gotten to. Was it possible that the news about Padric had already spread? *How?*

Monica and Alexis danced with excitement. "Who? Who? Ohmigod, who?" They were always bursting with energy. Sometimes Zoe wished they'd have a morose phase just for some peace and quiet.

"Padric Jeffers is back. Sailed right into the harbor as if he wasn't a world-famous rock star."

"Padric Jeffers is here?" Monica clapped a hand over her mouth, and Alexis gave a little shriek.

Then they both swung their gazes toward Zoe, as if waiting for her head to explode. She scowled at them and focused on the pizza she was crafting. They'd been barely more than newborns when Padric had left, but apparently they knew the gossip just like everyone else in Lost Harbor.

"You two seem awfully excited. I didn't know you liked angst rock."

"There's a lot more to him than that," Alexis corrected her. "Grownups just don't get it."

Zoe rolled her eyes. "He's the same age as me."

"Is he?" Alexis blinked at her innocently. "You seem so much older."

Zoe pretended to threaten her with a roll of pepperoni. Then something occurred to her. Padric being back—there were complications to that, things she needed to warn the twins about.

"Come over here, you two. I have to talk to you both." She beckoned to them, creating a cloud of flour in the air, almost like a smoke ring. They clustered into the cooking area, being careful not to get too close to the brick oven, which radiated heat.

"What's up, Zoe? Aren't you feeling well?" Monica's expression was entirely too concerned. If her imp of a sister was assuming she was going to fall apart because Padric was back, she had it all wrong.

"I'm perfectly fine. But Mama cannot find out about Padric. Seriously, not a word. You don't remember what the Scandal was like. She will flip out if she knows a member of the Jeffers family is here."

"She's probably going to hear it from someone," said Alexis, wide-eyed. "Like at stitch-and-bitch"—referring to a group of local knitters and crocheters.

"No, she's been skipping stitch-and-bitch. She's been sticking close to home and we need to make sure she keeps that up until Padric leaves. She *cannot* find out he's here. Promise me."

They nodded, although Monica wore a rebellious frown. "But the Scandal was so long ago."

"No no no, oh naïve one. Do you know nothing about the Bellini family? Mama is still upset about the British taking all the Greek sculptures out of the Parthenon. Something that happened fifteen years ago? Forget it. That's like yesterday to her. If she finds out he's here, it will be the freakout to end all freakouts. She cannot know, or our lives will become miserable. You understand?"

The twins nodded more seriously this time.

"Okay. Go, Monica, do whatever it is you were planning."

The twins exchanged a cautious look—the kind filled with communications only they could interpret.

"Actually, I'll stick around. I have a feeling it's about to get busy."

"Great." Zoe beamed at Monica. Maybe her sisters were finally starting to become more responsible.

Alexis went to take an order and Zoe got to work on the next pizza. The normal chatter of a busy lunch crowd took over, and Zoe could almost pretend that everything was back to normal.

Yeah, right. Nothing would be normal until she found out what Padric was doing here and, more importantly, when he'd be gone again.

CHAPTER TWO

Well, that definitely had not gone the way he'd expected. Padric steered the speedboat he'd rented in Aurora Bay into the temporary guest tie-up spot. He'd taken the long way to Lost Harbor—flown into Anchorage, then hired a helicopter to take him to Aurora Bay, then rented the *Jaunty* for the cruise to Lost Harbor.

Dodging paparazzi could be a full-time job sometimes, but it was worth it. He hadn't wanted to show up in Lost Harbor like an asshole with cameras trailing behind him. If they tracked him down, so be it, he'd deal with it then. But at least he had a head start.

As his boat nudged up against the float, he caught sight of someone running down the ramp. For a moment, he hoped it was Zoe, changing her mind about that cold shoulder she was giving him. He was here *for her*, after all.

Of course, she'd had no clue that he was coming. Maybe that explained her strange reaction. He hadn't expected her to flee at the sight of him.

He also hadn't expected her to look like...that. Like a stunning goddamn oil painting from Italy or something. She'd always been the kind of girl you couldn't look away from—or at least *he* couldn't. But her features had never quite fit right in her face—eyebrows too dark, nose too big, mouth too full, everything competing for attention. But now it all harmonized perfectly—beautifully.

Zoe was beautiful.

And just as proud as ever, judging by the tilt of her head as she'd watched him cruise in. She wasn't his awkward best friend anymore. Not awkward, and obviously not his best friend. She hadn't even smiled at him before she ran up the ramp.

But no, the new arrival wasn't Zoe coming back to say a proper hello. It was Nate Prudhoe, who reached the slip at a jog just as Padric turned off the engine.

"Nice timing," Padric told his old friend as he tossed him a line. Nate ran it around the cleat.

"It took exactly thirty seconds for word to get out," Nate said in his laughing way. "I figured you might need some backup. No entourage, no security, what are you thinking?"

"I'm thinking Lost Harbor doesn't give a shit about all that. Besides, who needs an entourage when I have you?"

He stepped off the boat and pulled Nate in for a hug. Padric didn't believe in man-hugs. With people he cared about, he went for the real thing.

"It's good to see you, man," said Nate, pounding his back. Nate was such a good guy—one of the all-around greats, and Padric had met a lot of people in his career. "Do you have bags? Where are you staying? You can crash on my floor if you want. Just like old times."

"Just one bag." He hopped back into the boat to grab his travel bag from under the bench. While he was there, he snagged a wide-brimmed fishing hat and his sunglasses. With those two items, he would look like any other visitor to the harbor.

But maybe not, judging by Nate's crossed arms and out-loud laugh. "You're not fooling anyone, superstar."

"You'd be surprised." Padric shouldered the bag and stepped back onto the float. The familiar harbor smells—fish guts, diesel, salt breeze—took him right back to his earliest days. His father had been a commercial fisherman, mostly salmon but some other varieties. Padric had helped out on the boat from the time he could haul in a net. He hadn't always loved it; it was boring and often cold and uncomfortable. His favorite part had been the slow times when he could watch the ocean and let images flow through his mind.

With the *Jaunty* secured, he and Nate walked up the ramp toward the boardwalk, which was much busier than Padric remembered. "How've you been, Nate? Haven't seen you since— where was that?"

"Houston. Great show."

"Thanks for coming. It was good to see a friend there." Padric noticed that Nate hadn't answered the first question. "You still with that girl, um..." The hell if he could remember her name, but the three of them had gone out for drinks after the show. He and Nate had spent the whole evening reminiscing about Lost Harbor, and he'd felt bad for...um...

Nate laughed. "Don't work too hard on her name. We broke up. But for your records, it's Mary Lou."

"Mary Lou. Right. Sorry, dude. You seemed like you had a pretty good thing going."

Nate shrugged lightly. "Things come and go, know what I mean?"

They reached the busy boardwalk, which was constructed with weathered planks that needed repairs every spring. A fresh white railing extended the entire mile-length of the boardwalk; both he and Nate had spent many hours volunteering with paint brushes every spring. Lost Harbor was an all-hands-on-deck kind of place.

"Business looks pretty good, I'll say that. I don't remember this place being so crowded."

"An article came out a few years ago in *Sunset Magazine*. They called us a hidden gem. Things haven't been the same since. Did you catch our *Trekking* episode a few weeks ago? That brought another wave."

"Missed that one." They ambled along the boardwalk, past kids with ice cream cones and tourists taking selfies with picturesque "bear-viewing" storefronts. The knot in Nate's stomach loosened just a bit. Being back wasn't...terrible.

"You gotta check it out. Zoe was in it." Nate shot Padric a curious glance. "Still an off-limits topic?"

"Nah. Actually, she's the reason I'm here. How's she doing?"

Nate dodged a kid on a skateboard. "Busy. That pizza place is a gold mine these days. She's training up her kid sisters to take some of the load off."

Huh. No mention of any health issues. Maybe Zoe's condition wasn't common knowledge yet.

He'd better not reveal anything—it wasn't his secret to share, after all.

"Do people still talk about..."

"The Scandal? Nah, not really. There've been several dozen scandals since then. Occasionally it comes up, because the Jeffers name is all over this town. And because you're, you know...you."

Padric cringed a bit inside. As an intrinsically introverted person, the spotlight aspect of being a singer always made him uncomfortable. Yeah, he'd gotten used to it. And it was a small price to pay for making his living as a recording artist. But it didn't come naturally to him.

"So anyway, you never said where you're staying."

"I was thinking I'd try out that candy-ass new hotel they built."

"New? You mean the one that's been here fourteen years?"

"New to me. I watched them frame it up that last summer I was here. Always wondered how it would turn out."

"Overpriced and overhyped. There, I saved you the trouble." Nate grinned at him.

God, it was good to see him. Nate was a salt-of-the-earth kind of guy. Loyal, solid, unpretentious, funny, good-hearted.

"Well, I figure I'll pump as much money into the local economy as I can."

"No one's going to argue with that."

A gap between two shingled buildings offered a glimpse of the road and the businesses on the other side. Which happened to include Last Chance Pizza. As usual, a line of customers clustered outside the front door. A chilly breeze cut across the bay, causing them to zip up their fleece jackets and tuck their hands in their pockets.

Padric couldn't help searching for a glimpse of Zoe. Steam fogged the picture window, with its view of the brick oven and the kitchen area. The painted words "Pizza," "Salad," "Wine and beer" got in the way too. But even so, he spotted Zoe's dark head bent over her work. She wore an orange bandanna that kept her curly hair in a wild pile on top of her head.

Then his view vanished when he tripped over the back wheel of someone's cruiser bike. He nearly took a header right onto the weathered planks.

"You okay there, man?" Nate grabbed his arm. "Wouldn't want to you to break a tooth, not to mention ten million teenage hearts."

"Cute." Padric regained his balance and adjusted his fishing hat, which had gone askew. "I'm good. Come on, let's get out of here." His little mishap had captured the attention of a few onlookers. If they looked too closely, he might be busted.

"Yeah, can't gawk at Zoe Bellini forever. Let's book."

"I wasn't—" But Nate was already a few steps ahead, charging through the mill of tourists like the first responder he was.

Whatever. Face it, he *had* been gawking. But who could blame him? Zoe had grown up...just...beyond his imagination, and he had a really good imagination.

They walked the rest of the way to the Eagle's Nest Resort and Hotel. Apparently the fact that the place had Jacuzzis meant they could call it a resort, because beyond that, it didn't resemble any of the high-end places Padric had stayed over the years.

The desk clerk didn't blink at the cash Padric offered for his suite, or at the name he provided. Gavin Strike happened to be his security guy. They had a name-sharing arrangement for those times when Padric wanted maximum anonymity.

It was probably pointless here in Lost Harbor, but in case any paparazzi were trying to pry names out of hotel clerks, he had a small layer of protection.

Nate whistled as they walked into the "Admiral Suite," which occupied the top ocean-side corner of the four-story complex. "Million-dollar view. Almost as good as mine."

"Nothing's as good as yours. But this ain't bad."

Nate had bought his parents' home from them after they'd retired to Arizona. It perched on a high bluff with a literal three-hundred-sixty-degree view.

Padric tossed his bag on the suitcase rack and sank onto one of the couches with a sigh. The suite had two bedrooms and a living area, a kitchenette and its own hot tub out on the balcony. And that view of Lost Souls Wilderness...icy white mountain peaks, deeply forested slopes with shadowed ravines, inlets glimpsed like secrets in the wild.

He wondered if he could spot the Larkspur Trail, the one he and Zoe had started to hike on that fateful day. Maybe it was just past that peak shaped like a perfect cone?

"Okay, dude." Nate dropped into the couch perpendicular to Padric's. "Want to tell me why you're staring at mountains when you're supposed to be on tour?"

"How do you know my schedule? You stalking me?"

"Don't fan-shame me. I follow you on Facebook." Nate's easy grin reappeared. "I happen to like teenage whiner music."

Padric clenched his jaw at the insult most frequently flung his way. He'd heard it enough, he ought to be used to it. "It helps people, okay?"

At least he'd thought so—until recently.

"Relax, superstar. I love your music. Like I just said. I might even follow you on Instagram. Not sure because I keep forgetting my password. Anyway, the question still stands. Why aren't you in Sweden right now?"

"I had a...voice thing. Nodes. Doctor advised a couple weeks of rest, and I couldn't think of a more restful place than here."

Nate stretched out his long legs and shot him a skeptical look. "It might be restful for some, but for a member of the Jeffers family? You might be better off at a Calcutta street fair."

"Oh come on. It was so long ago, and I wasn't even part of the Scandal. I was just caught in the crossfire."

"True that. Hey, I'm not complaining, just so you know. I'm glad you're here. How long do you think you'll stay?"

"I'm not sure."

That depended almost entirely on Zoe. If she truly wanted nothing to do with him, he wouldn't have much reason to stay.

"Are you supposed to rest just your voice or everything?"

Padric squinted at him. "Why? What are you getting at?"

"We're about to start a round of training for volunteer firefighters. If you're looking for something to do while you're here, come on by. Good crew, lots of fun, beers after every training session, and oh yeah, the occasional chance to save lives."

"Low on recruits?" he asked dryly.

"Always. This town is just too damn small. Anyway, just thought I'd drop that thought. I need to get going, my shift's about to start."

"But wait..."

He didn't want Nate to leave. Right now, Nate was a lifeline connecting him to *his* Lost Harbor, the real one, the one from his past, the one that didn't have a fancy resort with double couches and a plastic bouquet on the coffee table.

But Nate had a life that included other things besides playing entourage.

"We'll have to grab a beer sometime soon," Padric finished.

"You know it." Nate gave him a little salute and whisked himself out the door.

And just like that, Padric was alone. Actually alone—with no handlers or managers or publicity people or backup singers or roadies nearby.

The quiet settled over Padric like a suffocating blanket.

Nope. He wasn't ready to be alone. He wasn't used to it anymore. And now that he was...other thoughts crept into his mind.

Terrible thoughts.

Thoughts he kept trying to bury, but couldn't. Thoughts about the fucking trend that was spreading like wildfire through his fanbase.

Unable to stop himself, he pulled out his laptop and logged onto his private hotspot. He didn't trust other networks.

He'd bookmarked several pages where he could find new postings about what they were calling the "PJ parties."

Cute name for something so gross.

In one forum, someone named Tweenie45 had posted a video of her brand new "PJ." The raised mark, shaped like the Gothic letters of his logo, glared red against the inside of her arm. It made his own arm throb with sympathetic pain.

"*My mom's about to freak,*" she'd written as her caption. "*No *pain, no gain, amirite? This is for me and Padric, not her or anyone else, so she can suck it."*

Padric made himself look at the mark she'd put on her own skin—a permanent mark, not some kind of tattoo that could be removed when she came to her senses. No, these brands would be there forever. That was the point, according to their thought process. PJ Party 4EvR.

But these were *kids*. Kids who had taken one damn line from one his songs and twisted it into something he'd never intended.

It wasn't even a good line! *"You brand me with a kiss, your name on my skin, deeper than magic, undone from within."* One crappy line and hundreds of fourteen-to-seventeen-year-olds had decided they had to put brands on their skin.

He'd tried to stop it. At first he'd kept it low-key, simply posting messages on his social media pages.

"Lots of misinformation out there about my song 'Soul Brand.' Every phrase in it is purely metaphorical and was never meant to be interpreted literally. I would never want anyone to harm themselves; in fact, I condemn it. If a PJ party exists, it oughta be about love and kindness, not self-harm. Never self-harm."

When that hadn't stopped the viral trend from spreading, he'd made an official statement to the press, then done a televised interview. Nothing worked. These kids had convinced themselves that some magical thing was going to happen if they got a PJ brand. The worst part was that they were doing it to themselves or each other. Since no parent would allow it—and no professional studios would do it without parental consent—the kids took things into their own hands.

It was horrifying.

And yeah, he had a mild case of nodes, nothing he hadn't dealt with before. But he had a much bigger case of "what the fuck is happening right now" and "get me the fuck out of here so

I can figure out what to do next." Also, a case of "will I ever sing again without causing someone to hurt themselves?"

That was the worst part. He wrote songs because they ran through his head in wisps and snatches, driving him crazy until he could do the hard work of forming them into actual lyrics. He wrote songs because he loved music and wanted to share the joy.

He did *not* write songs so a bunch of emo kids could have an excuse to hurt themselves. He'd rather shut up until the end of time. Maybe those nodes knew what they were doing.

He closed his laptop and shoved it aside. *So quiet.* He used to love the quiet, even crave it. But now...fuck, he was a spoiled asshole too used to his fucking entourage.

He grabbed the binder labelled "Lost Harbor Sights and Adventures" that sat on the coffee table next to the plastic bouquet. Calla lilies—a flower that didn't even grow in Lost Harbor. Flipping through the pages, he saw flyers for fishing char-ters—the *Jack Hammer, Hooked, Aurora Bay Charters*—as well as adventure outfits offering everything from bear-viewing to kayak trips to nature tours. *Forget Me Not Nature Tours*, that was defi-nitely new.

Reaching the food section, he scanned through menus for Captain Crabbie's, the Olde Salt Saloon, Tremain's Fish and Chips, Soul Satisfaction Ice Cream—wow, was that Trixie Tran posing with an ice cream cone? Another local girl who had grown up right.

And then, there it was—Last Chance Pizza.

Family owned and operated for over twenty-five years, Last Chance Pizza brings the mouthwatering flavors of wood-fired pizza and real homemade Italian tomato sauce to your doorstep. Now offering delivery within a mile radius.

Delivery. Now that was an interesting thought. He wouldn't have to risk being recognized. He could call the shop and maybe hear Zoe's voice. She probably didn't deliver the pizza herself, but maybe one of her sisters did. If so, he'd get a chance to find out what was going on with Zoe. And he'd get to taste the best pizza in the world again.

Win-win-win-win-win.

He dialed the number and, sure enough, Zoe answered. Even though she was clearly busy—a din of voices hummed in the background—she came across as unhurried on the phone.

He'd always appreciated Zoe's refusal to be rushed. She moved at her own pace and no one else's.

"Last Chance Pizza, can I help you?"

He hesitated. Should he identify himself or not? Would she recognize his voice no matter what? "Hi, Zoe. It's Padric."

A frozen moment later, she spoke again. "Hi. Can I help you?"

"I...uh...saw that you offer delivery now. I'd like to order a pizza."

"What kind? Our menu's online."

"That's okay, I have it here." He fumbled with the binder. Damn, he couldn't detect one bit of warmth in her voice—and Zoe was fucking *made* of warmth. Sometimes it came in the form of fire, but that was good, too. "I'll take a Greek. Large."

"That's enough for at least two people."

Ha! Was she subtly inquiring as to whether he was alone or not?

"I'll eat the rest tomorrow. Actually, scratch that. You're right, I'll get a medium." That way he could order another pizza tomorrow. Maybe one for breakfast, another for lunch, then dinner. He'd wear her down with pizza orders.

"Medium Greek. Where are we delivering it to?"

So professional. So cool. Like one of those impossible peaks across the bay.

"To the Eagle's Nest, the Admiral Suite." He felt almost embarrassed saying the name.

"Okay then. The Admiral Suite. I guess the Emperor of All He Surveys Suite was already booked?"

Finally, a crack in her armor.

He laughed, a little too heartily. "Yeah, someone's getting fired for that."

But that sounded like an asshole thing to say, and it wasn't even funny. Face it, he was rattled. "Just kidding. No one's getting fired unless it's me for cracking a lame-ass joke."

"It wasn't that bad." The slight softening of her voice gave him a rush of hope. "It'll be about half an hour."

"I'll be here. Any chance you're playing delivery girl today?"

"No, I'm playing restaurant owner today." All the frost returned to her voice. "It's a fun game that keeps me extremely busy. Half an hour."

"Wait!" He stopped her before she could hang up.

"I mentioned the extremely busy part, right?"

"Forgot to mention that I'm booked under the name Gavin Strike."

"Gavin Strike," she repeated, laughter welling in her voice. Well, it was better than ice. "That'll be twenty-two fifty-five, not including tip, Gavin."

And she was gone.

His ear still vibrated from the sound of her voice as he put down his phone. He often heard color in sounds. His alarm always screamed in an obnoxious shade of yellow. His own voice sounded like various shades of blue to him. Zoe's voice, deep and rich and husky, held notes of violet and mahogany.

One thing her voice didn't show was any hint of illness. Whatever ailed her must be something not obvious.

Half an hour later, a knock sounded on his door. He opened it to find himself staring at a girl unnervingly similar to Zoe when he'd last seen her. This girl was slimmer, with shorter hair and eye liner—something Zoe rarely wore back then.

"You came!" she exclaimed as she pushed her way into his suite. "I can't believe it's actually you!"

"You're Zoe's sister?"

"Yes, I'm Monica." She thrust the pizza box at him. "Twenty-two fifty-five, please. It's quite easy to round up to thirty, of course."

"Math whiz, huh?" He handed over forty dollars. "Two twenties is even easier."

"Wow." Her eyes widened as she tucked the cash into the pocket of her denim leggings. "Do you need change?"

He waved her off as he opened the box and inhaled the divine scent of his favorite pizza. "Damn. Better than ever."

"It's probably about the same," Monica corrected him. "We haven't changed one single thing about the recipe in forever. My granny would freak if we did."

"Why mess with perfection?" His mouth was literally watering from the aroma of tomato sauce and melted cheese. But before he indulged, he had a few questions for Zoe's sister. "Come sit down. You can fill me in."

She danced from one foot to the other. Both of her wrists were loaded with friendship bracelets. Without thinking, he checked the inside of her forearm and didn't see any trace of a stupid PJ brand.

How screwed up was it that he'd automatically searched for one? God, he hated this.

"No, I can't stay," she said. "But I just wanted to say how incredibly excited we are that you actually came. Me and Alexis, I mean. My twin. There's something very important we'd like to discuss with you, so would you maybe have time—"

"Yeah, the stuff about Zoe," he said impatiently. "What's going on?"

Her gaze skittered away from his. "I can't get into that right now."

"You and your sister wrote me that letter. You're the reason I came all this way."

"Yes, we wrote the letter. We heard that you were really good friends with Zoe before the Scandal."

"Best friends."

"Yeah. Well, so, yeah, we thought you wouldn't mind if we contacted you, and…ohmigod, it's so great that you're here! It's really great!" Her phone buzzed and she rolled her eyes. "I have to go, but I just want to say welcome back, and hopefully we can talk really soon. Just—don't do anything until we explain."

"Do…what?"

"Anything! Especially about Zoe. Okay bye!"

The door closed behind her, leaving Padric staring at it blankly, pizza box in hand.

What the hell was that all about? The letter from the twins had motivated him to come all the way to Alaska. Now she didn't have time to talk about it?

Something was fishy. Aside from all the actual fish in this town.

He sank his teeth into a slice of pizza. Visceral pleasure sank all the way down to his bones. God, Zoe made good pizza. Had she made this particular pie? Had she thought of him while she'd sprinkled extra feta cheese and thyme on it? She'd remembered exactly how he liked his pizza. Was she really as furious with him as she'd sounded on the phone?

Why was she being so cold to him, anyway? He hadn't had a choice about leaving. His father had whisked them out of Lost Harbor so fast that Padric had even left his backpack in the locker at school. Nate had collected it and probably still had it somewhere.

So good, this pizza. Every mouthful tasted like his very best memories. Diving off the ramp on hot days, to the wrath of the harbormaster. Playing tag up and down the boardwalk—two points for every tourist who yelled at them. Bonfires on Seafarer's Beach as dusk turned to dawn, skipping night completely.

If Zoe really hated him, he'd be able to taste it in her pizza, wouldn't he?

He finished every last crumb, already looking forward to the pizza he planned to order tomorrow.

CHAPTER FOUR

"Mama, if you try one more time to get that blender down, I'll have to ground you." Zoe reached for the Vitamix in which Nicola Bellini made her daily doctor-recommended smoothies. Her mother stayed close to home these days, but she still hated admitting any kind of limitation. It was a game they played; Mama tried to do something she couldn't, Zoe helped her, Mama played the martyr.

"Ridiculous," snorted her mother as she sank back down into her favorite kitchen chair. Her fluffy white cat Athena jumped onto her lap and curled up. "My poor mother tried that and it didn't work. I ran off and got pregnant."

"Okay then. Please make sure to use protection, Mama. We can't handle any more kids in this family."

Her mother laughed until she coughed, while Zoe quickly put together a banana-kale smoothie for her. "Take your pills," she told her, then pressed the button on the blender to drown out her mother's protests.

She used the time to wrestle with the question that had plagued her ever since Padric had reappeared. Should she warn her mother that a Jeffers was roaming the streets of Lost Harbor? Or should she hope Padric was long gone by the time Mama found out?

Monica and Alexis were right; one of her friends would probably tell her. And maybe that would be best. The Scandal had been deeply humiliating to Nicola Bellini, and she hated talking about it with her children. In fact, the only thing she'd told Zoe was short and to the point. "Your father made a mistake with that devil woman, but he's apologized and that's the end of it."

"But what about—"

"Your friend is gone, and that's for the best."

Every time the topic of the Scandal came up again, her mother had a mini breakdown.

She released the button to find her mother glaring at her. "That's too long, it's going to be mushy."

"Smoothies are supposed to be mushy." She poured the green liquid into a glass and set it in front of her mother. With a hand that trembled ever so slightly, Mama picked it up.

That tremble wrenched at Zoe's heart. Her mother's health was so clearly degenerating. She didn't like to leave the house, and she used a walker when she did so. She still loved to cook, loved her family, but sometimes she slept through the entire afternoon. Nicola Bellini's passion had always been protecting and taking care of her family, and now it was Zoe's responsibility to take care of her.

What would be the most caretaking approach when it came to Padric's return?

He was a busy man. A rock star. He wouldn't be here for long. Why risk a breakdown when Padric might disappear at any moment?

No, she decided as she watched her mother take a shaky sip of smoothie and make her usual disgusted face. She wouldn't tell her mother. She'd just hope that Padric left as soon as possible.

Or she'd *try* to hope that. When she wasn't ogling the all-grown-up heartthrob version of her former best friend.

———

WITHIN A FEW DAYS, everyone working at the Last Chance knew that if Gavin Strike called for a pizza delivery, the order went to Zoe. She didn't want anyone else making pizza for Padric. She had a reputation to uphold, after all. He was a celebrity now, and one word from him could influence millions either for or against her pizza.

At least that was the reason she gave everyone. The real reason was...a big, hot, confusing mess. She didn't want anyone else making pizza for Padric. That was all there was to it. No need to overanalyze it.

Only the twins knew who "Gavin Strike" really was. They were more than happy to take turns delivering pizza to his fancy suite. He always gave them enormous tips and they always took much too long.

After two days—and six pizzas—he came into the Last Chance in person. He wore a thick hoodie with a fleece lining that made him blend in with the fishermen who came in for beer and pizza. No one looked twice at him, though she knew who he was before he even came through the door.

This time she was much more prepared for the sight of Padric. She'd spent the last couple of days lecturing herself on how to behave around him. Not hurt, for one. Grown-up. Businesslike. Mature.

"Confused" wasn't on that list.

"You seem to have lots of energy," he said to her in a low voice after he'd placed his order with Alexis and taken a stool at the counter.

"Um...yes. Thank you?" Confused, she pulled him a mug of ale and plunked it on the counter before him.

"You holding up okay?"

He sipped the ale, regarding her steadily over the rim. Those eyes—heart-stopping, that's what they were.

Alexis was obviously eavesdropping from the cash register. "Isn't it amazing?" she piped up. "Zoe always works through everything, no matter how bad she feels."

Zoe frowned at her little sister. What was Alexis talking about? She took days off when she got sick. She worked in the food industry, for God's sake. "So how have you been, Padric? I mean, besides the obvious." She lowered her voice. "World-famous and all."

"I wouldn't go that far." He seemed to hunch over the glass tumbler of ale. "But yeah, good. I'm good."

This was awkward. And the fact that it was awkward made it even more awkward. When had she ever felt awkward around Padric? Never. Until right this minute.

"Good." Businesslike. Cool. Mature. "How's your family?"

As soon as the words slipped out, she cringed. His family was not a good topic. The Scandal had nearly destroyed *her* family. Even though her parents had stayed together, things had remained tense between them, then Dad had died three years later.

"They're good."

Good. Everything was good, apparently. And yet nothing was.

"They retired to Florida. I mean, they already lived in Flor-ida, but they retired to another part of Florida."

He sounded just as awkward as she did, so that was some comfort.

"That's nice."

She had to serve a customer requesting more water. As she filled the pitcher, she took a few deep breaths. Padric was an old acquaintance, nothing more. After he'd left, she'd tried to call him. She'd also sent a letter and even an email through his new school system.

He'd never answered.

That silence had broken her heart, but she was completely recovered by now. There was no need for awkwardness.

Aa she handed the pitcher of water to the customer, she glanced under her lashes at Padric. How long was he going to hang out at the counter like this? She couldn't keep up "cool and professional" forever.

But he showed no signs of leaving.

"So you're working a pretty full schedule? Is that difficult?" he asked her.

She cocked an eyebrow at him. "What am I, a rookie? I've been doing this since I was what, twelve?"

"I think you were thirteen when you started. It was a week after your birthday."

Her mouth opened, then shut. Darn it, he was right. She'd started right after her thirteenth birthday, when she'd needed some extra cash for an art project.

"So what brings you back to Lost Harbor, Gavin?" she asked, a little extra edge of mockery in her voice. He deserved it, with his whole incognito act. "Are you trying to dodge your fans? You have a few here, too, you know."

"Why do you keep changing the subject?" He fixed her with a level, unwavering gaze that made her squirm. "You keep evading and dodging."

Dodging? She lifted her eyebrows at him. "I have no idea what you're talking about."

"See? *That's* exactly what I'm talking about." He pointed a finger at her in triumph.

Monica popped up next to her, babbling about a big order. She ignored her sister.

"You have a lot of nerve, Padric. I have no obligation to talk to you at all, so how could I be dodging?"

She poured a glass of wine for a customer, sloshing over the rim of the glass—probably because she would have preferred to toss it in Padric's face.

"Why wouldn't you talk to me? You can, you know. You can talk to me about anything."

"Yeah? How about the fact that you—" She cut herself off. No need to get into their personal history in front of her sisters and a bunch of hungry customers.

"I what?" His patient voice unnerved her even more, because it sounded just like the teenage Padric, who never got angry the way everyone in her family did.

"Look, Padric." She delivered the glass of wine and brushed away Monica, who kept trying to interrupt. Her sister was acting so strangely, like a mosquito buzzing around her ear. "Let's just keep things simple here. You're a customer, that's it."

"Right! Exactly!" Monica butted in. "I'll take over here. Zoe, you go make that order for the cruise ship. They want twenty pizzas and you're the fastest."

Zoe allowed Monica to hustle her over to the kitchen area. More proof that everything was upside down and inside out. She was supposed to be in charge here, not her sixteen-year-old sister.

On the other hand, it was a relief to focus on making twenty Surf 'n' Turf—halibut and sausage—pizzas instead of tangling with Padric Jeffers.

The next time she had a chance to look up, Padric was gone.

NOT THAT HE was *gone* gone. Oh no, that would be too easy.

Even though she tried to conduct life as normal, he kept popping up. Her life was pretty simple, especially in the summer. Pizza. Family (riding herd on the twins and keeping an eye on her mother). Her latest art project. That was about it.

Occasionally she squeezed in a drink or dinner with friends. Once in a while she went for a trip across Misty Bay. She still loved to hike over there, though she'd never been back to Larkspur Trail. She probably never would. When the salmon were running, she went fishing. When the blueberries and currants ripened, she went berry picking.

Every summer passed the same way, and now she was thirty. *Thirty*. How had that happened?

Padric was thirty, too. Their birthdays only nine weeks apart. But he was a world-famous, model-dating, successful thirty, while she was a still-doing-the-same-thing thirty. Or, more accurately, a crash-and-burn-every-time-she-got-involved thirty. Everyone in Lost Harbor knew she had the worst luck when it came to men; it was legendary.

The next time she ran into Padric, she was browsing the aisles at Misty Bay Art Supplies and Frame Store. She'd been working on a series of clay figures—animals and humans—with whimsical mutations she created from objects that had washed up on the beach. She'd enlisted a few local fishermen and tour guides to keep an eye out for interesting beach debris. She called the project *At Sea (Lost/Found)*, and it was supposed to be a commentary on how no one is immune from change.

Her secret dream was to submit her project for a fellowship in Banff. The Far North Arts grant was perfect for her. But chances were good that this dream would get torpedoed by her own self-doubt, as had always happened. She had yet to actually submit her work anywhere outside Lost Harbor.

Seeing Padric had inspired her to dive into the project again. He'd gone all out in pursuit of his music dreams. The least she could do was apply for one stupid fellowship. She already had a stockpile of found objects—pieces of buoys, aluminum cans, seagull bones, a Hello Kitty doll—ready to add to her figurines. But she'd run out of the fasteners she used to meld the debris to the clay.

So there she was in the "art tools" aisle when a familiar voice stroked every one of her nerve endings with a deep, "Hi, Zoe. It's good to see you still like art."

Using all her willpower to grab onto her "cool and professional" act, she calmly turned to face him. He looked scruffier than when he'd first arrived, as if he was avoiding his razor. He wore a simple t-shirt and flip-flops and looked relaxed and delicious.

"Hey, look at that, you can finally grow a beard."

"Yes, turns out you were right. It was just a matter of time."

Okay, that was a funny memory to hang on to. Beards, of all things, and his worry that he'd never achieve one.

"I was the expert, after all. I always had more facial hair than you. That's one thing our family excels at. Hair. It's a point of pride."

He laughed at the familiar joke. "And yours is still looking glorious."

"Thanks." Embarrassed, she turned to search for the right fasteners. He must have seen much nicer hair than hers in the rock star world.

"What are you looking for?"

"Oh, just something for a project." She found the fasteners and collected several boxes.

"What project?"

"Art." She stepped around him and headed down the aisle.

"Yeah, I figured. That's it? No details?"

"Why do you want details?"

"Because I'm interested? Is that so crazy?"

Interested? If he was interested, where had he been for the past fifteen years? She sighed, feeling cornered. She could either express her hurt at his disappearance or try to answer his question in a civil way.

"It's..." She stopped to face him. Luckily, the fellowship required an abstract, which she'd written and rewritten a few times already. "It's a mixed-media—clay and found materials—statement on the interconnectivity of humans and our environment, especially as relates to shifts in our ecology."

He looked momentarily stunned, his blue eyes electric against the slight tan of his skin. She noticed the first marks of laugh lines, and somehow that irritated her. Nice life he'd enjoyed since leaving Lost Harbor. Lots of laughter and fun and fame and fortune.

"Sounds...uh..."

"Fascinating, I know."

"Well, yeah, but also kind of...uh..."

"Bullshitty?"

"In the best possible way."

She grinned, feeling herself relax a bit. "It's a bunch of clay figures decorated with random ocean flotsam." She gestured with her box of fasteners. "And I'd better get back to it."

"Wait." He hurried after her. "Can I see it?"

"No."

"Zoe, come on. I was always your biggest art fan." A pause. "Only art fan. You never showed anyone else your stuff."

"That was a long time ago."

Mavis, who owned the store, was busy on a phone call and directed her to add the box of fasteners to her tab. Zoe scribbled in the ledger under her name, then stalked out the door. Padric followed her out.

"So you're saying you've finally started showing your work to the outside world?"

"Yes. I have." No, she hadn't. But she *intended* to. "As a matter of fact, I need to finish this project right away for this big competition I'm entering. So I'll see you around."

"Wait!" She turned to find him still on her heels. "Why do you keep running away from me?" He ran a hand through his shaggy mop of hair. Maybe shaggy wasn't the right word anymore. Or mop. Now it had a style to it, along with the perfect amount of scruff. "Why can't we have a normal conversation?"

"A normal conversation would have been nice. Maybe about fifteen years ago, that would have been good timing." She rubbed at the space between her eyebrows, where she felt tension gathering. "Now I'm not sure what the point would be."

"Zoe. Come on." She watched him swallow hard, the Adam's apple moving in his throat. "Things were so insane then. My family was falling apart. My mother was hysterical. My father was fucking furious. Mom begged me to keep my distance from you while they worked things out. I—I couldn't go against her. I tried to call you the night we left, but something was wrong with your phone."

Watching him speak his piece, she knew every word he said was true. Her parents had commanded her to do the same thing.

"My mother threw that phone into the garbage disposal," she admitted. "She was convinced Dad had used it for his 'dirty deeds.' It was a mess. Ruined our garbage disposal."

He gave a snort of laughter. "That doesn't surprise me. My parents went into a kind of cold war. I kept waiting for someone to tell me it was okay to say the word 'Bellini' again but no one ever did. We also had to avoid pizza."

"*Pizza?*" Zoe felt an oddly personal surge of outrage about that. "Pizza was entirely innocent in the situation. So were we, by the way."

"I know. I know. But you know grownups. Can't live with 'em—"

"Can't live without 'em." She finished the phrase with a smile. They used to say that in high school. "And now we're the grownups."

"And we're not acting like it. We're acting like them and not communicating. We were always really good at talking to each other, even when everything was shit."

"I know, I know. We were. Okay." She checked her watch. "I have to get to work, but we'll get together soon."

"When soon? I need specifics."

"Can't your people call my people and work something out?" she teased. It was so strange—even though they were completely different people now, that old sense of ease in his company was slowly coming back.

He lifted an eyebrow at her. "I can make this difficult if you want. I can keep ordering pizza until your delivery twins get fed up."

She laughed at the phrase *delivery twins*. "That will never happen. You tip them too well. I'm thinking I should confiscate those tips because I'm sure they're doing nothing good with them."

"Come on. Let's make a plan. I know—pizza. My place. Tonight."

A weird combination of panic and joy threaded through her at the thought of being in the same space with him, alone. "No, I'm working tonight. How about a jog first thing tomorrow? We can take the bike trail from Seafarer's Beach."

"So...you like to jog? That's...recommended?"

"Yup, doctor's orders," she said wryly. "They seem to worry about my pizza to white blood cell ratio."

She was simply making a joke about the hazards of being around so much pizza, but he reacted with surprising seriousness.

"What exactly did the doctor say?"

"What?" She frowned at him in confusion. "Which doctor?"

"So you have more than one?"

"I...what?" She checked her watch and realized she was late. "I gotta go." She gestured toward her Subaru, then headed toward it. "See you at Seafarer's parking lot tomorrow at eight."

As she zoomed out of the lot, she caught him staring after her with a puzzled expression. What on earth was up with him? Was it a rock star thing? Had the jet-setting lifestyle cost him a few brain cells?

Or maybe they simply didn't know how to communicate with each other anymore. They kept talking past one another, as if they were speaking different languages.

Ah-ha! That was it. He spoke "man language," which wasn't her specialty. If she understood "man," she wouldn't have such a disastrous romantic history.

Note to self: avoid that topic during tomorrow's jog.

CHAPTER FIVE

Padric got to the Seafarer's Beach parking lot half an hour before eight. He hadn't slept well—too much frigging pizza. He'd ordered one last night with the hope that either Zoe or one of her sisters would deliver it, but a different kid had knocked on his door instead.

The teenager had introduced himself as Joseph Kenai, and he'd issued an invitation along with the pizza. Or maybe more like a plea.

"I'm working with Monica and Alexis Bellini on the first ever Last Chance to Rock Music Festival later this summer—we're going to set up tents on Seafarer's Beach, we got a permit and everything—and when I heard you were here, I had to try and see if you might want to come."

"Sure, if I'm still here, I'll come." He'd handed over his usual forty bucks for the pizza.

"No, I mean...sing. Perform. It's a charity event," Joseph had added quickly. "For the Mariner's Fund. I mean, after we pay back all the expenses, then we give the rest away. It's just for fun.

It'd be so incredibly awesome if you wanted to sing, like, just even one song."

Padric had to laugh at the kid's chutzpah. "I'm supposed to be resting my voice. It's a thing called nodes."

"I know. I saw it on your Instagram. But you could sing *softly*. One of the low-key songs."

"I'll, uh, think about it. But chances are I'll be gone by then, so don't count on me."

The boy's face had fallen. He'd looked to be partly native Alaskan, with shoulder-length black hair, a death metal t-shirt and unlaced sneakers. "Thanks anyway."

Shoulders slumping, he'd let himself out of the suite.

Padric had felt like the ultimate asshole. The typical hotshot rock star refusing to perform if he didn't get paid his usual fee. He'd almost called the kid back, but he really was supposed to rest his voice, after all.

And he'd have no chance of anonymity if he performed on the beach.

And he probably wouldn't be here by then anyway, the way things were going with Zoe.

So now that he was here on a crisp morning at the water's edge, amid the lush midsummer growth of pushki and wild rose and cranesbill, he knew he needed a different approach with Zoe. He needed to corner her. Pin her down.

But when she parked her Subaru and climbed out in her curve-hugging track suit, hair in a braid down her back, deep smudges under her eyes, he forgot his entire plan.

"Zoe. Are you okay?" He strode to her side. "You look exhausted."

"Thanks. Always great to hear first thing in the morning." She propped one foot on the low railing that enclosed the parking lot. As she stretched her hamstring, she added, "You look fresh as a daisy. Those sheets at the Eagle's Nest must be topnotch."

"Stop trying to change the subject. Just be straight with me, Zoe. What's wrong with you?"

With her torso bent over her leg, she glanced over her shoulder at him. "Wrong with me? Jeez, that's two insults in less than a minute."

"I'm not trying to insult you. Why won't you talk to me?" His urgency rang in the morning air, startling a small flock of sparrows pecking at the gravel.

"Look, Padric, I get it. I've been a little distant. That's understandable, don't you think, considering the circumstances?"

"I get that it's very personal. But you used to trust me."

"I wish I still could." Her wistful tone made him want to tear his hair out.

"You can! I'm here to help in whatever way I can. Money, support, whatever you need. You just have to be honest with me."

"Excuse me?" Looking highly offended, she switched to the other leg. "Why would I need your money? You've seen the Last Chance. We're almost *too* busy. I'm really starting to regret the delivery option. Especially the last few days."

Maybe Zoe was in deep, deep denial. That would explain how casually she was treating the situation. "I'm sure the pizza shop is doing just fine, but big bills like this are different. You deserve the best, even if you can't afford it. That's where I come in."

"Wow, you are really arrogant. And really, really confusing. What big bill am I delinquent on? The house is paid off. My Subaru was a steal on Craigslist. I skipped college, so there's that. Maybe my tab at Misty Bay Art Supplies is getting out of hand?"

"Zoe!" He had to just come out with it. "Are you sick?"

She pulled her foot off the railing and planted it on the ground. Crossing her arms across her chest, she demanded, "Do I look sick?"

"Right now you look a little tired, and—"

"I was up late getting my application together. Also, I think I'm developing a cheese allergy, which is very awkward for a pizza maker."

"So...you're not ill?"

She finally picked up on his seriousness, and her ironic smile dropped. "Not that I know of. But I haven't seen a doctor in at least ten years, so I suppose I can't say for sure."

"You haven't been diagnosed with anything in the past couple of years?"

She flipped her braid over her shoulder. "I feel like these are weird and inappropriate questions, like where's my HPAA form? I didn't waive anything."

He was entirely out of patience. "Can you just answer the question? For me, your old best friend Padric?"

Slowly, shaking her head, she said, "I have not been diagnosed with anything other than a bruised elbow when I slammed it into the oven and multiple minor burns, also from the oven. All my medical issues are caused by that damn brick oven. What's this all about, Padric?"

He stared at her, his mind whirring. The letter from the twins. How strangely they'd been acting toward him. Zoe's perfect health. Monica urging him to avoid Zoe. The request from the kid last night—

The *music festival*.

Holy shit. He'd been played.

The laugh welled up from the deepest part of his soul, rose through his chest and burst out of his throat. He tilted his head back and laughed longer and louder than he had in many, many years. Maybe since the Scandal. Tears leaked from the corners of his eyes and ran down his face.

Zoe stared at him with a look of complete mystification. "Is my pizza oven that funny? Those burns actually hurt. I still have scars." She showed him the back of one hand.

He lifted it to his mouth and pressed a kiss to her skin. "You're not sick," he managed.

"Nope."

"And I got suckered."

"They do say the music world is ruthless—" she began, all sympathetic.

"By your sisters," he interrupted.

"Excuse me?"

"That's why I came back. They wrote me a letter saying that you were having a hard time with your diagnosis and that I should come support you. But you don't *have* a diagnosis."

She shook her head, folding her lips, mirth rising in her eyes.

"And they have a music festival they're planning."

She nodded. A flush swept across her face. "Oh my God. So you..."

"Got fooled by a couple of sixteen-year-olds. Yes."

And then they both burst into laughter and kept on going—endless waves of merriment rolling over them like a full moon tide.

Just like the old days.

IT TOOK Zoe a while to recover from the first laughing fit she'd had in years. Once she did, she wasn't so much entertained as furious.

"Those two are a menace to civilization." She busied herself tucking strands of hair back into her braid. "I feel like I should go drag them out of bed and smack their asses."

"Really? You can do that?"

"No. It's two against one. And I can't tell Mama because I don't want her to know you're here. Nothing personal."

His face shuttered, just a bit.

"Come on, let's jog while we figure this out. I want to know everything. Also, just so you know, when I say 'jog,' this is the pace I'm referring to." She set off down the trail at something between an amble and a saunter.

Padric easily kept pace. In fact, his biggest challenge would probably be slowing down enough to stay at her side.

"I'm pretty sure most people would call this more of a 'stroll,'" he teased.

"Mock me if you want. I'm at peace with my non-athletic nature. Besides, this way we can talk about my rascally twin sisters. What exactly did they say in this letter?"

He fumbled in the pocket of his hoodie and pulled out a piece of stationery paper. "I brought it in case you denied everything."

She took it and turned it over. The letterhead read "Misty Bay Regional Hospital."

"Sweet Lord, they went all out. Isn't this mail fraud or something?"

He laughed. She liked the confident way his body moved with each long stride. She found it wildly sexy. "It's just stationery, but it did add a little something to the whole effect."

She paused on the trail as she scanned the letter. The scent of alders and mudflats rose around her. The cheerful morning chirp of birds rustling in the alders added a soundtrack as she read the letter out loud.

"Dear Padric Jeffers,

"You might not remember us because we were just babies when you left Lost Harbor. Our names are Monica and Alexis Bellini, and we're writing to you because we know that you were good friends with our older sister, Zoe. We thought you should know that Zoe is struggling with some very serious issues and could use the support of an old friend. We don't want to reveal too

much due to family confidentiality. She doesn't know that we're writing to you.

"Damn right I didn't know, or they wouldn't have survived to put the stamp on."

"Keep reading," he said, with a grim chuckle. "I'm analyzing every word as you go."

"Our mother doesn't know we're writing to you either, and she would freak out if she did. So that's proof that this is really important. We know that Zoe will be really happy to see you. She's had terrible luck the past few years and she doesn't deserve it because she's a really good person. We all depend on her. Hoping to see you soon, Monica and Alexis Bellini

"Wow. I have no words." Zoe jabbed a finger at the piece of paper. "Did you notice how they never actually said I was sick? You jumped to that conclusion because of the letterhead."

"Exactly. And then they pulled the patient confidentiality card. Except they called it 'family confidentiality' and I just interpreted it as 'patient.'"

"That's just...diabolical. Seriously, I'm worried for them. Are they going to grow up to be criminal masterminds?"

She gave him back the letter and resumed her jogging—which was only a few degrees faster than standing still.

"What about the terrible luck part? Is that true?"

"Sure. That's more or less true. I don't think anything in that letter is a lie, really."

He waved the letter at her. "What about the line about you being happy to see me? That might have been a lie."

Actually, her sisters had been right about that, too. She looked over at him, at those dreamy blue eyes and rueful smile. "I wasn't happy at first, but I'm getting used to it. You've been excellent for business."

"I don't think you need any help in that area."

"You're right. The Last Chance is booming."

"And you're in perfect health."

"Perfect," she agreed. "I almost never get sick. Literally, I've missed maybe five days of work since I was thirteen. I think it's all the olive oil I consume. Health tip from my mother's side."

"Then what's the terrible luck part?"

And there it was, the one topic she wanted to avoid. Zoe shook her head as she brushed past an unruly alder branch. "Oh, no no no. We aren't done figuring this thing out about my sisters yet. So you think they did all this because of the festival?"

"That's my theory that I just came up with. Last night, one of your delivery boys asked if I'd sing at this festival. Your sisters never mentioned it to me, but they seem to be in charge."

"It's their baby, for sure." She waved away a mosquito. One consequence of her slow jogging pace is that insects had no trouble keeping up. "Of course. It all makes so much sense now! It's their obsession at the moment. They've gotten a few local bands to commit, but it's a small-town, low-profile thing. No A-list musician wants to be part of a first-time event put on by a couple of teenagers. Why on earth would they think you would be interested?"

He shot her a meaningful look that made her flush slightly. Was he implying *she* was the reason he would be interested?

"Okay, our former friendship, sure. But they had to basically lie...okay, I can see what they were thinking. Get you back here on false pretenses. Then you'd reconnect with your hometown and want to give back in the form of headlining their little project. Wow."

"Never underestimate the determination of a teenager," he said with a slight smile. "Remember how hard we fought to get permission for that lake house party?"

"I never got permission," she pointed out. "I snuck out."

"And there you go. This letter is the equivalent of sneaking out. You gotta give them credit for creativity."

"Oh, they're creative, all right." She felt like gnashing her teeth and brandishing her fist in the air like one of her Greek firebrand ancestors. "Ask them about their Moose Turd pizza. That doesn't make any of this okay. The worst part is, I can't figure out how to punish them for this without involving my mother. I'm just the big sister here. I'm not in charge of them."

He jogged in place, giving time for her to catch up. "Do they really need to be punished?"

"Of course they do! They manipulated a busy, world-famous singer into coming to Alaska. I'm sure you had better things to do than camp out at the Eagle's Nest and eat pizza."

"Hey, that's not all I'm doing." He looked wounded. "I'm working with the volunteer fire department. I'm helping the local economy. I'm *jogging*."

She made a face at him. "I believe the proper term is 'strolling.' Anyway, that's not the point. The point is, you could be anywhere in the world right now, and thanks to my naughty sisters, you're here."

"Is that such a bad thing?" He glanced over at her with a funny expression on his face—a mix of vulnerability and humor. Padric had always been the kindest person she knew, bar none. Her family members were generous, fiery, quarrelsome and full of pride. Padric used to be her refuge from all the Bellini drama. She'd go over to his house and they'd hang out, watch silly '90s comedies and play cards and talk about whatever came into their heads.

"No, it's not," she said softly. "I'm glad to see you."

His expression lightened. "You weren't at first."

"I was...hurt. We never even said goodbye. You were just... gone. And everything was so awful after your family left. Everyone whispered about us at school. My parents had terrible fights every night. I had nowhere to go because you were gone. Once, I snuck though the window of your house and just curled up in your old bedroom, even though all the furniture was gone. But at least it was quiet and no one was yelling at each other."

He stopped jogging and snagged her arm to bring her to a halt as well. "I'm sorry, Zoe. I'm really sorry."

She waved him off. "It wasn't your doing. I know that."

"Even so, I never thought about your end of things. You were stuck here dealing with the fallout. I got to move to Florida and start clean, like nothing ever happened. That's not exactly fair."

"Fair?" She snorted. "Since when does fairness come into it? It isn't ever fair that kids pay when adults screw up. Our friendship...well, we had a good run, I guess." She tried a cheeky smile. "Nothing says childhood friendships are supposed to last forever."

He touched her on the arm, a light, tentative caress that she didn't resist. He ran his hand down her arm and took her hand in his. It felt warm and familiar, and yet somehow wildly new and exciting at the same time. "It wasn't just a friendship, Zoe. It was a lot more than that."

Those words, in his deep voice, sent chills up and down her spine.

"One kiss." She shrugged.

"It wasn't just a kiss."

She ran her tongue along her lips, in a kind of sensory flashback. She remembered exactly how his mouth had felt against hers. The taste of honey and baklava and forest air and chapped lips came rushing back.

His eyes dropped to her lips and his pupils darkened.

A shot of wild energy swept through her, as if someone had just administered a dose of adrenaline. *She and Padric still had that core of attraction between them.* Holy shit. As if nothing had changed in the past fifteen years.

And if that was the case...a few other things made sense, too. Like her fiasco of a love life.

Shoving all those thoughts aside, she stepped back. "You're right. It wasn't just a kiss. It was two kids with no idea what was about to hit them. Not exactly a happy memory."

He narrowed his eyes at her, as if assessing how much she meant those words. Since she had the kind of face that revealed everything—she blamed her eyebrows—she quickly changed the subject.

"Back to the twins." She launched into a "fast walk," which was all she could handle at this point. "I'm going to withdraw our sponsorship of their festival."

"But isn't it called the Last Chance to Rock? I've seen the flyers."

"They ought to call it Last Chance to Live," she muttered, which made him smile. "I suppose they can keep the name, but that doesn't mean I have to support it. I'll withdraw our donation. I can't support something that causes them to act like teenage criminals."

"I get it. I do. But look, as a musician, I'm all in favor of music festivals. I hate to see their project suffer because your sisters messed up."

Why wasn't he more upset? He was the victim of their evil plan. Although "evil" might be overstating it a bit. Or maybe she'd think so after she calmed down. "Aren't you angry?"

"No. I'm not, actually. I'm glad to be here, and it's entirely thanks to them that I am. But I'm not in charge of their upbringing, so I get why you want to punish them."

"They need to understand what they did and why it's wrong."

"Absolutely. The worst part, for me, was that I was really worried about you. That's on them. They need to own that. So—I have another idea."

"What?"

"What if we turn the tables on them?"

She frowned over at him. The gleam in his eye told her he was concocting one of his especially fun schemes. "Explain, please."

"Well, due to patient and family confidentiality, do they actually *know* whether or not you have a medical issue?"

"Our family tends to know every little thing about each other."

"Not every little thing." He tapped the letter, which he'd put back into his pocket. "Obviously."

"You have a good point there." She tilted her head at him. "Okay. I'm listening."

CHAPTER SIX

It wasn't hard to find the twins. Padric tracked them down at Dark Brew, the coffee shop where the teenage crowd liked to hang out. Together with Joseph Kenai, the kid who'd invited him to sing, they huddled over a single laptop. Papers covered with sketches of logo designs littered the table.

He composed his face into the most serious expression he could manage. "Monica, Alexis, can I have a word?"

They both jumped to attention as if he'd used a cattle prod on them. "I better go anyway," said Joseph. Judging by his guilty expression, he was in on it, too.

"You can stay if you like. It's about the festival you invited me to."

"Oh. Nah, I'm good. They're in charge anyway. See ya!" He snagged his hoodie—with the Lost Harbor High sea monster logo —and hurried away. Did he mutter "wouldn't want to be ya" as he left? There was a good chance.

Padric pulled out a chair and spun it backwards. He sat down and rested his arms on the back. The girls watched him, wide-eyed, two slightly different variations on the theme of dark eyes and curly brown hair.

"I'm not sure you know this, but your friend Joseph invited me to sing at your festival."

They glanced at each other, torn between wariness and hope.

"I really wish I could," he said mournfully. "But with this news about Zoe, I just don't have the heart for it. Just between you and me," he lowered his voice, "I may need to take some time off. Please don't say anything to anyone, on social media or anywhere."

"Oh. Okay. We definitely won't. We wouldn't do that. But..." Monica chewed on her thumbnail, as if pondering the right thing to say.

Alexis stepped in. "Does, um, Zoe know about this?"

"No, I don't want to upset her while she's going through such a terrible time. Clearly she doesn't want to talk about it. Every time I try, she changes the subject."

Monica gave him a weak smile. "Well, that's Zoe for you. Work work work."

"Exactly. She really needs to get more rest. That's actually why I wanted to talk to you two. I've been watching her. I've seen how hard she works, even though she's ill, and I think it would be great if you two could give her a break at the pizza shop. You should take over completely, maybe for the rest of the summer."

"The rest of the summer?" The girls exchanged glances filled with panic. "But...um...we have so much to do still for the festival."

"The festival. Right. See, that's why it's a good thing you contacted me. You guys are so busy with the festival that you can't give Zoe all the care she needs. That's where I come in."

"You do?" Alexis was watching him like a deer in the headlights.

"Yes. I've decided I'm going to focus all my energy on Zoe's recovery. I'd like to take her somewhere warm, maybe the tropics, Hawaii or even Bali, perhaps. I'll rent a villa and hire some servants and treat her like a princess. What do you guys think about that plan?"

Monica was starting to look a little pale. "You're going to take Zoe away from Lost Harbor?"

"Just until she's healed. It would help if she'd tell me what's wrong, but she's being very private about that."

Alexis gulped and bit her lip. Ah-ha. She was the less nervy of the two. Monica was the instigator, as Zoe had guessed. "Yes, but—"

Monica elbowed her in the side and she yelped.

"But what?"

Alexis shot Monica a pleading glance, and the bolder twin stepped in to answer. "Everyone knows music is healing," Monica said. "This festival could be just what Zoe needs. Maybe you should both stay here."

He had to give her props for quick thinking on the fly.

"Interesting thought. Maybe we should consult with the doctors."

"No!" Monica's eyes darted this way and that. "Does Zoe know about your plan?"

"Not yet. That's why I'm here, to make sure you two can cover for her."

A spark of hope lit up Alexis' face. "Zoe would never go for that idea. She loves it here. She never goes anywhere. That's the reason at least two of her engagements ended, because she didn't want to leave."

Two engagements? Two of her engagements, meaning there were more?

This was big news. He'd have to get to the bottom of this bombshell. Some other time.

"I was worried about that, too." He pulled out the letter

they'd sent him and set it on the table where they could see it. "I have an appointment with the head of the hospital. I'm going to offer up a substantial donation in exchange for their help in convincing Zoe. Without breaking confidentiality, of course."

Alexis wrung her hands together, every line of her body screaming tension.

Padric almost felt bad for her—actually, he did feel bad for her—until he remembered the terror he'd experienced when he'd first read that letter. He steeled himself to continue the act.

Monica, proving her status as leader of the mischief, knocked over a glass of water, completely drenching the letter and nearly hitting the laptop. "Oh no!" She leaped to her feet and tried to clean up the mess. Of course, in the process, she managed to destroy the sodden remains of the letter.

"I'm so sorry. I hope you didn't need that."

Padric had to hand it to her. Without the letter, he didn't have much proof of their misdeeds. Luckily....

"I did, actually. Which is why I took a photo of it when it first arrived." He flashed his phone at them, then tucked it into his pocket. Of course he hadn't taken a photo of it. Why would he do that? "Anyway, what do you think about my idea? I'd like to call Zoe right away. Oh wait, here she is."

Right on cue, Zoe ambled into the Dark Brew in her usual relaxed way. She looked healthy as a horse.

"She's amazing, the way she puts on such a good front," he whispered to the girls. "You'd never know she was suffering at all."

Monica and Alexis were now too nervous to even laugh. They were watching Zoe close in as if she were a snake charmer they couldn't look away from.

"I'm so glad I caught you all together." She sat down and crossed one leg over the other. "I had a flash of genius this morning. You guys ready for this? I think that *Padric* should perform at the Last Chance to Rock festival."

The twins looked like their heads might explode.

"I know it sounds crazy, but hear me out. 'Hometown hero returns to his roots'—great headline, right? And obviously it would be great for our little festival. I know you're not here to work, Padric, but this would be a special occasion. What an incredible way to reintroduce yourself to the humble dot on the map where you were born. This festival would instantly become a worldwide sensation. Just imagine the possibilities!"

Wow, she was really piling it on. Monica's and Alexis' eyes were getting bigger with every word.

"What an amazing idea, Zoe. Why didn't we think of it?" Monica said innocently—the little scamp.

"I guess you've been preoccupied with mundane details like tent rentals." Zoe waved her hand grandly. "Sometimes it takes a grownup to see the big picture."

Poor Monica had to literally bite her lip to keep from protesting—Padric could see the white dent in her lower lip.

"You're a genius," she said reluctantly. "So, um, Mr. Jeffers, maybe you should consider Zoe's great idea—"

"No, I'm sorry, but like I told your friend Joseph, I can't sing anything unless my mind is at ease." Pulling the diva performer card felt...weird, since it was so against his nature. He'd performed with a hundred-and-four-degree fever once. He'd performed on painkillers post-knee surgery. He'd never missed a show, not once—until he'd asked his manager to postpone the Scandinavian leg of his current tour. "Zoe, I need to know the truth, no matter how painful it is to share."

Zoe looked appropriately confused. "Painful?"

"I can find you the best specialist in the world. We'll fly him or her to Bali, along with a traveling massage therapist I know. I'll bring a chef, too, so you don't have to lift a finger to cook anything. Everything will be taken care of. You can rest and focus on your recovery."

"My recovery..."

"Maybe you've just been working too much."

"Right. I suppose it could be that." Zoe looked under her lashes at her sisters. "I have been working a lot, haven't I, girls?"

"We all have," said Monica quickly. "It's summer. Goes with the territory."

"Then it's settled!" Padric exclaimed, slapping a hand on the table. "Bali it is. I'll call my travel agent and make all the arrangements."

"But...Zoe's idea...the festival..." The girls spluttered words like pellets from a BB gun.

"I wish we could wait until the festival, and I would love to make an appearance, but I don't want to delay Zoe's healing a minute longer than necessary. Right, Zoe?"

"Right. Healing comes first."

"Let me call my assistant." Padric picked up his phone and scanned through his contacts. Did someone say "entourage"? He didn't actually want to call any of his actual "entourage," because doing so would cause an uproar. Instead, he landed on Nate's number. Nate would get it. He would go with the flow and know what to say.

"Padric Jeffers here," he said as soon as Nate answered. "I need two tickets to Bali, a villa, a personal chef willing to drop everything, like right away, same for a masseuse, and whatever other entourage-type people you can think of."

"Hmm...personal on-call therapist?"

"Good. Put that on the list."

"How about your own personal first responder, just in case?"

"Excellent. Good thinking. Got a list going? Great. I need you to do some research, too. I need the best specialist in the world on..." He glanced inquiringly at Zoe.

"Overworking," she said promptly.

"Overworking," he repeated to Nate.

"So, uh…I'm driving to a small brushfire at the moment. Are you almost done?"

"Almost. You got all that? Thanks, Cindy. You're the best."

"You need to introduce me to this Cindy."

Padric hung up and brushed his hands together. "Now for a statement to the press."

"Statement to the press?" Monica went even more pale. "What about?"

"Oh, my PR person will know how to spin it. 'Padric Jeffers drops out of music to care for a childhood friend.' Man, it's really too bad about the festival. They could have done a press statement about that, too. Oh well."

He shrugged and picked up his phone.

"Wait!" Monica jumped to her feet. "'Drops out of music'? *Seriously*? Who would ever say that?"

"Like I said, she'll spin it better."

"No way, you're making all of this up." She snatched the phone from his hand and looked at his most recent call. "You called Nate!"

Busted. Still, Padric struggled to maintain the act. "He's a good friend, Nate. He's kind of my entourage here in Lost Harbor."

Monica wheeled on Zoe, who wasn't doing as good a job at hanging on to her poker face. "You guys are teasing us. You're not going to Bali, are you?"

"I'm totally up for a trip to Bali," Zoe said with as much of a straight face as she could manage—which wasn't much. "I do work a lot and I could definitely use a break. At this rate, I really might get sick."

Monica shut her eyes and seemed to utter a small prayer. Then she turned to Padric. "You know everything, don't you?"

"Yup. Everything."

She drew in a deep breath. "Okay. Let us explain."

Zoe stood up and widened her arms in a "halt" gesture. "The least you can do is spare us the drama. If you wanted Padric to sing at your festival, why didn't you just ask him?"

"Yeah, right!" Monica cried. "He hasn't come back here in all those years, why would he do it for some dumb festival? He needed a better reason."

"A better reason, like me being at death's door?"

"We never said that," Alexis interjected. "We never told any lies in our letter."

"Right, if you think about it, we really just did him a favor by giving him a good excuse to come back."

"Monica, you are really pushing it," Zoe warned. "I'm starting to think I need to take this to Mama."

"You can't," Monica said triumphantly. "She'll flip out if she knows Padric is here."

"Then what was your plan if Padric *did* agree to sing at the festival?" Zoe had her hands on her hips, eyes full of fire.

Padric grinned to himself with a sense of homecoming. The sight of a furious Zoe took him back to the days when Zoe would fight with her parents and the whole family would get involved. Everyone would air out all their grievances—allowance too small, too many chores, the sharing of rooms—and then it would be over and they'd all sit down to one of Mrs. Bellini's amazing spanako-pita meals.

"There's no way Mama is going to come to a beach festival," Monica scoffed. "You know she doesn't like outdoor stuff. And she has the walker now. We already told her that we'll record the good parts for her. The parts with us introducing bands and so forth. She hates our kind of music anyway."

"So you've thought of everything, huh?" Zoe demanded.

"We tried." Alexis perched on the tabletop so she could be

eye to eye with Padric. "Padric, we're really sorry that we misled you."

"Lied," Zoe corrected.

"We never lied. But we did mislead and that's pretty much the same thing." She said that last bit under the eagle-eyed stare of Zoe. "It was wrong. We kind of knew it when we did it, but we hoped that you would forgive us because you'd be so happy to finally come home."

She batted her eyelashes at him innocently.

"Aren't you glad to be home?" Monica asked him.

Under the weight of their pleading gazes, Padric couldn't quite bring himself to stay stern.

"I *am* glad to be back. But I'm not glad that I had to worry so much. That was definitely not cool. Imagine if someone did that to you— told you that your twin sister was sick, for instance."

Shamefaced, they both muttered, "We're really sorry."

Zoe cut in. "No, no, it's a lot more than that. You two messed with Padric's life. You made him cancel his tour."

"Postpone, and I do have nodes—" Padric tried to interrupt, but Zoe waved him off.

"No. They were thinking only of themselves, not of the thousands of people who would be affected. All those fans who bought tickets, all the other musicians, the crew members, roadies or whatever they're called. You guys didn't think of any of that, did you?"

Monica hung her head, and Alexis teared up—two pictures of mortification. "We didn't," Monica finally said. "We were being selfish."

"I feel so bad now," Alexis cried. "I'm so, so sorry. I wish we could take it back."

"Me too," Monica whispered. "It was my idea, so I'm even more sorry."

Padric exchanged a glance with Zoe. Did the twins actually

get it? Their regret seemed genuine, which was good enough for him. But he wasn't their de facto parent.

Zoe held on to her stern, big-sister expression. "I gotta tell you guys, I'm very tempted to withdraw the pizza shop's support for the festival."

Both heads shot up in alarm.

"But Padric doesn't want me to. I guess he's a sucker for music festivals."

"Thank you, thank you!" Alexis threw her arms around him, nearly toppling herself off the table. He met Zoe's gaze over her shoulder and crinkled his forehead in a "what do we do now" expression.

"But now I have to figure out something else, because I can't let this stand, and I can't tell Mama. Any ideas?"

"We'll work extra shifts!"

"For free!"

"Okay, done. That's a start."

"We'll write 'don't lie to rock stars' a hundred times on the blackboard at the Last Chance," said Alexis.

"No, we'll put it on a t-shirt and wear it to work," Monica chimed in.

And they were off, riffing on ridiculous punishments.

"We'll write it on the beach in rocks."

"We'll walk around with a scarlet PJ on our foreheads, for Padric."

And just like that, Padric's good humor vanished. The dark reality of kids maiming themselves with his initials rushed back, as if from another lifetime.

How had he managed to forget that nastiness in the short time he'd been here in Lost Harbor?

"That will definitely not be necessary," he said stiffly. Everyone glanced at him with surprise at his sudden seriousness.

"You guys figure it out. I gotta get going. Training shift at the fire department."

He stepped away from the group and gave them an awkward little salute. The three Bellinis watched him with expressions ranging from mystified to worried.

"So...about Zoe's idea," Monica began, until Zoe shushed her with a furious expression.

Never underestimate the determination of a teenager.

Those words echoed as he pushed open the door of the coffee shop and emerged onto the main street of Lost Harbor. Those teenagers putting marks on their skin...these teenagers dead-set on their festival.

So what about the teenaged Padric Jeffers? Where had his determination gone back when the Scandal erupted? Why hadn't he done whatever he could to stay in touch with Zoe?

He hadn't. Instead, he'd tried to forget her.

Footfalls behind him made him turn around. Zoe was jogging —okay, quickly ambling—to catch up with him.

"Are you okay?" she asked. For the first time since he'd returned, she was looking at him with concern instead of wariness. "What just happened?"

He looked at her, so lushly gorgeous with all that dark tumbling hair and those striking eyebrows and that full mouth, and understood why he'd never quite been able to manage the "forgetting" part.

"I fucked up," he said abruptly. "Back then, after we moved. You *should* be angry at me."

CHAPTER SEVEN

Startled, Zoe nearly tripped over an invisible crack in the sidewalk. Padric grabbed her arm to keep her from falling, but she waved him off. "Go on."

He ran his hand through his hair. "You were really important to me."

Past tense, noted. Her stomach dropped.

"You were important to me, too." She kept her tone as even and neutral as she could. "What's your point?"

"When we left...I was a mess. Dealing with my parents, the move, a new school. I had to get a job to help out with money. It was a lot. I had to shut everything out else out. I channeled everything into my music, and I shut you out. I got your messages, and I didn't answer any of them. I'm sorry."

She drew in a long breath, feeling a painful echo of that long-ago hurt. Had she really been so easy to forget?

"Things change. I get it." She aimed for a nonchalant shrug.

"No, don't let me off the hook. We were *best friends.*"

"Who kissed..."

"Once..."

"Right before all hell broke loose."

They looked at each other and laughed a little. Finishing each other's sentences, just as they used to.

"I was trying to survive," he said softly. "But I didn't forget about you. That's why I came. That's why the twins' crazy letter worked. Because I didn't forget."

How did he know that was exactly what she'd been thinking?

"I didn't forget you either." She heard the husky note of emotion in her voice and tried for something lighter. "It would be hard to do with all those headlines and tab—"

"Please don't mention tabloids."

They both laughed again. It felt so sweet to be on the same wavelength with someone again. She rarely felt that way with anyone. Somehow she and Padric always slipped into it so naturally.

It was unnerving. She needed to take a step back. Several steps. Back to teasing instead of confessing.

"Come on, I'll walk you to the fire station," she told him. "You probably don't remember where it is, you've been gone so long."

"It would be hard to miss it, since there're only about ten buildings in this town." They headed down the street toward the complex that held the police and fire departments.

"Oh, now you're mocking your own hometown? I guess that's what fame does to a person."

"Or maybe I've always been a jerk, did you ever consider that?"

"You are not a jerk. You never have been."

Padric had always been the sweetest guy she knew. He would never deliberately hurt her. Why hang on to a grudge—especially when he kept apologizing?

"Which is why I've decided to forgive you for ditching me back then."

"Really? Okay, cool. That was easy." He grinned at her. "All I had to do was wait fifteen years."

"And become a rock star. Once you get nominated for a Grammy, all grudges are forgiven."

"I knew it would all pay off someday." His smile broadened. "Damn, Zoe, it really feels good to be with you again. That's the killer…that I missed all that time being your friend. I could have used a friend."

They'd reached the fire station. The two garage doors stood open and a small group was assembling near the shining red fire engine. Zoe waved at Nate and a few other people she recognized. Lucas Holt was there—probably helping with the training, since he was an expert ocean rescue guy.

Darius Boone, the new fire chief, was shaking hands with the new volunteers. Zoe didn't know much about him, except that he came from Texas and all the single women in town were trying to find out everything they could.

"Could you still use a friend?" she asked Padric.

"I could," he said softly. A kind of sadness had settled over him. With his thumbs tucked in his pockets, he gazed down at her as if from a great distance. "Did you ever wonder…"

"What?"

"What would have happened if we hadn't gotten that call from your mother at that exact moment?"

Her breath caught. She hadn't ever allowed herself to think about that. "You mean, if we'd kept hiking?"

"And kissing. And if we'd gone back home and things had been normal."

She stood silent for a moment, digesting his words. Maybe it was thanks to her practical side, but she never had indulged that fantasy. She'd been too busy dealing with the wrenching battles that nearly tore the family apart.

"Did you?" she asked. "Did you wonder that?"

"I did. I wrote a song about it. It was one of my first hits."

"Padric! Get your ass over here," Nate yelled from inside the equipment bay.

Padric gave her one last lingering glance, then jogged off to join the others.

It took nearly the entire walk back to her car for Zoe to get her cool back. Padric *had* thought about her after he'd left. He'd even written a song about their relationship. She *did* matter to him.

All this time, she'd assumed he'd forgotten her because he ignored all her attempts to contact him. But that wasn't true—and it changed everything.

Now she had an urgent mission—figure out which song he was talking about!

BACK HOME, Zoe checked on her mother and found her snoozing in her recliner, her cat Athena purring on her lap. While it was technically true that Zoe still lived at home with her mother, the house actually belonged to Zoe. After Dad had died of a heart attack, Nicola Bellini had transferred the house and business to Zoe on the condition that Zoe take care of her as she got older.

Which Zoe would have done in any case, but putting it into a written contract eased her mother's mind. Her mother had a huge heart, but she worried a lot, especially about her family. Zoe was used to her mother's volatile nature and knew how to handle it. She basically let her say whatever she wanted, and then Zoe did what she thought was best.

It all worked out.

Even though Nicola Bellini was only in her early sixties, a lifetime of hard work and giving birth to six children had worn her out. She'd broken her hip a while back and never fully recovered. She still used a walker and refused to do any physical therapy or get any exercise. Without her husband to argue with, she'd lost much of her zest for life. Somehow arguing with her kids didn't give her the same charge.

Zoe wasn't the oldest child, but she was the oldest who had stayed. Her two older brothers were long gone—Homer had joined the Army, Theo had fallen in love with an Italian girl and moved to Italy. Her oldest sister Daphne lived in Las Vegas and claimed the desert climate had rendered her incapable of traveling back to Alaska. But really, she didn't want to risk the guilt trips their mother would inflict if she got a chance.

So Zoe and her rapscallion sisters were the last Bellinis left at home.

The bright side was that Zoe got to claim the best living space. Over the years her father had added more wings and additions to the house as the family grew. He'd converted the barn— once he abandoned his idea of raising farm animals—into an extra living space for the older kids.

Now, the barn was all Zoe's. Technically, the entire house was Zoe's, but the barn in particular gave her great joy.

Because it contained her studio.

She'd cleared out every speck of furniture and installed a long work table, extensive shelving, and tote bins that held her art tools. A small kiln took up one corner, and welding tools another. A stack of chairs leaned against one wall. She pulled those out for the art workshops for kids that she offered during the school year.

Once she was sure that her mother was fine, she closed herself into her safe haven and kicked off her shoes. She climbed the ladder to the loft, where she slept on a king-size mattress on the floor. A hexagonal window offered a sweet view of rolling hillsides, now covered with fuchsia fireweed blooms. From here, she could also survey her entire studio space. She often came up here to get a different perspective on her current project.

Or take a nap. Or both, sometimes. Since she had no aspirations to make her living with her artwork, she allowed herself to do things like nap or abandon a project if she wasn't enjoying it. This was for fun, right?

Only lately had she been wondering if she should send some of her art into the world and see what happened. Hence the Far North Arts Fellowship. Her application was allllmoooosst ready to go.

She found her laptop tangled up in the blanket she'd kicked off last night. Falling asleep to a Netflix show was more or less her routine in the summer. The pizza shop didn't leave room for much else.

Plugging in her earbuds just in case her mother decided to barge in, she searched on google for "Padric Jeffers' first hit." She'd deliberately avoided following his career and generally ignored his music. Petty, but necessary for her emotional balance.

She scanned through the list of his titles, focusing on the earliest. One possibility stood out: "Lost Chance."

Had he deliberately combined Lost Souls and the Last Chance, or was that a coincidence? Why had she never heard this song? She'd gotten her wish of a Padric-free life, but maybe she'd been missing out.

She clicked on the lyrics and read them quickly.

> A fork in the trail, one step to the edge
> Happened so quick, burned by a touch
> Don't know where we went, don't know why.
> Did I know we would break?
> Did I know you would cry?
> One chance, all we had. All we had, is goodbye.
> Nothing so cruel as a chance lost with you.

Tears came to her eyes as she read the song. Then, to torture herself further, she clicked on a YouTube video of Padric singing that song in a dark club. He sat on a stool under a single spotlight. Hunched over his guitar, he strummed the wistful melody that went with the lyrics.

The video was from ten years ago, so it must have been at the start of his career. That explained his casual clothes—a white t-shirt under a checkered overshirt that she actually recognized. He still had it, five years after leaving Lost Harbor! He still had the strong, tough physique that fishing had given him, but he looked like a young man rather than the quickly developing boy she'd known. His hands flew over the guitar strings with utter comfort and competence.

It was so sexy, watching him perform. She'd avoided his videos along with his music in general, so she'd had no idea how good he was.

But he was amazing. She never would have guessed from his performance that he'd always been on the shy side. He had so much quiet charisma that she couldn't take her eyes off him. And his voice!

As a kid, she'd heard him sing. He'd shared his first attempts at songwriting with her. But his voice had still been finding its true range. At twenty, in the video, he was fully in command of the rich resonance of his voice.

She sighed and closed the laptop. If she went down the rabbit hole of watching Padric Jeffers videos, she'd never get anything done today.

On impulse, she shot off a text to Padric. *Lost Chance?*

That's the one, he texted back after a moment. *Know it?*

No. I think I need remedial Padric Jeffers education.

Happy to oblige.

Happiness slid along her skin like honey. He was back. Her best friend was back.

YouTube is helpful that way.

Ugh, don't look there. Just listen to the songs. I'll make you a playlist.

Okay, I'll take a playlist.

How are the twins? We really had them going.

Wasn't that great? She cackled out loud, the sound bouncing off the low ceiling of her loft. *The best part is they actually volunteered for their own punishment of extra shifts.*

It's the least they could do.

Are you going to agree to sing at their festival?

Should I?

I'm staying out of it. You're on your own.

Heartless.

Impervious, she texted with a smile. If they'd been able to text back in the old days, they would have had so much fun. *I will say that I'd love to hear you live.*

That can be arranged.

No, no! I didn't mean that. I meant at the festival.

No private show?

She drew in a long breath. Was Padric *flirting* with her? How had they shifted from friendly gloating over their revenge on the twins to talking about a private show?

And how should she respond? She'd just gotten her friendship with Padric back. Should they really put it to the test with a flirtation?

Then again, it was just a text. *Don't get all crazy, Zoe.*

Has any woman ever turned down a private show from Padric Jeffers?

I feel like there's no right answer to that.

She laughed out loud in her cozy barn. Padric had always been able to make her laugh, no matter what drama was going on at home or at school.

Hey, we're friends again, right? You can tell me everything.

I'll tell you everything if you tell me everything.

HELL NO, she fired off right away.

She could imagine him laughing out loud wherever he was. Still at the firehouse? Or back at his hotel?

Where r u? She asked while she was thinking of it.

Boxers.

Was that a new bar in town that she hadn't heard about? She sent him a row of question marks.

Oh sorry, I thought you asked what I was wearing.

Haha. I guess I know what that private show is all about now. So we're on?

Man, that was fast. And now she had her answer. He was definitely flirting with her. But didn't he have any supermodel girlfriends waiting for him back in reality—aka the Lower 48? Maybe this was the right time to find out—via text—the coward's way.

No girlfriends to get upset about that? Or should I google you?

You haven't already googled me? I'm insulted.

She giggled at that. *Such a fragile ego for a superstar. Have you googled me?*

Should I?

Her smile dropped and she crawled across her bed for her laptop. Outside her window, evening was finally dimming the bright purple hills. Low clouds the shade of bruised plums were gathering on the horizon. The colors were so insanely vivid that she itched to memorialize them somehow. But she'd never had any luck painting the sunset—she never got the colors quite right. That was one of the reasons she'd switched to clay sculptures.

Tearing her eyes away from the sky, she opened her laptop and googled herself. Owner of Last Chance Pizza. Many TripAdvisor and Yelp reviews—mostly excellent. One angry complaint about the time Zoe had kicked a guy and his buddies out for harassing one of her waitresses. Her father's obituary had a mention of her. And then—oh cringe. Just what she didn't want to show up.

Local man sues over broken engagement.

Almost too afraid to read the whole thing, she squinted and forced herself to do so.

Reese Wirth, a Lost Harbor resident, filed an unusual lawsuit against Zoe Bellini for breaking their engagement. He's claiming emotional distress and the loss of other romantic opportunities during the time he was engaged to Ms. Bellini. According to the filing, she was never truly serious about the relationship and used it to extract goods and services from him in the form of dinner dates and other gifts. He's asking damages that amount to the sum of all his expenditures during their six-month engagement. Reached at his home next to Starling Lake, Reese said, "Women need to learn not to toy with men's futures."

Oh God, the mortification that she ever, for one second—let alone six months—was involved with that man! He was such a troglodyte, and he'd gotten so much worse after they'd broken up.

The reporter had called her for comment, but she'd refused. She didn't want to give the press any reason to pursue the nonstory. The case had gotten thrown out, but she'd had to hire a lawyer and the gossip around town had been *severe*.

She snatched up her phone and saw that Padric had texted again.

You just googled yourself, didn't you?

Maybe, she answered. Hopefully he wouldn't search past the initial page of Last Chance-related items. *I saved you the trouble. Nothing interesting there.*

Hmm.

Oh God. He knew! He'd probably googled her at the same time she was googling herself.

I can explain. It was a mistake. He seemed like a cool guy at first and my mom was pressuring me about settling down. So embarrassing.

Long pause. *I have no idea what you're talking about. What'd I miss?*

Nothing. I'm babbling. Ignore all that. DELETE.

Yeah, right. The word "delete" might as well mean "go back and read it again and try google while you're at it."

Also, no more googling!!!! An equally pointless thing to say.

How about I skip the googling and you tell me what you're talking about? In your own words?

Yes. That would be much better than letting him see Reese trash her without a response. *Good idea. Not by text, tho. Some other time.*

Holding you to it.

Da-dum-da-dum. (Theme song from Jaws.)

Don't worry. I just want to know what's happened in your life since I left. No judgy.

That used to be one of their phrases that they'd used as kids. For instance: "What grade did Ms. Fleck give you? No judgy." Or "That top looks weird on you. No judgy, but you should change."

It was a very versatile phrase, and she was glad to hear it again.

Holding you to that, she told him.

Had an idea. How about we go across the bay and go hiking? Say, the Larkspur trail? We never got to the high alpine. Perfect time of year for it.

Except for my work schedule.

Didn't you just get a bunch of free shifts out of your sisters? Better pounce while they're still feeling the guilt.

Good point. Based on her knowledge of the twins, their guilt had a half-life of a few hours. But it was worth a try, since they'd screwed up badly this time.

We'll see.

He sent her back a thumbs-up. *I have to check the training schedule too.*

How did it go today?

No judgy?

She smiled. *No judgy.*

Turns out I'm a spoiled diva who can barely handle a fifty-pound backpack. Where'd that fishing kid go?

He grew up and got an entourage.

Ouch. Okay I deserved that.

It was so good to have her friend back. Emphasis on *friend.* No more videos, she told herself. Her nerves couldn't handle it.

CHAPTER EIGHT

Padric dropped into another round of pushups at the command of the volunteer training leader, who happened to be Nate Prudhoe. His biceps were burning, not to mention his deltoids and his pecs, and his lats and really just every muscle in his entire torso.

"I thought you were supposed to be my entourage, not my personal torturer," he grumbled.

"That's personal trainer to you." Nate grinned and strolled through the motley group of volunteers. Two women and three men, ranging from eighteen to sixty-three. The youngest had just graduated from high school and the oldest volunteer was a retired longshoreman who was getting bored sitting at home.

Padric reached the end of the set of thirty pushups and sat back on his heels. When Nate made his way back toward him, he muttered, "This is about revenge for that time I kicked your ass wrestling, isn't it?"

"Yes, superstar, it's all about you." Nate didn't crack a smile. "I'm not at all interested in protecting Lost Harbor from a natural disaster."

"You know that's not what I meant. Fuck." Padric shook out his arms to get rid of a cramp starting in his forearm.

A blond woman next to him—she wore Carhartts and a ribbed tank top and would have caught his eye immediately, if he hadn't been so caught up with Zoe—finished her set. Sitting on her haunches, she shot him a curious glance. "You're the singer, right? The one who used to live here?"

"Yeah." Padric rubbed out the cramp in his arm. "And you are?"

"Carrie. Are you sure you should be working out like this? What if you hurt your hands?"

"Yeah, Padric, wouldn't want to hurt your moneymakers," Nate teased. "You're a delicate flower, man. Need some bubble-wrap?"

"Shut the fuck up. Not you," Padric quickly assured Carrie. "Just the commandant there."

"But I'm serious. I heard Katy Perry's legs are insured for two million dollars."

"Really?" Nate gestured for them to start another set. "I might amputate my own legs for that haul."

Padric and Carrie dropped down into another round of pushups.

"Do you know her?" Carrie asked. "Katy Perry, I mean. Or any of the big stars. Beyoncé, Madonna."

Padric realized that everyone in the grassy patch behind the firehouse was listening.

"I'm just a volunteer training like the rest of you," he said. "Here to haul hose and do whatever else Nate says."

"Nate says don't be an asshole and answer the question," said Nate.

Padric shot him a glare. "Yeah, I've met Katy Perry, and quite a few other big stars. But that's as far as it goes. They do their thing, I do my thing. I don't have any inside information. Anyone who reads *People* magazine knows as much as I do."

Carrie reeled off her pushups and sat up again. "I read that you dated Taylor Swift."

Not true. But he'd been requested to go along with that rumor, so he said only, "No comment."

"What about Toni Braxton? Did you date her? I read about that in *People*."

Damn it, this was worse than the red carpet at the Grammy's. At least there, his publicist shooed people out of the way when it got too much. "Can I just make a blanket 'no comment' about anything having to do with dating?"

"'No comment' means yes, right?" asked Nate, proving once again that he was useless as an entourage.

"Isn't there some important firefighting technique you're supposed to be teaching us?"

"Right. Of course." Nate clapped his hands for everyone's attention. The people still doing pushups collapsed gratefully onto the grass. "You guys," he pointed at them. "Pushups at home. It's important to build up your strength. Pushups, sit-ups, and cardio. Now. Let me clarify something for the group. This is Padric Jeffers. He's from Lost Harbor. He's not officially in training because he might not be here long enough to serve. But I saw that he was getting soft so I invited him to train along with us."

Padric gave the group a little salute. "Thanks for letting me work out with you."

Only Carrie seemed really excited about his presence. The others were more or less indifferent. Except, he noticed with a start, the sixty-three-year-old longshoreman, Willie, who wore a suspicious scowl.

Then again, that might be his normal expression, since he

was scowling the same way at Nate. A lifetime of squinting at the sunlit ocean could do that to a person.

Nate continued. "We really appreciate you all applying to volunteer. As you know, in order to go out in the field as a firefighter, you'll have to pass this course, which is a hundred-and-ten hours long. However, there are other ways to volunteer. Some might be more suitable for you, so listen close. We need people for all of these functions. Number one: office help. Always very important. Number two: maintaining and cleaning the equipment. Number three: dispatch and cleaning of the vehicles. We pride ourselves on how well we take care of our gear and rigs because our lives depend on them out in the field. Very important. We're isolated out here, as you all know, and we have to rely on ourselves. We do that by training until our ears bleed and by keeping our gear in tiptop shape. And by being studs."

Nate grinned and the others laughed along with him.

"That's kind of sexist, isn't it?" said Carrie.

"Point taken, but women can be studs too," he said promptly. "Have you met Officer Badger? I mean that as a compliment, in case you wondered. Maybe the word I should use is badass instead. You okay with 'badass,' Carrie?"

"I can live with that."

Padric laughed to himself. Nate had his own style, that was for sure. But it worked for him; everyone was paying close attention.

"And now the final way that you can help the Lost Harbor Fire Department. Fundraising."

For some reason, all eyes swung toward Padric. He narrowed his eyes at Nate, who winked at him.

Holy shit. He'd been played. Big time.

Nate continued innocently. "Now, we could do a bake sale. Those are always...okay, sometimes...occasionally...effective.

Maybe a car wash, that works for the high school kids. I don't know, does anyone else have any ideas?"

Padric sat on his butt and rested his elbows on his bent knees. This was going to be interesting. And by interesting, he meant excruciating.

"We do have the annual fire department auction coming up. Maybe certain people could offer a date with themselves," said Carrie, with a sidelong glance at Padric. "Especially the single men."

"Good idea," Nate said promptly. "I'd volunteer for that."

"Count me in," said Willie the longshoreman. "We got a lot of widows around here. I'll be a hot ticket."

"Yeah, you would be. Anyone else?"

Everyone looked at Padric, who dropped his head in his hands. He could just imagine the circus that would erupt if he put himself on the auction block as a date.

"I'll match whatever anyone bids on you guys," he said.

"Accepted."

Still, no one seemed satisfied by that offer. Padric felt the weight of their expectant stares. Would anyone really notice outside of Lost Harbor if he joined in on this crazy idea? Alaska was so far away to start with, and Lost Harbor perched at the end of a long road through mountain passes, at the very edge of Lost Souls Wilderness. It was rare that anyone in the outside world paid attention to Lost Harbor.

"How about this? I'll put up a serenade for auction."

"A serenade?" Nate cocked his head. "How would that work?"

"I'll sing a song to someone. Privately or publicly, however the bidder wants. It's not a date. It's not dinner or anything like that. I'll show up wherever they want, sing a song, and leave."

Carrie was nodding excitedly at that idea. "That way, a dad

could bid for a song for their kid, or a husband could bid for their wife."

"Exactly. It has a broader appeal than a date."

Also, he wouldn't have to risk winding up in the tabloids.

"Win your own personal serenade from the world-famous Padric Jeffers," mused Nate. "I like it. A lot. Thanks, Padric."

"Thank *you*, Nate, for offering me the opportunity to serve the community." Was that a little *too* sarcastic? Or not sarcastic enough?

"You're very welcome," Nate said smoothly, ignoring his sarcasm completely. "The auction is about two weeks from now, but there's still time to get your items listed. I'd like everyone to get creative and think of something to put up for auction. A boat ride, a dog-sled ride," he glanced at the other woman, who hadn't said much to this point.

Padric looked at her more closely and suddenly realized who she was. Alison Raines had competed in the famous Iditarod race several times, even came in second one year. In his opinion, her celebrity counted for much more than his.

Alison shook her head. "You're shameless, Nate."

"I'll take that as a yes. Now grab a pack, everyone, and see what fifty pounds of fire gear feels like on your back!"

For a hot moment, Padric wondered if he should just walk out. If Nate had wanted his help with fundraising, why hadn't he just said so? Instead of grabbing a pack, he stepped to the edge of the grass and grabbed his water bottle.

Nate appeared next to him, his commandant expression in place. "Slacking, superstar?"

"Not slacking. Just second-guessing. What am I really doing here, Nate?"

Nate switched from his training-leader voice to his old-friend voice. "Hey, don't be mad. I thought you might want something to do besides hang out in your hotel room eating pizza. The auction is extra."

"Really? That's not how it feels. It feels more like being used. I should know, I get that feeling a lot."

"Sorry, man." Nate looked more than sorry; he looked horrified as he scrubbed a hand through his hair. "Really, I am. I'm always looking for ways to promote the department and get funding. But that's not why I invited you to train with us. I thought you'd like it. You want to back out?"

"I didn't say I wanted to back out," Padric snapped. "I just don't like being manipulated. Just be straight. If you want something, say so."

If only Monica and Alexis were here for this lecture. It applied to them even more.

Nate nodded soberly. "I hear you. You probably get asked for stuff all the time."

"And that's fine. It goes with the territory. Just be straight about it, that's all I ask."

"Message received. Actually, there is something I want to ask."

"Seriously? There's more?"

"Yeah. How about a beer after we're done here? I told you we go after every training session. This one's on me, as an apology."

Padric relaxed. "Sure. Sounds good." He bent to pick up the heavy backpack. "I still think you just wanted a chance to boss me around."

"There's that, too."

CHAPTER NINE

The Olde Salt Saloon was one of the oldest structures on the boardwalk, an original fish house dating from early in the last century. An earthquake and subsequent shifts in the ground had given it an off-kilter slant, and its cedar shingles had been hammered by winter storms. By now the poor building looked as if it had been constructed by drunk carpenters.

Which, quite possibly, it had been.

Inside, the low ceiling sagged so much that taller customers had to duck. The walls were covered with old photos and newspaper clippings and posters from various events over the years. It was a historian's dream.

The lights were kept very low in the Olde Salt—no doubt because of what full illumination would reveal. Old ship lanterns swung from the ceiling, occasionally bonking people who forgot how low it was.

Many tales of drunken misdeeds at the Olde Salt had echoed through the decades. Padric's father had spent many an hour there drinking with Jack "Hammer" Holt and Old Crow and the other fishermen. One night, they'd all accepted a dare to swim through the harbor naked. Legend had it that Old Crow's balls had been blue ever since.

As a teenager, Padric had always looked forward to his first legal beer at the Olde Salt, but they'd moved away before he got a chance.

He and Nate peeled off from the rest of the volunteer fire-fighter group and settled onto stools at the bar—scarred dark wood with some kind of thick, ancient, discolored varnish. They both ordered drafts from the bartender, a pretty brunette. She spoke with a slight Hispanic accent as she repeated the order back to them.

"I thought the Olde Salt bartenders were always crusty old men."

"Times change. Toni's been bartending here for the past three years. She's a black belt, which comes in handy here."

"Black belt in what?"

"Kicking ass. That's all I know. She looks sweet, but she can pin a guy to the ground in half a second."

"Noted."

He eyed Toni warily as she brought over their beers. She didn't look like a fighter, but he'd take Nate's word for it.

"So. You and Zoe," Nate said, as soon as she left. "Picking up where you left off?"

"I don't know exactly what we're doing," he admitted. "But it feels good to be talking again. It's not like I've been thinking about her a lot the past few years, but she was always there in the back of my mind."

"Well, as your friend, and more importantly, as *her* friend, I think you should step carefully."

Padric bristled. "I don't need your advice, Nate. I can handle my own life."

"I'm not worried about you. This is about her. Zoe is…she's a very proud person, you know that."

"So?" That was certainly true.

"She's had the worst luck of anyone I know. It's almost like she's cursed. The last thing she needs is you coming along and piling on."

"Cursed? What are you talking about?"

Nate set down his beer and fixed Padric with a serious look. "First of all, this isn't gossip. It's history. I'm only telling you what everyone here already knows, and the only reason I'm doing it is so you understand what Zoe's been dealing with."

"Jesus, Nate, you're scaring me now."

"Dealing with" sounded like it could be medical. But that was off the table, right? Zoe had told him she was healthy as a horse.

"It's not like that," Nate said quickly. "She just has bad luck with men. First off, there was the Scandal, which obviously you know about. Then her dad died. You probably knew about that, too."

"Yes."

"A few months after that, she got engaged. But it ended in disaster. Her fiancé disappeared."

"What do you mean, disappeared?"

"He stole her car and drove to Canada. Sent her a postcard breaking it off."

Padric took a long swallow of his beer. Damn, that must have hurt. He hated thinking about Zoe pining over some guy who stole her car. "That's low."

"Yeah. Took her a few years to start dating again. Then she got together with a new guy in town, a reporter at the newspaper. He wanted to further his career in the Lower 48, but she didn't want to leave Lost Harbor. He broke off the engagement and spread all kinds of rumors about her in revenge. It was a rough time for her. Eventually, we all told the dude to knock it off and he moved away."

That was one great thing about Lost Harbor. When they

weren't feuding, people watched out for each other. The community usually came together in the face of outside threats.

"That's some pretty bad luck."

"That's not even the end of it. She got engaged *again,* but changed her mind almost right away. This time *she* broke it off, and the guy sued her. It was ugly. The town took sides, because he's a well-known mechanic, and you know how hard it is to hold on to decent mechanics here. Eventually the suit got tossed out of court but poor Zoe was traumatized. I brought her here one night for a break and she had a mini meltdown. Told me she was through with men, that every single one had let her down. She didn't mention you by name, but I'm pretty sure you're on that list."

"Fuck. I bet you're right. I'm probably at the top of the list. The first one to screw her over."

"I wouldn't go that far. You were a kid, too. But she definitely changed after all that went down. She kept to herself in school, she didn't hang out. It didn't help that the whole town was buzzing about the affair, and how suddenly your family left."

Poor Zoe. What that must have been like for her...Padric could hardly imagine. In those days, she was still awkward, still getting a grip on her curves and her striking features. To be constantly the subject of gossip...well, he actually understood how that felt, now that he was in the public eye. It sucked. And Zoe didn't have fame and fortune to make up for the suckiness.

"Thanks for telling me all this, Nate."

"Yeah? I wasn't sure if I should."

"No, it's helpful. Seriously. This is the kind of thing I would have known about if we hadn't left. Or if I hadn't dropped the ball on keeping in touch."

"*We* kept in touch," Nate pointed out.

"That's different. That's because you stalked me once I made it big."

"True that." Nate clicked his glass against Padric's. "And see? It paid off. Now I'm hanging out with a superstar at the Olde Salt. Buying *him* a beer. Something's wrong with this picture."

"Right? I'll have another, since you're buying and all."

THREE BEERS LATER, Padric practically stumbled onto the boardwalk. Nate was still inside playing darts with Darius Boone, the fire chief. Nate claimed he had to suck up to his new boss, but really he just loved to play. The hour was late, although plenty of light still lingered in the sky. The sun had dipped below the clouds and a chill rode in on the wind coming off the ocean.

The boardwalk had cleared of tourists; everyone was snuggled in their B&Bs, their VRBOs or their AirBnBs. Only a few locals were left—the "harbor rats" who made everything run.

Something flew through the air at him. He sidestepped it just in time, and it shattered against the railing of the boardwalk.

A beer bottle, judging by the yeasty smell of it. It had almost hit him instead of the railing.

He swung around, looking for whoever threw it. "Hey!" he called. "You could hurt someone like that."

Peering into the deepening shadows near the Olde Salt, he thought he saw a stocky shadow. "Someone there?"

But he must have imagined it, because nothing moved. After a moment, he shrugged and turned back around. Damn, he was wobbly on his feet. He ought to get back to the hotel before he passed out on the boardwalk. Not that he would be the first to do so.

Instead, he peered south, toward the Last Chance. The pizza shop was closed, of course, but one light was still on. Someone must be cleaning up.

Zoe?

Instead of heading for the Eagle's Nest, he lurched the opposite direction, toward the Last Chance. He might be shitfaced, but he hadn't forgotten the stories Nate had told him about Zoe's doomed love life. He'd put something together in his head about that. He had to tell her, and what better moment than while he was plastered?

He crossed the road and loped down the empty boardwalk on the other side. The ocean to his left slumbered like a gray beast, heaving occasionally as a swell came through. The stench of a rotting sea creature—a washed-up jellyfish, maybe—made his nostrils twitch. Overhead, an enormous lone eagle perched on a lamppost and peered down at him over his sharply curved beak.

Eagles didn't generally fly at night; maybe this one was looking for one last snack before dark. Something in its posture and bearing made him think he was quite old.

Crazy thought—had this eagle been around when Padric and Zoe were growing up? Eagles could live a long time, he knew. Twenty to thirty years.

"Yo, eagle!" he said to the bird drunkenly. "Didn't we used to know each other back in the day? Good to see you again, old friend."

The bird cocked his head, then returned its attention to the ocean.

"So that's how it is. Don't you know I'm a superstar now?" Padric rolled his eyes at his own drunken boasting. "For what that's worth."

A bit of liquid dropped from the bird and landed a few feet ahead of him. Great. An eagle just tried to poop on him.

"I get the message. You did that on purpose, didn't you?"

The eagle studiously ignored him—either that, or he was tracking a source of food that Padric couldn't see.

"I'm going to put you in a song, just you wait and see. And it won't be one of the patriotic ones."

The eagle unfurled its wings and lifted off from the lamppost in a powerful swoop that sent a cloud of dust Padric's way.

"Damn. I think that eagle got the last word."

"Are you arguing with the wildlife?" The sound of Zoe's voice made him jump about a foot in the air.

While he'd been occupied with the eagle, he'd reached the rear entry of the Last Chance. They kept an outdoor refrigeration unit back there, next to an enclosure to store their garbage bags until someone could make it to the dump.

Zoe carried one garbage bag in each hand. A red kerchief held her hair away from her face, and an apron covered her curvy figure. A smudge of flour marked her cheek as her dark eyes sparkled with amusement.

"Someone has to," said Padric. He cocked his head, assessing his statement for accuracy. "I don't know what that means."

"Are you coming from the Olde Salt?" She waved her hand on front of her nose. "I can smell the decades-old beer."

"You're taking out garbage," he pointed out.

"I'd recognize Eau de Olde Salt with my eyes closed." With a practiced motion, she heaved a garbage bag over the white slats of the enclosure. "Did you have fun?"

"Fun" didn't seem to be exactly the right word. "I heard some stuff. About you."

Her face changed, the amusement fading. "Oh." She started to lift the other bag over the side, but he hurried to stop her.

"Let me. It ain't a fifty-pound backpack, if you know what I mean."

"I really don't, but sure. Go ahead." She stepped back and folded her arms across her chest as he flung the bag into the enclosure. "How drunk are you, anyway?"

"Drunk enough to tell you something. About you."

Impatiently, she turned away from him. "You already apologized. There's no need for anything more."

"No, not that. You think everyone rejects you, don't you?"

"What?"

"All your bad luck. Your breakups. The lawsuit."

He noticed that every word made her wince.

A gust of wind tumbled through the narrow gap between the pizza shop and the fish cleaning station. It blew her hair over her shoulders and made her shiver. She was scowling at him. "I'm freezing out here, and you're listing all my most embarrassing moments. What is your point?"

"You doubt yourself. And it all started with me. Am I right?"

She blew out a breath, as if trying to hang on to her composure. "I don't know. Maybe. I was easy to forget, so there's that."

"No, you have it all wrong. All wrong. You know how I reached out to you? Do you know?"

She shook her head, eyes wide, arms still crossed defensively.

"I wrote songs. That's how I dealt with it all. You, the Scandal, the move. Me missing you. It's all there in my music. But you didn't listen to any of it, did you?"

Tugging her lush lower lip between her teeth, she shook her head. "No."

He shook his head, then stopped when the motion made him queasy. "You should have. You really should have. Shit. I need to lie down."

She shook herself to attention and briskly wiped her hands on her apron. "I'll drive you back to your hotel. Sit tight. Oh, and Padric?"

"Yeah?" He clutched his head, which felt as if it might split apart.

"We should talk more about this when you're not drunk. Like maybe, say, on the Larkspur Trail."

He gazed at her blankly for a moment, too plastered to put it together.

"Our hike, remember? You wanted to try the Larkspur Trail again?"

"Right. Our hike. Is that a yes?"

"Yes, let's do it."

"Now?"

She laughed, then came forward to take his arm. The gesture was probably to keep him from falling, but it felt like more. "In a couple of days when you've slept it off."

"It won't take a couple of days," he grumbled. "I'm a rock star, I'm used to... Ah, who am I kidding. I never could handle more than a few drinks."

She led him to her car, an older model Subaru, and opened the passenger door for him. "I'll finish closing up and be right there."

From the comfort of her passenger seat, he watched her hurry back into the pizza shop. She was so beautiful with her firm calves and rounded ass. And they were going hiking! They'd finally be alone together across the bay, the way they'd always dreamed about.

An eagle—the same eagle, Padric recognized him by his size—landed on one of the garbage bags.

"Guess I got the last word after all, dude," he told him through the front windshield. "I have a date with Zoe. So there."

CHAPTER TEN

"I'll take you," Megan Miller declared as soon as Zoe told her about the planned trip across the bay. "You need a chaperone. Rock stars can't be trusted, everyone knows that."

"That's a stereotype." Zoe scoffed as she served up two slices of pizza to Megan and her daughter, Ruby. Megan had moved to Lost Harbor recently and, after a rocky start, had fallen madly in love with Lucas Holt. They made an adorable couple that actually made Zoe rethink her attitude towards men. Megan didn't have the best luck in that area either, with a divorce under her belt. But she and her ex worked quite well as co-parents. It was rather inspiring, actually.

Still, Megan's bad luck didn't begin to compare to Zoe's. Zoe's was epic. Legendary. And it had all started across the bay.

"I knew Padric before his voice broke. Do you know there was a point in our friendship when I was six inches taller than him and thirty pounds heavier?"

"Those days are long gone. I've caught a few glimpses of him." Megan put up a hand to shield her mouth and whisper. "He's *hot.*"

Zoe felt color rise in her cheeks. She knew perfectly well how hot he was. The details kept her awake at night. That hard body, those confident hands, those dreamy eyes. He made her feel like one of his crazed female fans.

"He's an old friend, and we're simply rekindling our friendship. You don't have to worry about a thing."

"I like his songs, but I don't like his music," Ruby declared through a bite of her pepperoni pizza.

"How can you like one but not the other, you confusing child?" Megan asked her.

"I like the words because they're kind of like poems, but his music sounds like a seal who got caught in a net. Like crying."

Zoe hid a smile, grateful Padric wasn't here to witness that blunt assessment of his art. "It's a whole genre, kiddo. Wait until your first breakup, then you'll be glad he wrote all those songs."

"I don't know his music at all," Megan confessed. "I got through my divorce with a lot of country songs."

"To be honest, I don't either." Zoe waved at a customer trying to catch her attention. "I was going to do a binge listen before the trip, but I haven't had a chance."

Also, she was afraid of the effect his music would have on her. He was already easing back into her heart, whether he knew it or not—or wanted to or not. And she didn't know what his intentions were. He didn't live here anymore, and she would most likely *always* live here.

"Changing the topic, did you send off your submission?"

Megan was one of the few friends she'd told about the fellowship. "I finally did. Just last night." She wasn't sure what had finally inspired her to press "send," but it had something to do with Padric. That thing he'd said about her doubting herself had really struck home.

She knew why she was afraid of rejection in her personal life. But why should that transfer to her art? She'd never even *tried* to get rejected. Surely that was even worse than rejection—it was self-rejection.

Clicking the "send" button had been so difficult. She'd actually closed her eyes and said a little prayer as she did it. Her heart fluttered every time she thought about her work—photos of it, anyway—flying out into the world on the wings of the Internet.

"Congratulations, that's awesome," Megan was saying. "When will you hear?"

"I have no idea. I'm not thinking about that part. The only way I can handle this is to pretend I sent the application into some kind of cosmic black hole."

"You're a nut," Megan scolded. "They're going to love it. And if they don't, someone else will."

Zoe smiled at her friend affectionately; she was always so supportive. She had other friends in Lost Harbor, of course, people she'd known all her life. But she would always be glad that she'd taken Megan under her wing when she'd first arrived and the other "harbor rats" had resented her

At that point, she got busy with other customers and didn't have time for more than a wave goodbye when Megan and Ruby left. *Three hours to go.*

Yup she was counting down the hours to their hike. How pathetic was that?

Padric texted. *Three hours to departure.*

She laughed out loud. How about that? Still in sync after all these years.

Megan just offered to take us in the Forget Me Not.

No way. I rented that cabin cruiser and I want to use it. It's a sweet ride, you'll see.

That's fine. Should I bring snacks?

I got this. Relax. You spend all your time feeding people, it's my turn.

Warm little thrills of happiness danced through her heart.

Padric had always been the *sweetest guy*. And now he was so many other things besides sweet.

Like hot.

Megan definitely wasn't the only one who had noticed that fact.

ZOE GOT another dose of that reality when she met Padric at the float where his boat—called the *Jaunty*—was tied up. The engine was on, warming up, and he was swabbing off the deck with a bucket of water. He wore a soft checkered shirt with the sleeves rolled up, and each movement emphasized the corded muscles of his exposed forearms.

She sighed to herself, remembering the days when she'd just started to notice Padric as a "cute boy." When she'd glance over at him while they were studying and his wrist would catch her eye, or his bouncing knee under the table. Or his long eyelashes, so absurdly extravagant for a fisherman's kid. Or the Adam's apple popping up in his throat, or the new way that his chest filled out his clothes.

Now he was full-grown, one hundred percent adult male, packed with dreamy sexual charisma. He probably kept it dialed back in everyday life. From that one tiny clip she'd watched on YouTube, he had plenty more he could unleash when he chose.

He glanced up as she reached the *Jaunty*. Their eyes met, and a strange sensation traveled through her, as if a time shift had occurred, as if they'd always been looking at each other just like this, even when they were apart.

She shook it off. "Hey, sailor, got room for one more?"

"Come on in. The champagne is chilling."

Champagne? Was this some kind of rock-star seduction?

"That's funny, on our last trip all we had was orange soda and a gallon of water."

He reached out a hand to help her over the railing. "If you want to recreate that trip exactly, we have to get some of your mom's baklava."

She held up her backpack in triumph. "Way ahead of you. I raided the freezer. She makes it in bulk."

"No way. Hand it over." He snatched the pack from her and plunged his nose into it. "Oh my God," he groaned. "That honey smell, it's the best thing in the whole fucking world."

She laughed and stepped onboard the *Jaunty*. Should she tell him she hadn't enjoyed baklava since their last hiking trip? "I'd pass that along to my mother but she already knows. Humility is not her thing."

Padric stowed her backpack in the little cabin, which was upholstered in the softest vinyl she'd ever touched. Two cushioned benches sat on either side of the cabin, along with a deluxe swivel chair for the pilot. Everything was so clean it sparkled— which meant that this boat had probably never seen a fish.

"This is a lot different from the boat you grew up with," she commented as she gazed around at the grunge-free interior. "I don't see a single fish scale or bloodstain."

"It's almost unnatural, isn't it? I feel like I'm eating at my grandmother's house with the best china. Like I have to sit up straight or I'll get a ruler on my knuckles."

She snickered and settled onto the bench in a comfortable lounging position. "Guess I'm just a rule-breaker."

"I'm not complaining."

She caught his quick glance along the curve of her hip, to her legs. After a lot of debate, she'd dressed in a pair of athletic leggings that clung to her body. Now she was glad she'd opted for the sexiest of her mostly non-sexy hiking gear.

Electricity throbbed between them and jolted her to her feet. "Want me to cast off?"

"Sure." He didn't react to her obvious skittishness.

She stepped out of the cabin and tried to collect herself. Face it—this situation made her a little nervous. What was the right way to act around an old friend who you'd kissed once and who had now grown into an international celebrity? Was there a guidebook for this?

She lectured herself as she unwound the lines from the cleats and hopped back onboard. *It's just Padric. He's just a person. I was there when he got his first pimple. I watched him pop it.* Holding on to that slightly disgusting thought, she was finally able to relax as they cruised out of the harbor. *If nothing else, it's a day off,* she reminded herself. *A day off in the summer. With a handsome guy and a fancy boat. And champagne.*

A huge eagle perched on the rocks watched them as they passed the breakwater and the buoy that marked the harbor entrance. Zoe caught its golden eye for a moment. This particular eagle must be an older one, though it was hard to tell an eagle's age once they grew into their adult plumage. As soon as they cleared the breakwater, it spread its wings and lifted into the air.

Zoe wanted to fly, too.

"How fast does this thing go?" she asked Padric.

"Let's find out, shall we?"

He opened up the throttle and the boat lurched forward like a panther trying to find its footing. They cut across the waves, skipping along the surface, barely touching the water. "Whoop," Padric yelled out loud. "Now that's what I'm talking about!"

Zoe grabbed onto the dashboard with one hand, a grip bar with the other, and relaxed her knees. She too shrieked into the wind, spray spangling her face. "You're crazy!" she yelled. "I love it!"

They skimmed across a wave that a heavier boat would have

had to cut through. *Up on step*, that was the phrase, the point at which a boat was barely held by gravity anymore, and simply skipped across the tops of the waves.

Seabirds floated past, not at all disturbed by their headlong rush across the water. She spotted Arctic terns and cormorants, and the curious head of a sea otter. The wind blasting past them felt like life itself—brushing away every cobweb, every doubt and fear. *This is now*, it seemed to say. *Everything is new. There's only now.*

Padric was saying something, but she couldn't make it out over the purr of the engine and the rush of the wind. Or maybe he was singing—yes, that was probably it. He was singing into the wind, or *to* the wind, or maybe back at the wind. You never knew with him.

And in that moment, she realized that her old friend Padric and rock star Padric weren't really so different. They both loved music and dreams and imagination.

She was still smiling about that when they entered the more sheltered inlet on the other side of the strait. This inlet was one of the most-used entrances into Lost Souls Wilderness. It contained dozens if not hundreds of coves and pebble beaches, and a few actual sand beaches. Not that anyone would consider swimming there, except for the occasional daring young person. She and Padric had challenged each other to a swim during a school camping trip once. It had taken hours to warm up by the fire afterwards.

Padric steered the boat past a narrow privately owned beach where a tire swing dangled from an overhanging branch.

"Remember when we—" he began.

"—pushed Deke so hard he fell out of the swing and got a concussion? Yes."

"Poor guy. Last time he invited us out."

"Come to think of it, has there ever been a single time someone didn't get hurt on one of our trips across the bay?"

Padric cocked his head. "Nicks and bruises. Nothing serious."

"True, but still. Good thing I brought my first-aid kit."

He gave her a delighted glance as he steered into Glacier Cove, where the Larkspur trailhead began. "The same one?"

"No, I've upgraded. That ibuprofen expired years ago."

Watching the depth finder, he throttled down to an idle. "This is a good place to anchor. Want to do the honors?"

She made her way to the bow and tossed the anchor overboard. The anchor line was so new it showed no weathering at all.

A fresh start all around. Maybe this time no one would get hurt. Maybe this time everything would be perfect.

When the line went slack, she headed back to the cabin, where Padric was unfastening the Zodiac that was stored along the outer wall of the cabin. He slid it over the side with a splash, then gestured for her to get in.

As if they boated together all the time, they worked together in silent harmony. He handed her both of their backpacks, then lowered himself into the boat and took up the oars.

Happy to let him do the work, she sat back and gazed up at the clouds dodging the mountain peaks and casting shadows on the snowy cornices. "What a glorious day for a hike. It's so peaceful out here, I always forget what quiet sounds like."

The drone of a small plane interrupted her, and they both laughed.

"It's probably headed for Glacier Lake," she said. "Or maybe just flightseeing. Everyone wants to see bears."

"From a distance, you mean."

She laughed. "Exactly. Remember the time—"

"—you tripped and fell in a pile of bear scat and were terrified the bear would be mad about it and come after you?"

"No. I was afraid the bear would think *I smelled* like a bear. Which I did, for about a week, no matter how much I showered."

"No, you didn't. You just felt like you did."

"I could still smell it." Her nostrils twitched. "I think I *still* smell it, fifteen years later."

"Has nothing changed in fifteen years?" He lifted his eyebrows at her as he stroked through the water. His eyes caught an extra shine from sun reflecting on the ocean. His broad shoulders flexed with each stroke of the oars. Her mouth watered.

"Maybe a few things have changed," she murmured, helpless to stop her gaze from drifting across his body.

He caught her meaning and his eyes darkened. She felt herself respond in a very primal way, deep in her belly, like the vibration of a cello string. She swallowed, and knew that he *saw* her swallow, and that he knew exactly how to interpret that.

The Zodiac crunched onto the rocky shallows. Padric, who was wearing water boots, jumped out and brought it broadside to the shore. She scrambled out, doing her best to keep her good hiking boots from getting immersed in the ocean.

He handed her their things, one by one, then the two of them carried the Zodiac to high ground and beached it.

"Should we have a snack before we hit the trail?" she asked. Nothing else was going to distract her from Padric's edibleness, so she might as well eat.

"I thought we could have a picnic once we get to the first ridge. Better view."

She kind of liked the view she had—his strong hands adjusting the straps on his backpack, his eyes alight with the joy of being in the wild.

"Good plan." She tilted her head to look at the tall spruce

trees piercing the sky, crowding thick as soldiers up the slope. "So, here we are again. The Larkspur Trail."

"You nervous?" He picked his way through the driftwood and seaweed that marked the high tide line.

"I am, a little. My whole life changed the last time I was here."

"You know what I think we should do? Just walk right past that spot. It's not far from the beginning of the trail. Once we pass that boulder, the rest will be new territory."

"Are you being metaphorical right now?"

"Maybe a little." He grinned. "But also literal. I've never hiked past that spot—did you?"

"No, I've never been back to this trail until now."

Their gazes met and held, then he reached for her hand. "Come on. We got this," he said softly.

CHAPTER ELEVEN

Silent now, they stepped into the deep quiet of the forest. To Zoe, It felt like entering the house of an ancient being. A wise being. As if the forest had an identity of its own, a way of communicating through its atmosphere. Hadn't she and Padric been talking about forest spirits that last time? She couldn't really remember the conversation, except that she'd scoffed at the concept and he'd shrugged off her skepticism.

She didn't feel so skeptical now. The deeper they walked down the trail, the more she felt enveloped by mystery. Did she really know everything about what was and wasn't real? Could anyone really say that?

They didn't even speak as they passed the boulder she'd leaned on after she'd twisted her ankle. They paused for a moment, as if honoring their past selves, then continued onwards. *New territory.*

She soaked in the details. Moss-draped nurse logs with baby spruce trees sprouting from the generous decay. A mushroom with flared flanges. Crisp lichens the color of celery. The scurry of voles in the underbrush. The quiet flap of an owl disturbed in its sleep.

She held her breath as she took in the wonder of this hushed place. In the coolness, Padric's hand felt warm and alive in hers. As far as she knew, they were the only two humans in this deep wilderness, with only a sketchy trail to prove anyone else had ever been here.

The trail headed upslope and she had to breathe again. She let go of Padric's hand so they could hike single file. This time he took the lead, which meant she had an excellent view of his rear. She tried not to focus on it as the grade steepened and her breath grew ragged.

It didn't work. Instead, other fantasy images flitted through her mind. Naked images. The flex of his buttocks as he turned to face her. His hips moving as he braced himself over her in bed. The glow in his dream-blue eyes when he entered her.

Distracting thoughts like that kept her occupied until they reached the ridge and the view opened up to show the slopes of the next mountain beyond, and a river cutting through the valley. In the other direction, they could see across the inlet to Driscoll Cove, one of her favorite spots for gathering debris.

A short spur trail took them to an overlook with a flat rock perfect for a picnic.

"Wow." Zoe panted as she tucked her thumbs under the straps of her backpack. "We did it. We made it past the..."

"Past?" Padric smiled at her and offered his hand for a high-five. "How does it feel?"

"Glorious." She shaded her eyes and gazed out over the wooded slopes, miles and miles of spruce dotted with birch and alders. "Not a soul to be seen except us."

"Do you know how rare this is for me? Normally I'm surrounded by people. I miss having time alone."

Time alone? That was a strange comment, and she felt her

joy dim. "Do you wish you were alone right now?"

"No! No, that's not what I meant. I meant, alone with my choice of person to be alone with."

She cocked her head at him. "I don't get it. What's the point of having all that success if you can't do what you want and be with whoever you want?"

He shrugged slightly. "It's...complicated, I guess. I feel like I owe everyone whatever they want from me." He slid off his backpack and propped it against the rock. "You must know what I mean. You do everything your family needs. Do you ever think about what *you* need?"

The way he was looking at her implied that he knew what she needed—even more than she did.

She wetted her lips and glanced way from him. If he kept looking at her like that, she might do something crazy.

"If you keep doing that, I might do something crazy," he said, his gaze fixed on her mouth.

Her lips parted in surprise. How on earth—how could they be *that* in sync after so many years apart? "I was just thinking something similar."

"Were you?" He stepped to her side and helped her slide her backpack off her back. His closeness made her tremble. "Funny how that still happens."

"I was thinking *that*, too." A smile sketched across her lips, which drew his gaze again. Her tongue tingled.

"Is that a fact? Well, I *really* hope you're thinking the same thing I'm thinking now." He took her hand again and gently tugged her against his chest. Fire flashed up and down the entire front of her body. "Since we've broken the curse and made it all the way up here."

"They say there's only one thing that can really break a curse." She leaned closer to him and tilted her head. Her lips parted all on their own under the magic of his attention. Always, from the beginning, she'd felt the most *herself* with Padric. The most strong, the most confident, the most sexy.

Okay, the sexy part was new, but very real. Under his gaze, she felt like a goddess, because that was what she saw in his eyes.

He bent his head so he could reach her lips, and there it was—like a key in a lock—instant, glorious rightness. The touch of his mouth, the scent of his skin, the sound of his breath drawing in—everything new and yet already written.

He ran his tongue along her lower lip, eagerly tasting the flesh he'd been eyeing a moment ago. "So sweet," he murmured. "And lush. So beautiful."

She closed her eyes under the combined pleasure of his kiss and his words. For a moment suspended in time, nothing else existed. Just her and Padric and skin and touch and this *kiss...*this lingering, exploring, opening *kiss...*

A whining drone caught her attention, and her eyes fluttered open. She spotted it immediately, the same twin-engine plane from earlier, now headed back toward Lost Harbor. But something was wrong.

She drew away from Padric and shielded her eyes against the sun so she could see better.

"What's wrong?" Padric asked.

"Not sure. That plane is flying funny."

He turned to look where she was pointing. "Maybe they spotted a bear and are trying to— Oh my God."

Zoe cried out at the same time. As the plane banked, black smoke poured from the right engine. The wings tilted sharply.

"They're looking for a place to land," said Padric.

"There's nothing out here. Oh my God! They're going down!"

With smoke spiraling behind it, the plane plunged at a terrible angle toward the forbidding wilderness below.

And then disappeared into the trees.

CHAPTER TWELVE

Padric snatched up his backpack and dug around for his binoculars and phone. He handed the binoculars to Zoe.

"Keep your eye on the spot where they went down. Is there still smoke?"

"Oh yeah." She scanned the surrounding area while he turned on his phone. "I think they're near the Hope Trail, the one that wraps around Lookout Mountain. This trail intersects with the Hope Trail. Probably an hour hike away."

"They need emergency help, not us." He dug out his phone; no service. "Fuck, we're out of range here."

"They probably sent out a mayday."

"I hope so. Come on, let's get to higher ground so we can get a signal."

"What about going back down? There's a signal at the beach, I think."

"I'll run back down and make the call, you go on ahead. If we can help on the ground, we should try."

"Good." She held her hand out. "I'll take your pack so you can run faster."

Before giving her the pack, he grabbed her hand and pulled her against him for a hard kiss. "Someday we'll get to finish a kiss right," he murmured against her lush lips.

She smiled—he felt the motion against his own lips—then shooed him away. "Go make the call. I'll be jogging up the trail, and you know what my idea of 'jogging' is. So I'm sure you'll have no trouble catching up."

Briefly, he cupped her face in his hand. So beautiful and *real*. So actually here instead of slumbering in his memories.

He launched himself down the path, leaping over patches of exposed rock and the occasional fallen branch. Every muscle of his body was sore from the training workouts, but also stronger, so on balance it was a win. *Thank you, Nate, you commandant bastard.*

As he ran, he kept checking the signal, and as soon as a bar appeared—a short distance from the beach—he stopped and dialed Nate's number. Not that he didn't trust the dispatchers, but he could communicate more quickly with Nate.

"Yo," his friend answered. "How's the big hike—"

"We saw a plane crash. One of the twin-engine bear-viewing planes, it went down on the west slope of Lookout Mountain, about a mile in."

Nate was instantly all business. "What else did you see?"

"Lots of smoke coming from one of the engines. We're going to hike down and see what we can do."

"I'm on it. Don't do anything crazy."

"We won't."

Nate ended the call, and Padric filled his lungs a few times before heading back up the trail. Would it make more sense to bring the boat around to the Hope Trail, in case anyone needed transport back into Lost Harbor?

He dismissed the idea. He could always come back down for the boat, and he didn't want to leave Zoe alone on the trail.

Hiking alone was never a good idea. Not that she couldn't handle herself, since she'd grown up hiking in Lost Souls Wilderness. But if there were injured people on that plane, it would take two of them to deal with the situation.

He loped back up the trail, once again passing the infamous boulder where they'd kissed the first time.

Why did every goddamn kiss get interrupted by some kind of disaster? It had to be just a coincidence, but it sure was a strange one. The old local proverb drifted through his mind. *Strange things happen around Lost Souls Wilderness.*

Add another strange thing to the long list.

He caught up with Zoe about half a mile past the overlook. Even carrying two packs, she was making pretty good time.

She stopped to catch her breath while he jogged the last few yards to her side. He reclaimed his backpack and slid it over his shoulders. "You got farther than I'd expected."

"See, that's my secret. It looks like I move slow, but I get there."

That sounded almost metaphorical.

"Did you call for help?"

"Nate's on it. They'll probably call in a chopper with a rescue rappeler crew."

Zoe nodded. "I was thinking the same thing, but the closest crew like that is an hour away. We should still see if we can help."

"Agreed." As one, they set off at Zoe's fastest pace down the trail.

That feeling of being exactly on the same page with someone —he loved that. The only other time he felt that was when he was jamming with a group of skilled musicians. Listening, respond- ing, creating, until all boundaries disappeared and the flow of music was like a river carrying them all to the promised land.

They saved their breath for the exertion of tackling the steep switchbacks of the Larkspur Trail. The trees thinned out as they reached the higher elevations. Up here the blueberries grew thick on the ground, and low alders clung to the thin soil. Patches of snow glinted from the rocky cliffs higher up.

In a few months, all of this would be covered with a thick blanket of snow, and the only people who would come here would be heli-skiers dropped from a helicopter.

"There!" Zoe pointed to a trail that forked off to the west. "That's the Hope Trail. There's supposed to be a sign, but I heard it got stolen."

"Who the hell would steal a trail sign?"

"Probably the twins," she said wryly.

He laughed, as much as he could while being completely out of breath. They took a short break while they both took a drink of water. Zoe reached into her pack and pulled out a foil-wrapped package. "Baklava? We have to keep our blood sugar up. It has protein, too, with all the nuts."

"Sure." He accepted a small piece from her and let the divine combination of honey, walnuts and pastry melt on his tongue. "This really takes me back."

"Yeah." Zoe delicately placed a bit of pastry in her own mouth. "Did you know I haven't had baklava since you left?"

He took in her averted face, her lowered eyelashes. "Why would you deprive yourself of something so delicious?"

"I just...it reminded me of that day. I hated thinking about that day. So I just avoided it."

She swallowed it down, her throat muscles moving under the tender skin of her throat. The sight was disturbingly erotic.

"So...how does it taste?" His voice held a rougher-than-usual edge.

"Nostalgic. High-caloric. Also it tastes like home. Oppressively loving with lots of high drama." She sighed and brushed off her fingertips. "Come on. Break's over."

They hurried toward the Hope Trail fork. *Oppressively*

loving. Quite the phrase. And from what Padric remembered, it described the Bellini family perfectly.

They were halfway down the trail when they saw the smoke rising over the treetops deeper in the valley.

"We're going to have to bushwhack," said Padric. "They went down off the trail. Let me go first."

She didn't protest. Bushwhacking through alders took a lot of energy, and they didn't have any tools to work with. A machete would come in handy right now, or a hacksaw or a chainsaw. He thought longingly of all the fire mitigation tools at the fire station. Why hadn't he brought something like that with him?

Nope, instead he was reduced to ducking under bushes, snapping branches, clearing just enough space for him and Zoe to squeeze through.

The stench of the smoke grew stronger the closer they came. Padric knew enough about fires to know that the consistency of the smoke depended on what was burning. Thick and black, like this smoke, meant that metal was involved instead of wood.

At least the crash wasn't lighting the forest on fire.

"Did you hear that?" Zoe asked at one point.

They paused, listening for sounds coming from the crash site. Was that a voice? The light wind snatched the sound away, lost to the wilderness.

"Let's go," he said grimly. "If there are survivors, they might not have much time.

He picked up the pace, ignoring the branches scratching at his face and the burn in his muscles. The world telescoped down to one step at a time. Hack away at the undergrowth. Listen to Zoe's ragged breaths behind him. Fear that they wouldn't get there in time.

And then they burst through a grove of alders into a clearing that hadn't existed before, because the smoldering, deformed broken hulk of a plane had created it. Still smoking, it lay on its side like a toy someone had thrown away. One wing pointed toward the sky and the other shattered on the ground.

Scorched alder branches rimmed the perimeter of the crash site. The plane had ignited a fire, but it hadn't spread far. Lucky —if that word could be used in this situation.

"Over there!" shouted Zoe. She pointed to the far perimeter on the other side of the plane. "I see some people. Hello!"

The wind was blowing the wrong way and they couldn't hear her. They jogged around the plane, giving it a wide berth. Padric peered into the cockpit as they passed, but he didn't see any movement inside. Had everyone managed to get themselves out? It was possible to survive small plane crashes, but quite often they were fatal. Every year in Alaska, dozens of people died in crashes just like this one.

As they rounded the smoking tail of the plane, they spotted two men and a woman, all sitting or lying on the ground. Blood flowed from the woman's head, while a man held a balled-up t-shirt against her wound. His left pant leg was rolled up to expose the purple, swelling mass of his lower leg.

Definite fracture. Padric didn't need to know much to figure that out.

The third man lay unconscious on a jacket spread out on the ground.

"Hey there!" Padric hailed them. "We saw you go down. Emergency rescue is headed your way."

The two survivors looked so dazed they barely reacted. "You're not here to rescue us?" asked the woman. She was middle-aged, in a loose floral-print jacket and very white cross trainers.

"We're here to do whatever we can. Is everyone out of the plane?" Padric knelt next to the unconscious man and felt for a pulse. Very faint. Barely there.

The man next to her, who had a salt-and-pepper brush cut—

nodded. Sweat beaded his face; he must be in terrible pain from that leg.

Zoe crouched down next to them. "My name's Zoe. This is Padric."

"I'm Mary and this is my husband, Ronnie. That's the pilot, his name is..."

"Art. I know," said Zoe. Padric glanced over at her. Her face had gone several shades paler. Of course she knew the pilot; she knew everyone in Lost Harbor. This had just gotten much more personal for her.

"He's alive," he told her softly. "Barely. What happened?" He didn't see that there was much he could do for Art, but he draped his jacket over him to keep him warm.

"He said we lost an engine," Ronnie explained. "He told us we were going down, but he did this thing where he tried to get the treetops to break the impact. It must have worked because we didn't die. Blacked out for a minute, then my wife woke me up."

Zoe dug through her backpack. She pulled out her first-aid kit and opened it up. "How about some ibuprofen for that pain?"

"Oh thank God," the man groaned. "I'll take anything right now. Hurts like a motherfucker."

His wife rolled her eyes as Zoe tore open a packet of the painkillers for him and handed him a bottle of water.

"He's been swearing since I woke him up."

Zoe took Ronnie's place so he could deal with the ibuprofen. "Mind if I check out your wound?"

The poor woman winced as she shook her head. "It hurt at first, but now it's just numb."

Zoe lifted the t-shirt and examined the gash. Padric left Art's side and hovered over her, ready to get her whatever she needed.

"I'm not a nurse, but I have first-aid training," she told Mary. "I can bandage this up if you like."

Mary squinted at her. "Aren't you the girl at the pizza shop?"

"Yes. I'm the owner."

"Your mushroom gorgonzola pizza is amazing."

"Thank you." Zoe lifted her eyebrows at Padric. He knew what she was thinking. Shock? Concussion?

"Do you have any with you?"

Definitely concussion.

"No. No, I don't. But we do have plenty of food, so if we're here for a while, no one's going to starve. Actually..." She shot another questioning glance at Padric and jerked her head toward her pack. He got it—she was asking about the baklava. Blood sugar was important, right? On the other hand, people in shock weren't supposed to eat or drink anything.

He shook his head no. Mary's gaze swept in his direction, and stopped there. She frowned as Zoe carefully dabbed at the blood still seeping from her scalp.

"I know you. I know your face. Who are you? You're some kind of celebrity. Am I crazy? Am I seeing things?"

"You may have seen me somewhere," Padric reassured her. "But I wouldn't say I'm a celebrity, just a singer."

"He's too modest," Zoe said. "That's Padric Jeffers."

"Padric *Jeffers*? My daughter's crazy about you! She loves your music. Can I take a selfie with you?"

"Mary, don't be ridiculous," her husband said. His eyes were drifting shut—the effect of the ibuprofen, or was he going into shock? "We came here to get pictures of bears, not goddamn singers."

"Nan would kill me if I didn't get one!" She was starting to get agitated, and Zoe put a hand on her shoulder to calm her.

"How about you take a selfie at the hospital?" she suggested. "After you get cleaned up. Padric can sign something for your daughter."

"You bet," Padric said. "Let's focus on getting these wounds patched up. I need to save my phone battery. Ronnie, you're not looking so great. How about you lie down and we keep you warm until the cavalry arrives?"

Ronnie didn't object, and Padric helped him lower himself into a prone position, with a rolled-up sweater under his head. Zoe offered up her jacket and he spread that over him.

"When...are they coming?" The poor man's voice came out strained and raw.

"We called almost an hour ago, so it should be soon." He glanced up at the sky, but saw nothing but a mass of puffy clouds, innocent as cotton candy.

"This is taking forever. Can we call again?" whimpered Mary. "What's wrong with this place?"

Padric exchanged a quick glance with Zoe; they had to get her to calm down. "Alaska has some of the best rescue crews in the country," he told her. "I'm sure they're coming as fast as they can."

"Well it's not fast enough, is it?"

"On the bright side," Zoe dug into her first-aid kit for a large bandage, "you survived the worst part."

"All we wanted was a bear photo," Mary moaned. "And now we're stuck here with no one but a pizza waitress and...you. Oh my God. It's you!"

Padric looked up to find her glaring at him with the force of a million suns.

"I know you! You should be ashamed of yourself!"

Zoe paused in the midst of applying the bandage to her head. "Mary, I think you have a concussion, you're not making any sense. Try not to move around too much."

"I am making sense!"

"But you said your daughter was a fan of Padric, and now you're yelling at him."

"Yes, but I got it confused. He's the other one." Mary gripped her by the wrist. "PJ. My daughter went to a PJ party and nearly came back with one. She didn't because she has more sense than that, but her friend did."

Padric felt frozen, rooted to the ground. He always dreaded meeting one of the "PJ parents," people whose children had managed to sneak around their rules and get the brand. Whenever one wanted to meet with him, he did so. He felt it was the least he could do. But he'd never imagined running into one here, in the middle of the wilderness, at the site of a plane crash.

"You much be hallucinating—" Zoe began. He cut her off.

"It's all right," Padric said. "She's not hallucinating. Let her talk."

"I would never take a selfie with you," Mary spit at him. "Never. I take it back."

Zoe attached the bandage to her head and sat back on her haunches. "Lady, you have some nerve. We're just trying to help you, and now you're yelling at Padric and saying crazy things."

"Stop saying I'm crazy!" She rubbed at her face, where blood had dried next to her ear. "I'm furious, not crazy."

Zoe glanced at Padric, her expression one of utter confusion. He cleared his throat and told her in a low voice, "I'll explain later. This isn't the best thing to talk about right now."

"You know what you should do?" Mary tugged her jacket tighter around her and shivered. "You could stop writing your horrible songs, you devil. Just stop. For good."

Padric couldn't think of a good response to that. His brain felt numb and slow, as if he was the one who'd been through a traumatic fall from the sky.

"You leave him alone, you awful woman," Zoe told her sternly.

"*What* did you just say?" Mary drew away from her with an offended glare.

"You heard me. You're *awful*. What about all the people who love Padric's music? He brings people joy with his songs. Who are you to tell him to stop?"

"I was in a plane crash! You're supposed to be nice to me!"

"I already told you I'm not a nurse," Zoe snapped. "I'm a pizza shop owner. I don't have to be nice."

"Then I'll leave you a bad review."

"Go for it. I'm too busy as it is." Zoe rose to her feet. "The one thing I won't stand for is anyone insulting Padric. He's the kindest, most goodhearted person I've ever known. Stop saying that stuff."

Padric would have laughed if he wasn't still struggling with the strangeness of this encounter. Zoe held the same fierce hands-on-hips posture as that time in fifth grade when a bully kept saying he smelled like fish bait.

"It's okay, Zoe. She can think or say whatever she wants."

"You should be ashamed—" Mary started up again.

The drone of an oncoming helicopter interrupted her rant. Thank God. Padric had never been so grateful for a giant metallic mosquito to show up. He wanted to tell Zoe about the PJ parties in his own way.

He jumped to his feet and shaded his eyes so he could watch the chopper hover overhead.

"Wait!" called Mary.

He looked down at the angry woman. "Yeah?"

"Can I still get a selfie?"

"Of course not—" Zoe began hotly.

He shushed her with a gesture. "Rescue first, selfie later. Okay?"

CHAPTER THIRTEEN

It took over an hour for the rescue crew to get all three of the crash victims into the helicopter. Zoe forced herself to be pleasant to the horrible woman who'd yelled at Padric. What was she even talking about? What could cause that level of anger toward a songwriter? Zoe kept turning it over in her mind as the rescue crew strapped poor unconscious Art onto a gurney. She didn't recognize the paramedics, so she filled them in on his information, yelling over the whir of the hovering helicopter.

"This is Art Dinty, owner of Black Bear Flightseeing. He has a wife, Marge, so someone should call her."

"Will do, Miss. Now back away, we got this."

The paramedic signaled to the chopper pilot, who maneuvered the controls to hoist the gurney up. A third crew member crouched in the open hatch, waiting to receive the gurney.

In the meantime, the paramedic got Ronnie ready for transport. He stabilized his leg with a brace, and when the gurney came back, he gestured to Padric to help him roll the man onto it. Apparently, Nate had relayed the fact that Padric was in the midst of volunteer firefighter training.

The charming and oh-so-pleasant Mary went up last, since she was the least injured. She actually did manage to shoot a selfie with Padric just before the paramedic strapped her into the rescue harness.

"You guys want to ride along, too?" The paramedic asked them before signaling to the pilot.

Zoe had to admit the idea was tempting. They'd hiked a long way to get here, and that was under the influence of adrenaline. Getting back was going to be twice as difficult.

"No, you'd better get these guys to the hospital," Padric told them. "The pilot never regained consciousness, so he could be in bad shape."

Which was a very good point. Zoe suppressed her sigh. They watched the helicopter ascend, its blades batting the air, sending wind rushing past their faces.

And then they were alone in a clearing with only a smoldering wreck of an airplane for company.

And a bunch of unanswered questions.

Padric stretched his arms wide. "I don't know about you, but I'm starving."

She narrowed her eyes at him. "Are you going to tell me what that was all about?"

"Yes. I am. But I know you, Zoe. You're going to want some food first."

She laughed, the sound echoing in the sudden absence of the helicopter's roar. "Fine, you're right. I'm starving, too."

They found a downwind spot at the very edge of the clearing, where they could barely smell the smoke. It had to be the weirdest picnic spot ever, but she knew they needed a break before they hiked up that mountain. Padric brushed away rocks and other debris to make a comfortable sitting spot, then spread out his jacket. She sank down on it with a sigh and gazed at the wreck of the plane while Padric rummaged through his pack.

She'd seen that plane fly over the harbor at least a hundred times. And now it was nothing but a pile of twisted metal parts. Poor Art. He had three kids, at least one in college. Black Bear Flightseeing had an impeccable reputation, but a crash like this could destroy that.

Her heart twisted as she thought of the way he'd lain unconscious on the ground. Those passengers—as annoying as they were—had saved his life.

"Do you think Art's going to be okay?"

"He's alive. I didn't see any obvious injuries. But we'll have to see what the doctors say. Pretty fucking lucky, all three of them."

"Do you think they know it? They didn't exactly seem grateful for our help." She looked up at the sky, where the helicopter was little more than a fast-disappearing dot.

"They were in shock. Don't hold it against them. Besides, it was sweet, the way you stood up for me without even knowing the situation."

She shrugged, since to her it was no big deal. "That's what friends are for, right?"

"Or maybe *this* is what friends are for."

She looked around—and gasped with pure joy. Padric had spread out a magnificent feast. All of her favorite picnic foods were laid out on a soft blanket—olive tapenade spread with crackers, chocolate-covered strawberries, onion rings from Tremaine's food truck, a hunk of brie cheese, salted pistachios, an entire filet of smoked salmon, dark rye bread from the Sweet Harbor Bakery.

Granted, many of the items looked like they'd had a rough day. The onion rings were soggy, the brie was squished nearly flat, half the crackers were broken. But none of that mattered. It all looked delicious. And it was incredibly thoughtful of Padric.

"This is...amazing, Padric." She crawled across the few feet between them and gazed at the spread in awe. "This is my dream feast. How did you know?"

"Monica and Alexis. I wonder how long I can play the guilt card. It's really working for me."

She smiled, her mouth watering. "Milk it for all its worth. Those girls...honestly, I'm surprised *they* know my favorite foods. I didn't know they were paying attention."

"Never underestimate a teenager." He spread tapenade on a cracker and handed it to her. She snatched it from his hand and popped it into her mouth so quickly, he burst out laughing.

"Oh my God," she moaned through a mouthful of salty deliciousness. For a short period, the two of them concentrated on gorging themselves on all the treats he'd assembled. The tiny bit of baklava they'd eaten several hours ago hadn't held them for long, and in the meantime, they'd hiked several miles and hacked their way down a mountain.

Finally she took a break with a long, happy sigh. "Nothing has ever, in the history of the world, tasted this good."

"Really? Not even Last Chance pizza?"

She shook her head and popped a chocolate-covered strawberry into her mouth. "Not even close."

"Not even baklava?"

"Nope." She bit down on the strawberry and tasted juice running down her tongue.

"Not even a kiss spiked with baklava?" His eyes gleamed mischief at her, and she couldn't resist.

"I might have to run a comparison test," she told him after she'd swallowed the last bit. "My memory's a little foggy."

"Really? Mine's perfectly clear."

Oh Lord, the look in his eyes. Direct, honest, straight from the heart. Or maybe from another part of him.

Her belly filled up with butterflies. Was this really happening? Did the intense connection she and Padric had always shared still exist?

Judging by the reaction of her body, which was going

haywire, it did. Her nipples hardened as their gazes held, and her lower belly clenched.

"Zoe," he said again. "About the things that Mary said..."

She reached across the blanket to touch his hand. "Does it really matter? I know you, Padric. You're not the way she made you sound."

"Are you so sure you know me? I disappeared on you."

"But that wasn't your fault. I know that, but I think I was angry at you because," the truth slid into place, "because it was easier than being angry at my father."

As soon as she said that, it made total sense. If she held on to her grudge against Padric, she wouldn't have to face the fact that her beloved dad had betrayed her mother.

Padric picked up her hand and brought it to his mouth for a kiss. He brushed his lips across her knuckles. "The thing is, it's one thing to blame me. It's another to blame yourself. I don't want you to do that anymore. I want you to see yourself the way I see you. You're incredible, Zoe."

Her heart skittered past the next few beats. What she saw in his face was much more than a light flirtation or an urge to explore an old attraction.

"Stop it," she whispered. "This can't go anywhere."

His eyes darkened. "Why not?"

"Because it can't. Because you're *you* and I'm...here. Not going anywhere." Even though it wasn't the most articulate way to describe the situation, hopefully he knew what she meant.

"I'm still the same Padric Jeffers. You're still the same Zoe. We're just...more than before. Older, more experienced. More."

Her heart did another somersault at his mention of more experience. The hairs on the back of her neck prickled as she thought of what his "experience" would be like in bed.

No. Bad direction.

"Your experiences include conquering the world and dating

supermodels. Mine are more along the lines of crashing and burning every time I get involved with someone. How can we ever make that work?"

"There's only one way to find out." He touched her face, running his thumb across her cheekbone. The invitation in his eyes made her shiver deeply.

God, it was tempting. But what if it went wrong? What if the same thing happened that *always* happened? Rejection and disappointment.

"We just got our friendship back," she whispered. "I don't want to lose that."

He looked at her for another long moment, then nodded and sat back on his side of the blanket. "I don't want to make you uncomfortable. You know where I stand. The ball's in your court."

But *did* she know where he stood? What was he offering, exactly? A brief trip to bed, just to satisfy the chemistry buzzing between them? Or an actual—if impossible—relationship?

Couldn't she just ask him? This was Padric, after all. She and Padric had always been able to talk things out. But now the "things" were piling up like a highway collision.

"Maybe you should tell me about this PJ party thing."

CHAPTER FOURTEEN

Back to reality. Padric braced himself for his least favorite topic in the world. He'd much rather keep watching that flush flood Zoe's cheeks every time he flirted with her. He'd rather keep exploring the chemistry that flared between them. Find out how much of it was real. After his time as a star, he craved real more than anything.

But if he was going to be real with her, he had to start with this. He didn't want any barriers or secrets between them.

"I wrote a song that some teenagers decided to interpret as a call to...brand themselves."

"Brand themselves? Like...cattle?"

He cringed at the image. "No, not like that. It's a thing that some frats do. It's a sign of loyalty and...belonging, I guess. I have no problem with adults doing it, but these are kids. A lot of my fans are in that age group between middle school and high school. It's a tough age and they need something to bond over. This PJ party thing started on one of my fan forums and just took off."

Zoe, bless her heart, didn't react with the horror he'd feared. With a thoughtful expression, she sliced up the brie and filled a paper plate. "I can't imagine the twins doing that, but some of their friends...yes. I can see it. They identify so strongly with their favorite bands or comic books or games."

"Yeah, until they grow up and regret it, and hate my guts."

She offered him some cheese and a sympathetic look.

"So how is it *your* fault? You didn't tell them to do anything like that."

He waved away the brie. The topic had soured his appetite. "I feel responsible. When I first heard about it, I wanted to come forward publicly and condemn it. But my management team thought it would be a mistake. They said it would give the story oxygen and make it bigger than it was. Their advice was to let it blow over. So I stayed quiet until I finally couldn't take it anymore."

"You think you could have stopped it earlier?"

He jumped to his feet and paced restlessly around the picnic blanket. "I *still* haven't fucking stopped it. It has a life of its own now. But maybe I could have if I'd tried when it first got going."

"Maybe. But you don't really know that. What's that phrase you keep saying to me? Never underestimate the determination of a teenager? If these kids really see it as a bonding thing, it's not really about you, is it? They're bonding with each other."

"I never said it was 'about me.'" He scrubbed a hand through his hair in frustration. "I don't care about being a rock star. I never have."

"That's not what I—"

"I write songs so I can reach people. To connect, to share the pain. I remember what it was like being a teenager, how fucking confusing and exhilarating and terrifying it was. I want to reach out a hand and say 'I get it. You're not alone. It gets better.' That's what I want to say. Not 'put my initials on your skin and you'll have friends for life.' That's not my fucking message, and it kills me that it got twisted that way."

Zoe was watching him with wide eyes. "Oh wow, Padric," she said slowly. "I wondered if there was another reason you left your tour. Are you hiding out in the Eagle's Nest questioning your music career?"

He hadn't thought of it that way, but Zoe had a way of putting her finger on things. "I question it. Yeah. Why write music when it's actually hurting people? I'd be better off fishing for a living. At least then I'd only be hurting the halibut."

She laughed a little at that. "Well, I'm sure the harbor rats would welcome you back. And they're more into tattoos than brands."

She didn't seem to be taking this as seriously as he would have thought.

"That's your advice? Quit and start fishing again?"

"I didn't say that. You're the one who mentioned fishing."

"You didn't think it was a bad idea."

She squinted up at him from her kneeling position by the blanket. "Are you saying you want my advice?"

"Maybe."

"Like, my honest advice as your friend? Or some feel-good advice to make you feel better?"

Ouch. Zoe's directness had always been one of his favorite—and most challenging—things about her. "As a friend," he muttered.

Hopefully he could take it.

"Okay, as your friend, it seems to me that you're kind of feeling sorry for yourself and that you need to snap out of it."

"*Snap out* of it?"

"Yes. You're a world-renowned recording artist. Millions of people listen to your songs. I mean, not me, but I'm probably one of the few." She wrinkled her forehead at him, trying to soften her words. It didn't really work. "You can't control how *millions* of people interpret your songs. Every person has their own reaction. Once you release it, it's out of your hands. Right?"

She was making a certain amount of sense. He'd seen such wildly different reviews of his work that he knew it was true. But it didn't absolve him.

"Yes, in a way, but these are kids."

"Kids have brains, too, and willpower. A lot of willpower, take it from me. You've seen the twins in action."

He couldn't argue with that.

"Good judgment, on the other hand..." She shook her head. "Don't get me started. The point is, if you've publicly stated that you don't support these PJ parties, and you want them to stop, what more can you do?"

"What Mary said. Quit writing."

"Okay, Padric Jeffers. I'm about to tell you something about yourself. Are you ready for this?"

He braced himself, because he remembered that tone of voice. This was Zoe Bellini's "deliver harsh truths" voice. "Bring it, babe. I can take it."

"You can't stand being the bad guy. You never could. You have the kindest, sweetest heart, and you always loved making people happy. Remember that time Mindy in fifth grade had a crush on you? She kept leaving notes on your desk, and you made me steal them. That way you wouldn't have to reject her, you could just tell her you'd never seen any of her notes. She really hated me for that." Zoe rolled her eyes at the memory, which he'd completely forgotten about.

"But Zoe, I knew she was having trouble with her stepdad. I didn't want to make her life worse."

"Which was very sweet and kind. But reality isn't always sweet and kind. The truth was, you didn't like her the way she wanted you to. And instead of telling her that, you got me to play the bad guy. The note-thief."

Now it was all coming back to him. The way Mindy's hopeful eyes had followed him in class. Her two braids swinging against her coat as she searched for an answer to her note. The crushing disappointment on her face when her desk was empty.

Okay, so it hadn't been his finest moment. "I was only eleven."

"I know that, but have you really changed that much? You say you write music to make people happy."

"I do."

"And you've made so many people happy. So many! But now not everything is perfect in rock-star land. Some of your fans are making you feel like the bad guy. And you're not used to that."

He turned away from her, feeling as if each word was chasing him like a heat-guided missile. "I've had bad reviews, people who hate my music. Doesn't bug me."

"That's different. A bad review doesn't make you the villain."

The villain. Images of various PJ brands flashed through his mind, reddened skin and raised scar tissue, each one like a brand on his own soul. He felt each one down to his bones.

"But if you're going to put your art out there," Zoe continued, "you have to take the bad with the good, don't you?"

He wheeled on her. "How would you know? You aren't putting your art out there at all."

Her entire body winced as that blow landed. Instantly he felt like an ass. He fucking *was* an ass. "Sorry," he muttered, digging the heel of this hand into his forehead. "That was out of line."

"No. You're absolutely right. I haven't put my art out there." She almost said more, as if there was something else to add, then stopped herself. "As long as we're sharing truths, you are correct."

She crumpled up her paper plate and stuffed it into a pocket of her backpack. Then jammed the remaining crackers back into their plastic tray.

"Zoe—"

"It's fine. Don't stress about it. Point taken." She tossed the rest of the picnic remains in his pack. "But attacking me doesn't change your problem. Which is that you're feeling sorry for yourself and hiding away in Lost Harbor, and that's selfish, because you're letting a few people deprive everyone else of your music."

Selfish? Zoe had never paid one bit of attention to his songs, and now she was accusing him of being *selfish?* "You haven't even listened to my music. Don't you think you should before you spout off about it?"

Fire filled her eyes, and all of a sudden she was every bit the Bellini. "I don't have to listen to it to know that people love it. You asked for my honest advice, remember? If you don't like it, that's on you."

She jumped to her feet and shouldered her backpack.

In mutually agreed-upon silence, they set off up the mountainside. The air was beginning to chill down; evening was approaching, although it wouldn't get dark until sometime around midnight.

What a disaster this trip had been. Instead of bringing him and Zoe closer, it had pushed them apart. The best friend he'd ever had was now stomping up the trail ahead of him.

Looking sexy as hell, with her wild dark curls flowing over her shoulders and her backpack bouncing just above her round ass.

Fury became her. Even though the things she said still rankled, he wanted her just as much as before. Maybe more.

No one told him the truth anymore. Only Zoe. No one else had the nerve.

That was one thing that hadn't changed in fifteen years.

CHAPTER FIFTEEN

Zoe's anger, as always, burned hot and fast. By the time they reached the top of the ridge, most of it had drained away. But she knew that Padric didn't operate that way. Whenever they'd fought in the past, he took longer to work through it. She'd be ready to forgive and forget, and he'd still be nursing the wound.

Besides, she was in the right. Wasn't she? He'd asked her opinion and she'd given it.

Though, she hadn't really thought of how it must feel to *be him.* Instead she'd jumped right to the "selfish rock star" interpretation.

But he wasn't being selfish. He was being human. Which was what made him such a beloved singer in the first place. Because he genuinely cared about people. She would never want to change that about him.

As they wound their way down the Larkspur Trail, the light turned the deep gold of late evening. It hung in the branches like mist, as if the ancient spruce trees knew magical secrets barred to humans. Squirrels chirped as they passed and migrating songbirds chittered back and forth. The fresh breath of the forest felt like a kiss.

Zoe replayed their conversation over and over again. And she realized even though they'd had a fight of sorts, it felt *so good* to be talking again. SO GOOD. Really, she'd rather quarrel with Padric Jeffers for a week than spend an hour with any other man.

Crap.

She realized something else as well. He'd made a couple of really good points.

She stopped abruptly. He nearly collided with her, and swore.

"Everything okay?" He steadied her with one hand.

"Send me a playlist," she said. "As soon as we get back."

"Okay. But Zoe, just because I—"

"Just send it. Promise?"

"Sure."

She threw up a hand so he wouldn't say any more before she got her apology in. "You were right about something. I should listen to your music. But you're wrong that I haven't heard any of it. I watched a video of you singing 'Lost Chance.'"

"And?"

"It was really great. If I'm going to be honest with you, I should also be honest with myself. I was jealous. You put yourself out there and share your art with the world and the world loves it. And I can barely bring myself to show one piece to my friends."

"Including me."

"Including but not limited to you. So I guess from my perspective, you're complaining about something I can only dream about. So my advice was worthless. At least, it's worthless until I listen to more of your music."

Padric touched her arm gently, as if not entirely sure of his welcome. "Your advice was not worthless. It was just hard to hear. I'm not used to people laying it all out there like that. People tend to pussyfoot around me."

"Well, I'm not a pussyfooter, I guess."

"That's for damn sure." His lips quirked up in a smile. They stood on the trail, energy vibrating between them. Wind whispered in the treetops and made the giant ferns edging the trail quiver.

Her breath caught in her throat, and she remembered what he'd said—*the ball's in your court*. Did he still mean it?

"I submitted an application for an art fellowship."

His face lit up. "You did?"

"I did. Just the other day. Actually, you inspired me to do it."

He touched her cheek, so lightly she almost thought she'd imagined it. "I shouldn't have lashed out at you," he said softly. "I'm sorry."

"I'm sorry too. I should have thought more about what it's been like for you."

"I'm a big boy. You were right. I've been licking my wounds here."

"You're entitled to do that. You care about people. You don't want them to hurt themselves. That's completely understandable."

Now the apologies were coming fast and furious, from both of them.

"But then I turned around and hurt *you* instead of just listening to you. That's fucked up. I'm sorry."

"I'm more sorry. If one of my sisters hurt themselves because of me, I'd want to tear the world apart. Just because you're a—"

"Spoiled rock star?" he said dryly.

"I did not use those words. I was going to say 'beloved mega-star.'"

"'Beloved mega-star.' It's kind of a turn-on when you say that. Can you say it some more?"

All the anger between them had vanished, as if whisked away by the evening wind. A kind of wild flirtatiousness took its place.

"I could probably be talked into it," she said. "With the right kind of persuasion."

His eyes flared and he took a step closer. "More snacks?" He gestured with his head toward his backpack.

"Mmmm, no. I'm pretty satisfied on the hunger front."

"Champagne? Somehow it didn't feel right bringing out the bubbly at a crash site."

She lifted her eyebrows in astonishment. "I forgot you still had it. You hauled a bottle of champagne down a mountain and back up?"

"Not just any champagne. Veuve Clicquot."

"I almost want to pop it just to see how fizzy it got with all this hiking."

"Sure, we can—"

"No. Not really." She slid one step closer to him. "You're leaving out the most obvious thing."

"Oh yeah?" The gleam in his eyes told her she was going to have come right out and say it.

"Court, meet ball," she said.

He laughed, releasing the tension between them as if he'd snipped a cable in two. "You are something else, Zoe Bellini. There's no one else quite like you. And I know, because I've been everywhere."

With that, he closed the remaining distance between them and crushed her against him.

The hardness of his chest and thighs took her by surprise. Had she been fooled by his kind eyes and general restraint? She shouldn't have been. He was a fisherman's son, and he'd worked his body hard his whole life. And no matter how sweet-hearted he was, no one got to be a beloved mega-star without being tough.

He was showing off that toughness now. She sensed it in the

way his hands ran all over her body, in the way he claimed her mouth in a deep, passionate kiss. *Experience.* Yeah, he had his share, she knew it the second he cupped her ass as if he knew exactly what to do with all her curves.

She sighed against his mouth and melted against him. He plundered her mouth with smooth sweeps of his tongue that left her panting and wild. With strong hands, he shaped the upper slope of her hips and the indentation of her waist, then slid up her torso and spread his hands across her back. With his thumbs, he flicked the straps of her backpack off. For a moment, her arms were pinned behind her by the pack, and he dropped his gaze to her chest.

Under two layers of clothing—a thermal hiking shirt and a light fleece jacket, her nipples hardened into tight peaks. Every rapid breath made her chest heave and her breasts push against her clothing. They seemed to get harder every micro-second he spent staring at them—until they wanted to burst free.

Then he lifted one hand and brushed his thumb against her right nipple.

A sharp bolt of sensation reached all the way through her, all the way down to her sex. She made a sound, something weird and probably embarrassing, but he didn't seem to mind. He unzipped her fleece jacket and reached inside to touch her through her thermal top. It had a built-in bra, with an extra layer of support fabric, but even so she felt his touch like an earthquake.

"Mind if we..." he asked in a rough voice.

Even though he didn't finish the sentence, she shook her head. She didn't mind anything he did at this point. He trundled her backwards a few steps so she leaned against a boulder. It still held heat from the day's sun, and its firmness relaxed her. He gently got rid of her backpack and set it aside. Her arms were free now, but she still felt as if he'd taken the reins. She let them dangle as she gave herself up to him.

He lifted her shirt up to expose her breasts. They spilled out into the cool air. It was wildly erotic to feel so exposed, even though the only one here was Padric. With a reverent appreciation, he thumbed her nipples again, flesh on flesh this time. Strong, warm, skilled, those hands worked magic on the tight peaks. She tilted her head back and arched to give him all the access he needed.

He filled his hands with her aroused flesh, and then bent to work her into an even wilder frenzy with his tongue. He sucked hard on one nipple, creating a deep throb direct to her lower belly. She cried out and clutched at his strong back, feeling his muscles clench and flex.

"I'm going to make you scream, Zoe Bellini." He left her nipple and nuzzled her neck. He bit the tendon there—gently but with just enough force to make every nerve in her body respond.

"Please," she whispered. "Please." She wasn't pleading for anything specific—just more touching, more stroking, more of this command he had over her body.

"I'm going to put my hand down your pants now," he warned, panting slightly. "And I'm going to see how wet you are. How much you want me. Then I'm going to stroke you until you come so hard, you'll never be the same."

Oh, she was wet, all right. She knew what he was going to find when he touched her. His fingers were going to get drenched with the evidence of how freaking aroused she was right now. Her entire body throbbed and hummed with wild excitement with every move he made. Her fingers trembled against his back. She wanted to bite his neck. She wanted to scream into that perfect nook between his collarbone and his throat. She wanted to burst into flames and soar through the treetops.

And that was before he slid his hand under her leggings and right to the heart of her aching desire.

As soon as she felt his fingers touch her clit, her body

clenched against the pleasure shooting through her. She was about to go off like a rocket, but she didn't want to. She wanted this to go on and on, she wanted to lose herself in it, glory in the sensations.

"God, you're beautiful, Zoe," he whispered roughly in her ear. "You're like honey. I wish I could put my mouth on you and feast until dawn. I wish we could stay here all night, me touching you, fingering your sweet pussy. Will you come for me, honey? I want to see you come apart against my hand. I want to feel this hot, plump little clit go wild for me. Can you do that?"

She gasped something incoherent—it was meant to be along the lines of "can I stop myself"—and then she *couldn't* stop herself. She came hard, the pleasure waves seizing her body with ruthless, relentless force. The orgasm felt obliterating as if it wiped her clean, blew away everything meaningless, and left behind only the core of her. Only what really mattered.

Her and Padric, and the forest of Lost Souls.

She sagged against him, panting and weak as a kitten. He delicately withdrew his hand from between her legs. The scent of sex wafted into the forest atmosphere. A brush of cool air made the skin of her abdomen quiver.

He saw the goose bumps and gently put her top back into place.

Okay then. Had she really just experienced the hardest orgasm of her life up against a boulder on the Larkspur Trail?

She opened her eyes to see Padric watching her with calm eyes and a tiny smile at the corner of his mouth. "That was the most incredible thing I've ever been part of," he said softly. "I'm not even exaggerating."

An embarrassed flush spread across her cheeks. "What, because I came the second you touched me?"

"No, just...everything. You take my breath away."

She slid her hand across the front of his pants and noted the very clear bulge, which she'd felt pressed against her as she came. His eyes half-closed as she caressed him. The hard outline of his erection gave her another jolt of arousal.

"Look, Zoe." His voice came out rough. "I have a pretty nice bed waiting for me on the other side of the ocean. How about we pick this up again there?"

"But it's so far. We have to row out to the boat, we have to cross the strait, enter the harbor at a torturously slow pace, tie up the boat, get off the boat, drive to the Eagle's Nest, take the elevator up to your room…"

With each phrase, she escalated her stroking, until his erection was about as hard as the boulder at her back.

He groaned loudly. "You're torturing me, aren't you? You're still mad about the Scandal and you're getting revenge."

She gave a husky laugh. "I think you just made up for all of that. I just feel so good right now, I want you to feel it, too."

"I feel it," he promised her. "I was right there with you." He curled his arms around her. "I can *still* feel it, the way you shook and moaned. It was everything I wanted."

"Not *everything*."

"All in good time. I'm a spoiled rock star. I like my thousand-count bed sheets," he teased.

"Oh, so a random boulder in the forest is good enough for me, but not for you?"

"It's not a random boulder. Don't you see where we are?"

She leaned back in the circle of his arms and gave their surroundings a closer look. "Oh my God. This is the same spot—"

"Where you hurt your ankle. Over there is where we kissed." He gestured down the trail a few steps.

"If my fifteen-year-old self could see me now…" She laughed and stepped aside to comb her fingers through her hair. "Well, she'd be pretty freaking shocked. She was such an innocent."

"I remember," said Padric softly. "That was your first kiss, wasn't it?"

"Of course. Wasn't it yours?"

She picked up her backpack and slid her arms through the straps. Those thousand-count bed sheets were starting to sound pretty good to her. She was so sure of Padric's answer that when it came—"No"—she spun around, shocked.

"Who, then?"

He fastened the hip strap of his pack as he laughed down at her. "Mindy O'Reilly. Remember the one who kept sending me notes?"

"You *kissed* her?"

They headed down the trail.

"I did. At the movies. It was a group, and I was sitting next to her, and as soon as the lights went down, she turned to me and said, 'Do you want to kiss?' She smelled really nice and her hair was soft, and so I said, 'sure.' That was that. It was so unspectacular that I decided kissing wasn't really all that. I didn't try it again until we kissed here." He waved at the trees towering on either side of them. They seemed to be leaning in, almost as if they were listening to his story. "When we kissed that first time, it blew my mind. I finally got it, why people kiss. It was a completely different experience."

"I can't believe you never told me! I thought we were best friends!" She was torn between laughter and indignation. "All this time I thought we were mutual firsts."

"You're telling me you'd never kissed anyone else, even as a kid just checking out how things work?"

"I didn't. The boys were kind of scared of me, I think. I was always about a foot taller than everyone and kind of..." She made a gesture meaning *curvaceous*. "I was too much woman for those elementary school boys who happened to be my age."

"It took a while for them to catch up with you, huh?"

She shot him a sidelong glance. "They're mostly still trying."

He tilted his head back and let out a long laugh that resonated in the still forest. "I get the message. I'll keep working on it."

She smiled along with him, without telling him the truth: that of all the men she'd known, he was the only who *didn't* need to work on it. Actually, she might be the one with some catching up to do.

CHAPTER SIXTEEN

Padric could barely keep his hands off Zoe's shapely body during the trip across the strait to the harbor. The taste of her, the feel of her, worked like a drug on his system, and all he wanted to do was get her naked. In a private place. With sheets. He'd always be grateful for Lost Souls Wilderness for providing such an inspiring location to take things further with Zoe, but he wanted the next part to happen indoors.

He wasn't exactly sure when getting closer to her had become so important to him. Maybe once she'd relaxed and stopped resenting him? Maybe when he'd tasted her baklava? Or maybe when he'd first spotted her on the float when he cruised into Lost Harbor.

It didn't really matter. Now that he'd felt her shatter in his arms, he had one goal in life. To make it happen again, but this time while he was deep inside her body.

He kept up a constant flow of conversation as they zipped across the darkening bay. He was afraid that if he stopped talking, she'd think better of his invitation. She'd remember that he was a rock star and therefore untrustworthy, or she'd get mad about the sixth-grade kiss he'd never told her about.

Once again, they were in weirdly perfect sync.

"So why didn't you tell me about kissing Mindy?" she asked, just when the topic surfaced in his own thoughts.

"I was afraid you'd disapprove," he admitted to her. "You knew I didn't really like her. It seemed like such a typical boy thing, and you always thought I was better than that. Apparently I wasn't."

"Did I think that?" She lifted an expressive black eyebrow at him. "Are you so sure?"

"You didn't?"

She tilted her head, considering. "I knew other girls liked you. Lots of them. More than you knew about, by the way. But my older brothers thought you were gay."

"*What?*" That was news. News that almost threw him off course.

"They said there was no way a straight boy would be okay with being friends forever."

"Who said I was fine with being friends forever?" He shook his head, bemused by this new information. Zoe's brothers were big macho guys several years older than them. Had they really thought he was gay? "I was pretty much always interested in girls. My first big crush was all the girls in Destiny's Child, for God's sake."

"I knew you weren't gay. But I let them think that you were."

He quirked an eyebrow at her as he steered past the breakwater that marked the entrance of the harbor. To his right, a red marker blinked. To his left, the shadowy structures of the fuel depot loomed. "Okay. That might explain a few things, looking back. Why did you do that?"

"So I could come over whenever I wanted." She gave him a cheeky smile from her perch on the padded bench. "Didn't you ever wonder why my conservative Greek Orthodox parents gave me so much leeway when it came to you? They figured you weren't a threat to my virginity."

"True, as it turned out," he said ruefully. "Due to circumstances out of our control."

"Circumstances *they*—" She broke off. "Well, you know. We don't have to rehash the Scandal."

"Do you know that my family never mentions it? Ever. They never talk about Lost Harbor. It's almost like we never lived here. It's strange, but I've learned to just go with it."

"My mother generally doesn't talk about it either, but she completely loses her shit if anyone mentions the Jeffers name or anyone in your family."

"Loses her shit how?"

"Cries. Throws things. Takes to her bed for a day."

"Jesus." He wondered if it made things worse that he'd become famous.

"You know my mother. Drama to the max."

He nodded, remembering some of the scenes he'd witnessed when he'd hung around Zoe as a kid. Sometimes it had been like watching a soap opera, or maybe a real opera. "I'm really sorry about your dad. He was always nice to me."

Zoe nodded but didn't answer. Maybe that wound still hurt, so many years later.

He aimed the front-facing light toward the temporary guest slip that he'd been assigned. As he maneuvered the *Jaunty* into position, he thought about what Zoe had told him about her mother. Mrs. Bellini still couldn't stand even the sound of his name. That didn't exactly bode well for any future for him and Zoe.

"So she doesn't know I'm here?"

"I haven't told her. The twins haven't told her. One of her friends might have, but I haven't witnessed any explosions yet, so they probably haven't, either. It's best all around if she never finds out."

The side of the *Jaunty* bumped against the float. Zoe hopped off the boat and dragged the line to the nearest cleat while Padric shut down the engine.

No future. That sad truth kept echoing in his mind.

He and Zoe had no future. How could they if Mrs. Bellini couldn't tolerate even hearing about him—let alone seeing him or welcoming him back into the family?

No future. Until a few days ago, he and Zoe had lost the past, too. Finally, after their trip to Lost Souls, the past had returned to them. It was no longer in timeout, like a misbehaving child. They had the past and they had the present. Was that enough?

Face it—he'd take what he could get.

Zoe leaned over the railing to grab her backpack. Her firm curves were silhouetted against the fluorescent glow from the tall utility poles spaced along the boardwalk. A yellow wedge of light spilled from the pottery studio, where someone was working late. Low laughter floated from the balcony of one of the B&Bs over-looking the harbor.

Zoe was so much a part of this place. And he...wasn't. Not anymore. His parents had made sure of that.

WHEN THEY REACHED the Eagle's Nest, the late-night desk clerk lifted his head from his folded forearms and waved him down. "Message for you, Gavin."

Everyone at the hotel knew who he was by now, but they gamely kept up the fiction. Padric stepped to the desk to pick up an envelope with his name handwritten in block letters.

"Thanks, man. Back to that nap."

"Good idea. Good night."

He rejoined Zoe at the elevator, where she was waiting with her back turned to the desk, as if they were doing something shady.

"No one cares," he whispered. "That desk clerk was half unconscious. For all anyone knows, you're just hanging out with an old friend."

"Yes, but I know what we're really up to, and my face isn't good at hiding guilt." They stepped into the elevator and she pressed the button for the top floor.

He cocked his head at her choice of words. "What's there to feel guilty about? We're grown adults. Consenting, or at least we'd better be. If not, tell me now."

"It's not that. It's the whole 'sleeping with the enemy' thing. The Scandal. All that." She stretched her arms overhead. "But honestly, right now, mostly I just want a shower."

"Amen to that. I have a Jacuzzi, did I tell you that?" Barely paying attention, he opened the envelope. It held a folded piece of paper.

He opened it and white powder spilled into his hand.

The piece of paper read, "Die PJ."

CHAPTER SEVENTEEN

At first he could only stare at the powder in shock. It looked like baking soda, or maybe cocaine. But was it something worse? News stories flitted through his mind—anthrax, toxins, nerve damage. His heart froze, then started beating double-time.

"What on earth?" Zoe was leaning over his arm to peer at the powder.

"Get back!" he barked at her. She jumped backwards and a puff of the powder wafted into the air.

"We need to go back down. Call 9-1-1. Or Nate. Yeah, call Nate. Tell him someone sent me some suspicious-looking powder. Then call the front desk and tell them not to let anyone on the elevator."

"Oh my God, do you think that's..."

"Why are you still next to me?" Panic threaded his voice. He didn't want Zoe paying the price for his crazy life.

"Because I've probably already been exposed by now. Just... don't move, Padric. I got this." She slowly backed away so as not to disturb the powder and dialed a number. "Hi Nate, this is Zoe and Padric. Yeah, I know. Again. We're just trying to keep your life interesting, sorry. We're in the elevator at the Eagle's Nest, and Padric just opened an envelope that has a white powder in it and a threatening note. Yeah. Okay. Yes, I've heard of 9-1-1. We just like you better. Yes, we'll do that. Thanks, Nate."

She hung up and gently touched Padric on the back. "He's calling everyone on the biohazard team. He said just stay right here and don't move and don't let anyone else get exposed. He's going to call the desk clerk and tell him what to do. Also, he said you're going to owe him several dozen beers at the Olde Salt after today."

"I hear that." He tried to talk without emitting any breath that might stir up the powder. It wasn't easy. "Jesus, Zoe, I'm damn sorry. You shouldn't have to deal with this."

"I definitely had something else in mind for the rest of the evening, but I'm glad you're not alone. I'm sure we'll get that shower at some point. Probably Silkwood-style, or a fire hose behind the station, but that works, too."

In Padric's experience, very few people wouldn't be freaked out about the situation. "How are you staying so calm?"

"You try making pizza for a screaming mob of hungry fishermen. You get used to keeping your cool."

An endless moment passed until they reached the ground floor. The door opened, then closed again. The desk clerk stared at them as he spoke on the phone.

"Did they say how long they'd be?" Padric asked.

"No, he just said as soon as possible. Only a few of our first responders are familiar with the biohazard protocol. They probably have to dig out the gear from under someone's cot."

"Don't make me laugh," he warned her.

"Do you really think it's something dangerous? I can't believe anyone actually wants to kill you. Why would anyone want to kill you?"

"You heard that woman, Mary. I'm sure it wasn't her, but

people can get angry and vengeful. I never realized it until I entered the public eye."

She leaned against the back of the elevator. The door stayed closed, which probably meant that the desk clerk had gotten the word from Nate and had disabled the elevator.

"Do you like being a rock star?" she asked. "I mean, besides this part of it. But the rest of it? Is it everything you dreamed?"

"Are you trying to distract me?" He actually found himself smiling at her. Turned out being with Zoe improved every kind of situation.

"Yes. I know, you could sing me a song."

"How about one of the songs about you," he said without thinking.

She gave a double take and stood up straight. He noticed the dark circles under her eyes. She was exhausted, and now she had to deal with this crap. So unfair. "*One* of the ones about me? What do you mean?"

"Forget it. I wasn't serious."

"Yes you were. I know you. Did you really write more than one song about me?"

"Oh, only all the early ones," he said uncomfortably. "Songwriting is how I process things. You were a big part of what I was processing. I told you that, remember?"

"Yes, but I didn't realize that the songs were about me. I thought they were about you."

He cocked his head. "They're both. Those early songs were like…letters, kind of. Except in song-language, so more metaphorical and poetic. Or at least my version of poetic."

She was still staring at him in astonishment. "So there are songs about me out there and I've never listened to them? I'm such a dumbbell."

"They aren't going anywhere. It's not too late. Well, I

suppose it might be, if..." He gestured to the white powder in his cupped palm.

She paled. "Don't joke about that. My God, Padric."

"Sorry." He hadn't really been joking, but decided he shouldn't mention that.

"You weren't joking, were you?"

He gave the faintest shrug of his shoulders.

"You know," she said slowly. "There's something I should tell you, too. Especially given the circumstances. In case I don't get another chance."

They looked at each other, the potential gravity of the situation sinking in.

"What's that?"

"I did a lot of processing, too. Mine was in the form of letters."

"I never got any letters."

"That's because I never sent them. I didn't have your address, and I wouldn't have mailed them anyway. Too personal. But I still have them."

"*You still have them?*" This felt like huge, important news. Almost important enough to make him forget the possibly deadly powder in the palm of his hand.

"Oh, somewhere. Maybe under the bed. Or in my shoe closet."

He shot her a death glare.

"Don't get excited and start throwing that powder around like flour at a cupcake fight."

"Fine, as long as you let me read those letters."

"I'll think about it." She winked at him, her dark eyelashes fluttering up and down. He realized again that she was trying to distract him, to keep him from losing his cool. And that made him fall a little more—

Holy shit. *In love* with her.

That was what was going on here. That was why he'd been so single-mindedly focused on spending time with her. Holding possible death in his hand brought it into crystal-clear focus. He was falling in love with Zoe.

"That's not fair," he managed. "I wear my heart on my sleeve. I put it all in my songs."

"Yes, but my letters aren't exactly works of art."

"If we survive this, do you promise to let me read them?"

"If we survive this, do you promise to let me have a shower in your fancy hotel suite?"

"Done. I mentioned the Jacuzzi, right?"

"You did. And the thousand-thread-count sheets."

"I'll even throw in some pizza delivery."

She laughed, then immediately covered her mouth with her elbow to stop the puff of air.

Someone knocked on the elevator door. A muffled voice called to them from the other side. "We're opening the door now. Can you hold your breath while we're prying it open?"

A few moments later, the door slid open and two people in white biohazard suits and gas masks stood before them. Behind the masks, he saw Maya Badger and a paramedic he'd seen around the firehouse.

Officer Badger stepped to his side. "You doing okay? Any symptoms?"

"I feel like sneezing," he told her. "But I refuse to."

"Good. Nothing else? Sore throat, nausea, shortness of breath?"

He shook his head.

"Is paralysis a symptom? He hasn't moved a muscle since he opened that envelope." Zoe's voice wavered even as she attempted a light tone.

Officer Badger looked over at her sternly. "How about you,

Zoe? Any unusual symptoms? Like joking at inappropriate moments?"

"I'd say that's normal for me, so no. Nothing unusual. But I didn't get as close to it as Padric has been."

Maya—Padric remembered her from school—opened a white plastic bag and carefully slid the envelope and its contents into it. She swabbed his hand with something like a Q-tip, then handed it to the other paramedic, who held some kind of testing kit.

"We should know in a minute if it's toxic."

"You mean, anthrax?"

Officer Badger nodded calmly. "Anthrax is one of the substances we can detect. There are a few more as well. Lucky for you, Lost Harbor got a grant for a pilot biohazards program. Otherwise you'd be up shit's creek."

"Good to know," Padric muttered. "Are you always this diplomatic with panicky people who might be holding anthrax?"

"You don't seem panicky to me. You're holding it together really well. And my point was, you're *not* up shit's creek. We got this."

"Negative," said the paramedic.

"No, we do. Sure, this is our first actual biohazards event, but we've trained for this and so far, it's textbook—"

"No, I mean, the sample is negative. It's not anthrax or any of the other major toxins."

The tension in the elevator deflated with a collective "whew" of relief. Officer Badger lifted Padric's hand and cleaned it with a baby wipe. He realized his entire arm was trembling from the effort of holding all that adrenaline at bay.

"Mind if I keep the envelope and the note?" Officer Badger asked. "We'll open an investigation into who sent it."

"No, that's great. I'm glad not to be poisoned, but that was scary as shit, especially since Zoe was here."

"I wasn't scared," she insisted.

"I was scared *for you*," he told her. "It's one thing if someone comes after me, but not you. That's not okay."

He caught the surreptitious glances from Officer Badger and the other paramedic. Well, the word about him and Zoe would definitely be getting out now, unless he stopped it now.

"Any chance we could keep this very quiet? I don't want the media getting ahold of it." He held Maya's gaze. "Paparazzi are a public safety issue."

"Good point." She turned to the paramedic and said sternly, "Not a word to anyone about this. Whoever left this was probably local. We don't want to tip them off about anything. As far as the perp knows, Padric never got the envelope, he never opened it, and we never came here. Got it?"

The paramedic nodded reluctantly. That was a lot of juicy information to keep to himself.

"I'm deadly serious, Mike. If anyone finds out, I'm going to blame you. Chief Boone will hear about it, and you don't want that smoke. Zoe, Padric, that goes for you, too. No one can know about this. He'll probably try again, so Padric, if you get any other mysterious communications, call me immediately."

"Yes, ma'am." He'd always liked Maya, who'd been quiet but cool and confident even in her student days. He wouldn't have pegged her as a police officer, but she wore the badge well. "Thank you for coming out so quickly."

"We aim to serve here in Lost Harbor." The two of them collected their gear and turned to go. "Loved your last song, by the way. Kick-ass."

"Hey, thanks." Her compliment gave him a surprising amount of gratification. She was a grownup, not an angst-ridden teenager. "Nice of you to say."

"Keep singing, Padric. Ignore the haters. And the powder-senders."

And she and the paramedic were off.

He caught Zoe's gaze. Wow. What a crazy experience. What an endlessly long day. He punched the button for the top floor. "Okay then, where were we?"

"I think you were saying something about a Jacuzzi?"

Light-headed from the release of all that tension, they held each other and laughed helplessly all the way to the top floor.

CHAPTER EIGHTEEN

Over the past week or so, Zoe had done her share of fantasizing about what spending the night with Padric would be like. Bare skin, flexing muscles, dreamboat eyes blazing above her.

The reality was nothing like her imagination.

They were both so exhausted from the long day that he fell asleep in the armchair, fully dressed, while she showered. She gently woke him up so he could take a shower. Wrapped in a gigantic fluffy bath sheet, she sank onto the couch just for a moment—which turned into a sleep so deep, she barely felt him lift her up and carry her into the bedroom.

Her eyes drifted open as he tucked her into his bed. She certainly noticed that he was bare chested, with only a towel wrapped around his hips. Even half asleep, she took note of his rippling chest and the old fishhook scar he'd gotten at age twelve.

She realized that he was going to leave her alone in the bed, and grabbed his wrist to make sure he didn't do anything of the sort. "Stay," she murmured.

After that, she sank into a deep, exhausted sleep that lasted until late the following morning.

Strange dreams flitted through her mind like mist in the forest. A twin engine plane vanished with a burst of white powder that showered through the air. The full moon rose above the trees—a pepperoni pie, by the looks of it. Padric strummed on a guitar, a single spotlight illuminating his strong form. He sat on a boulder and sang to a gaggle of squirrels, who ignored him as they feasted on baklava.

She woke up with a start. All those images were so clear in her mind that she wanted to memorialize them. A painting? Paint was not her strength. She'd always preferred to shape things with her hands. Maybe that was thanks to her pizza-making background.

But clay...yes, she could make a clay display of Padric serenading the squirrels. That would make a whimsical addition to her figurine project.

Padric.

She glanced to the other side of the bed and saw that it was empty. A note sat on the pillow.

Had to go tend to a few things. There's fresh coffee in the kitchenette. I'll be back soon.

Great, they hadn't even had sex and she was getting the brushoff. She knew this feeling all too well. One moment it seemed that everything was going along fine. The next, you were getting a text—"we should talk"—or a phone call—"I don't know how to say this, but—"

Why was she such a magnet for rejection?

She pushed aside the covers and swung her legs over the side of the bed. Naked in Padric's fancy hotel bed, and he hadn't even waited around to take advantage of that.

Fine. Time to go home and put this whole crazy experience behind her. Handling rejection was her superpower. She knew how to do this. The trick was to get back to work and carry on as if nothing was different. As if she hadn't had the most intense orgasm of her life on a remote trail in Lost Souls Wilderness. As if her childhood friend hadn't just returned and turned her life upside down.

She wrapped herself in the bath sheet that Padric had thoughtfully folded for her. Her clothes were also folded in a tidy pile, but they were so grungy and smelly that one sniff made her toss them aside.

Maybe she could call a friend and get them to bring her some clothes. A very discreet friend. Megan Miller owed her a few favors.

She pulled her phone from its waterproof pocket in her backpack.

Shocked, she saw that it was nearly one in the afternoon.

Luckily it was Sunday, and the Last Chance was closed. But when was the last time she'd slept this late into the afternoon?

She wandered out of the bedroom, chasing the scent of fresh coffee. Rain pattered against the windows and clouds of mist drifted above the bay like smoke. A gray day matching the heaviness in her heart.

As she was dialing Megan, the door to the suite opened and Padric stepped inside. Her heart turned over at the sight of his vivid blue eyes and freshly shaven face. Droplets of rain clung to his tousled hair. He carried a bouquet of peonies in one arm and a bag of groceries in the other. A tote bag hung from the crook of his elbow. *Her* tote bag.

"I brought some clothes for you." He set the tote bag on the kitchenette counter. "I figured you wouldn't want yesterday's gear anywhere near your body."

"My clothes?" she said blankly.

"I hit up Monica and Alexis."

"Oh no. What did you tell them—"

"Nothing. I bribed them," he admitted with a grin.

Zoe rolled her eyes at the thought of her shameless twin

sisters charging Padric for their silence. "They're impossible. What's in the bag?"

"Thought you might be hungry." He opened the grocery bag so she could peer inside. Her stomach whined at the aroma of freshly baked sweet rolls from the Sweet Harbor Bakery.

"Oh my God," she moaned.

"Still your favorites?"

"Absolutely." She inhaled the steamy, sugary fragrance and nearly cried with joy. "You keep bringing me food. Yesterday's picnic, now this. Usually I'm the one feeding everyone."

"I know." He said it so simply, as if it was perfectly obvious that she must need a break from being pizza-provider to one and all. "That was my thinking. Also, I know how much you love food." He winked at her. "Figured that's the way to your heart."

She picked a flake of sugar off the roll and nibbled at it. "When I saw you were gone, I thought you were blowing me off."

"Really? Why? I left you a note."

"Yes, but the note was kind of...impersonal."

"Was it?" He gave her a tender smile and handed her the bouquet of peonies. "Sorry. Conveniently, I happen to have some apology flowers. My note was meant to be informational, that's all."

She took the flowers and breathed deeply of their fresh scent. Between the cinnamon rolls and the flowers and the scent of Padric's clean skin, she was in sensory heaven. Her heart glowed. He'd brought her flowers. And food. And that smile.

"It's me. I'm an idiot. I've just had a few bad experiences, that's all, so I automatically jump to conclusions. It's not your fault. Your note was perfectly fine."

He took the bouquet from her grasp and set it on an end table. Then he cupped her head between his hands and brushed his lips ever so lightly against hers. "I get it. I won't write any more impersonal notes. Hell, I'm a songwriter. I should have written you something more poetic. But you looked so delicious, I had to get out before I woke you up with my giant hard-on."

She laughed, a flush sweeping up her face. "Now that's my kind of poetry."

His eyes darkened as he tugged her lower lip between his teeth. The light scrape triggered a dazzling burst of sensation.

"Eat your sweet roll," he commanded in a gruff voice, his forehead touching hers. "You're going to need your strength."

"Oh really?" she managed through her suddenly tight throat. "What for?"

"For the world-class fucking we're about to lay down," he growled.

She swallowed hard and realized she was swaying slightly on her feet. Low blood sugar? Or had her blood suddenly drained from her brain?

He tore off a piece of a cinnamon roll. "Open your mouth," he ordered.

She did as he said, her mouth already watering with anticipation. He placed the flaky pastry on her tongue. The taste of sugar flooded her senses and made her eyes close halfway. She moaned with joy—the kind of joy only delicious food delivered.

Other kinds of joy had their place too, but food would always be close to her heart.

"More," she told him—her turn to give orders.

"Of course, my queen." With a glimmer of a smile, he gifted her with another bite. "Feeding you could get to be an obsession. I love how you enjoy yourself when you eat. And while you come."

Heat burned in her cheeks. "You liked that?"

"I *loved* that. I was dreaming about it all night. Woke up with the hardest erection of my life. Do you know what it took not to wake you up with my throbbing cock?"

The rough edge in his voice, the blunt words, sent a jolt of heat to her sex. She shifted from one foot to the other. He noticed the movement. Probably knew exactly what it meant, because his eyes went even darker. They were barely blue anymore, more of a deep midnight.

"So..." She moistened her lips with her tongue. He noticed that too. "What's going on with that situation now?"

"The hard-on situation? Feel for yourself."

She eased her hand along the front of his jeans. Her pulse raced as his bulge swelled against her palm.

"Eat your roll," he told her again. Goose bumps rose along her skin.

She held his gaze. As good as the roll tasted, she didn't think she could eat another bite. Not while these wild cravings were flying through her. "I'm not hungry anymore."

"You sure?"

"I'm sure."

He set the pastry bag aside, next to the peonies. *Should put them in water*, she thought vaguely. Then forgot about them entirely when he continued.

"In that case, drop your towel."

CHAPTER NINETEEN

Zoe's dark eyes widened, the wings of her eyebrows rising over them. Was he being too bossy? He got that way sometimes. But he knew Zoe, knew that if she didn't like it, she'd let him know. Hell, she'd complained about his damn note.

"I will," she said in a husky voice. "As soon as I see a little Padric Jeffers skin."

He traced a finger across the creamy curve of her cleavage. Zoe's body was just as generous as her nature. He loved the way her flesh plumped over the edge of the towel. He saw goose bumps rise wherever he touched. Her breath shifted.

He hooked his finger behind the knot she'd tied in the towel and drew her a step closer. "My skin isn't a work of art like yours."

She didn't protest as he teased apart the knot. The towel fell to the floor and Zoe's glorious naked body stood before him. Breasts proud and full, nipples ripe, each curve melting into the next, all of her encased in the rich buttercream of her skin. He wanted to drop to the floor and worship her, press his face into the dark nest of curls between her thighs. Fill his hands with her ass and delve into her most intimate secret self.

He reached for her, but she danced away. "Oh no. Fair's fair."

"All's fair in love and war, don't you know that?" He grabbed her hand and tugged her toward the mirror that hung on the wall next to the door. "Just take a look. Is that fair?"

He positioned himself behind her so that his clothes—he wore a sweater the color of burnt mahogany and black jeans—set off her pale skin. The contrast was wildly erotic. He shaped her waist and hips, then spread one hand across her lower belly, just above her curls, while the other cupped one breast, as if displaying it for the mirror.

Her lips parted and she rested her head against his chest.

"How is it fair that you're so fucking beautiful? That your nipples look like perfectly ripe raspberries? How is it fair that you can get me this turned on just by dropping your damn towel?" He pressed his erection against her ass to make his point.

She wriggled that fine ass against him, nearly making him come on the spot.

"Now that is definitely not fair. Bad girl." He bent his head to gently take the lobe of her ear between his teeth. A shudder when through her.

He spread the fingers of his lower hand wider and tangled his little finger in the soft hair just above her clit. When he gave a light tug, she gasped. In the mirror, he caught the gleam of moisture springing between her thighs.

A kind of wild need gripped him. He had to touch her everywhere, feel everything. His hand around her breast, her nipple rising between his fingers. The knobs of vertebrae under the soft skin at the back of her neck. Her tumble of dark hair against his cheek, fragrant from her late-night shower.

She convulsed at one point, when his hand glided between

her folds to the hot nub of her clit. An orgasm? Not quite—just the sharp pierce of pleasure when his hand met her flesh.

"Padric," she moaned. "I need you. You're making me crazy."

That was what he wanted. Crazy. Crazy as he already felt. Crazy as the wild impulses tossing him this way and that. *Bend her over. Fuck her from behind. No. Too much. Bed. Too far. Couch. Right here. Wall. No. I want her. So bad. Somewhere. Somehow.*

Then she took things into her own hands by reaching behind her and undoing the snap of his jeans. She lowered the zipper, pushed aside his boxers, and wrapped her hand around his member. "This guy needs to be inside me," she murmured. "Before I lose my fucking mind."

Enough said. "Don't move. Stay right there." Hands shaking, he reached inside his pocket for a condom and rolled it on. He tilted her hips so he could reach her entrance more easily, then plunged his hand between her legs again. She jumped and a little rush of hot liquid touched his hand.

"Not yet," he told her. "Just wait one second."

"Then stop touching me there," she gasped. "I can't help it."

He eased up on the friction but kept his fingers where they were. She felt too good to let go—juicy and slick and steam-heated.

With his other hand, he held her hips steady while he eased his rearing shaft into the shadowed entrance of her channel. Just like steering a boat, he thought crazily. Out of the storm and into port. His cock was so hard and thick that he had to pause and let her adjust. She did so easily, deepening the arch of her back to make the angle more accessible.

He pinched her clit lightly, feeling it swell against the pressure. She gasped and wriggled harder against him. "That feels so good. Rub just a little harder, could you?"

God, he loved a woman who knew what worked for her. He

increased the pace and friction of his stroking, even while continuing to work his way inside her. Her lush body gave way beneath him, inch by inch, opening to his penetration as if the two of them had been made for exactly this moment.

And maybe they had been.

When he was fully seated inside her, he forced himself to take a long breath and control himself. Her inner channel held him like a hot fist, and the sensation was so outrageous, he could barely cope.

Hot, juicy flesh filled his arms and surrounded his cock. He watched her in the mirror as he stroked into her, one hand deep between her thighs. God, she was so fucking sexy. Hell, they both were, together. He looked like another person entirely with his head bent over her and his body impaling her like a beast.

Her clit surged against his fingers the more he caressed. She ground against him, then quivered as he thrust again, deep and long. He wanted to bite the soft tendon between neck and shoulder, like a lion subduing its prey. But he kissed her instead, a long suckle that sent another deep shudder through her body.

Her nipples...they called out to him, so proud and erect, so neglected. He slid his hand up her body, along the deep curve of her waist, to the heavy globes of her breasts. As soon as he brushed his thumb against her nipple, she cried out.

"Oh God, Padric. Do that. Do it again."

He smiled to himself. That was his Zoe, direct and sensual. She'd always been that way about food, so why not everything else as well? He licked his thumb and circled it around her nipple. Her eyes fluttered shut as she gave herself over to the pleasure. For a moment he concentrated only on her, stilling himself inside her so he didn't come too soon.

She gave a low moan and clutched his hand tighter against her breast. With her other hand, she touched her own nipple, and the sight of that in the mirror was the last straw for him. He pushed into her, burying himself deep, just a breath before she erupted with a long cry. He held on one more minute, gritting his teeth against the orgasm building at the base of his spine. He kept his hand clamped onto her pussy, milking every last wild spasm from her climax.

Only when her moans had shifted from desperate to satisfied did he let the reins loose on his own orgasm. It exploded out of him, ripped right from his core. His vision blurred at the edges and he had to hold on tight to her warm body to keep from keeling right over.

As the last waves faded, he found himself hunched over her, panting as if he'd just finished an especially wild concert.

"You okay up there?" She reached up and tenderly touched his cheek.

"No. I'm not okay. You fucking rearranged my atoms." He laughed down at her.

"Is that why I saw stars? Atoms rearranged?" She turned and wrapped her arms around him, pressing her soft flesh against him. "I guess that would explain things."

"Like what?"

"Like how I feel like I've never done that before. Even though I have. Of course. But not *that*." Her tongue stumbled over the words, and he knew exactly how she felt. That no matter how many times he'd had sex—and he'd had plenty—it had never touched him like this.

"I think I need to sit down," he murmured.

She laughed. "Right behind you."

With one last kiss on the top of her tangled dark hair, he shifted his attention to the condom. He got rid of it quickly, then refastened his clothes.

Still naked, Zoe crossed over to the tote bag he'd dropped on the counter. Riveted by her flushed sensuality, he couldn't tear his eyes away from her as she sorted through the clothes from Monica and Alexis.

"Okay, those two are going to pay for this." She held up the top they'd sent. It was a crop top that said, "Hot to Trot," over a glitter-maned pony.

"Oh hell. I didn't even check what they gave me. I just grabbed the bag and went."

"Where did they even get this underwear?" She displayed a pair of leopard-print panties. "I better have a talk with those two."

"I don't know, those are pretty hot," he told her.

She spun them around to show off the writing on the back. "*Back off, I'm farting,*" it read.

He burst out laughing. "Are they teenagers or nine-year-olds?"

"A little of both, I think. Also they might be blind. In what world would these shorts ever fit me?"

She held up a pair of cutoffs that barely had a crotch, they were so short. She put her arm through one of the leg holes. "It hardly fits over my arms, let alone my legs. Those two are dead to me. Oh, and check this out."

From the bottom of the tote bag, she pulled out one more item. A hot-pink condom package. "Those girls are in big trouble."

"They probably got that in health class or something. People hand out condoms like candy these days. It's a good thing."

"I know it's a good thing. But they're my little sisters, and they cause enough trouble as it is," she grumbled. She turned the "Hot to Trot" shirt inside out and pulled it on. It barely fit over her breasts, and he felt a stirring in his cock at the sight.

"I guess this could get me home," she said dubiously.

"How about this? There's a washer and dryer for guests. I'll wash your clothes while you drink your coffee. It's raining and miserable outside, why not just hole up here for the day?"

She cocked her head, considering. "Is there breakfast involved in this scenario? Those three bites of cinnamon roll got burned up by all that hot sex."

"Oh yes. I bought enough for an army."

"So." She ticked items off on her fingers, one by one. "Flowers. Pastries. Orgasm. Coffee. Jacuzzi. Laundry. Anything else you want to throw in there?"

"Is there anything else you need?"

"Yeah. Answer a question for me."

"Shoot." He picked up her pile of grungy hiking clothes.

"Will you be my best friend? Again?"

CHAPTER TWENTY

Zoe would have expected things to be awkward after having sex with Padric for the first time. But the only awkward thing was that she wanted to do it again almost as soon as he left the room with her laundry.

She felt too good to worry about the fact that they'd tossed a big grenade into their friendship. This was Padric, someone who knew her flaws intimately. He knew she could be hotheaded, and that her pride got in her way sometimes. He knew she feared rejection—or at least he knew that now. He knew she occasionally said things without thinking, and that she was stuck here in Lost Harbor for the foreseeable future. He knew she had disastrous romantic luck. He knew she held grudges. He knew she believed in revenge. He knew that she couldn't jog much faster than a freshwater snail.

And he still wanted her.

And she wanted him, despite the fact that a rock star and a pizza shop owner had no chance of a future.

Did the future really matter?

Truth was, she already knew what her future would consist

of. She already owned a home and a business. She'd probably be making pizza until she was an arthritic old lady.

Why not grab this opportunity for something special and fleeting? It would be gone soon enough, when Padric went back to his jet-setting lifestyle.

A knock on the door startled her. "Hello? Padric?"

"It's Officer Badger. Is Padric there?"

"He'll be back in a minute."

"Can I come in? Official police business here."

"Hang on."

Oh great. Padric had taken all her real clothes. Her choices were a bath sheet, her sisters' joke clothes, or stark nakedness.

She pulled on the leopard-print undies, surprised they actually fit. They were stretchier than they looked. Instead of the micro-shorts, she darted into Padric's room and found a pair of workout pants. The crop top matched it well enough, and at least it was inside out. Unfortunately, she looked nearly pornographic without a bra. She wrapped a towel around her shoulders.

Ridiculous outfit for a police interview, but it would have to do.

She opened the door with as much dignity as she could manage. "Hello, Officer Badger."

"Hi, Zoe."

Officer Badger—Maya, as Zoe usually called her—swept in. Ever the professional, she showed no reaction to Zoe's bizarre outfit.

Strangely, that made Zoe nervous, and she started to babble. "It was such a scary thing, I mean we were pretty rattled last night, so I decided to stay here instead of trying to drive home and—"

Maya threw up a hand. "Don't care. Not my business."

Zoe relaxed with a whoosh of relief. "Of course. It's just—"

"Not. My business." Maya pulled out a notebook. "I need to interview you both again about the envelope."

"Shouldn't you talk to the desk clerk? He probably saw who left it."

Maya blinked at her, a single sweep of her curly eyelashes that conveyed every bit of her unspoken "do you think I'm a moron?"

"That's being investigated," she said briefly. "But I need to talk to both of you, too."

"Right, of course you do. Go ahead. Ask me anything."

"Are you two back together?"

When Zoe did a double take, Maya laughed. "I'm just teasing. Like I said, it's not my business. But here's the thing. Someone in our town has it out for Padric. And you know him best, except maybe for Nate Prudhoe. And now you're spending lots of time with him, hiking across the bay—"

"How'd you know that?"

"The plane crash."

"Right. Of course."

"And now you're here at his hotel."

Good point. How was she supposed to keep any of this private when they had to keep calling 911?

"So it'd be real helpful if you could keep your eyes open and do some thinking about who might be pissed off at Padric, and why."

Suddenly it clicked, and Zoe understood what she was getting at. "You're thinking of Reese."

"Thought crossed my mind."

Zoe swallowed hard. Was it possible that her nasty ex was trying to scare Padric? "He doesn't even live around here anymore. He moved to Dillingham."

Maya wrote that down. "He's a mechanic, right? He might

come down this way for parts or jobs. I'll check into his travel schedule."

Zoe nodded, twisting her hands together. "It's possible."

"I'll need contact information for your other ex-fiancés, too."

Okay, this was officially mortifying. "I'll give you what I have, but it seems like a reach. Are you sure it's about me and not something in his life? Oh! You should ask Padric about the PJ parties."

Maya made a note. "We're going to look at everything, including some bad blood regarding the Scandal and the Jeffers family."

Alarm bells clanged. "Maya, for the love of God, ask me or my sisters or my exes anything you want. But *please* don't bother my mother. She doesn't even know Padric is here. If you need to talk to her, just let me tell her first. It'll be better coming from me."

Maya's serious face relaxed into a sympathetic smile. When Maya dropped her severe police business expression, she was gorgeous. "I'll do that, but it's very unlikely I'll need to talk to her. It's just an angle I need to consider."

"Do you think...do you think I'm putting Padric in danger by spending time with him?"

"In danger from baking soda? Yeah. Flour, too, and tomato sauce."

Zoe couldn't quite manage a laugh. "You know what I mean."

"I do. Since we don't know what's going on yet, it's hard to say. There's just as good a chance that Padric is putting *you* in danger."

"That's not exactly reassuring, Officer Badger." Zoe attempted a smile that went wrong somewhere around the middle.

"Yeah well, it's the truth. I'm not here to sugarcoat anything. You both need to be watchful and keep your eyes open and call me if something seems off." Maya tucked away her notebook and swung toward the door. "Notice that I said to call *me*, not Nate. He's not your personal 911 service. Call him too often and he'll get a big head." Her wry smile was the last Zoe saw of her as she slipped out the door.

She must have intercepted Padric somewhere between the laundry room and the suite, because it took another half an hour for him to get back. In the meantime, Zoe paced around the suite in her crop top and leopard-print undies and tried to sort out what to do.

Screwing up her nerve, she called Reese. He'd changed his number when he'd moved to Dillingham and his lawsuit got thrown out of court, but he'd called her a few times—always hanging up when she answered. She'd kept the number just in case she needed to report him to the police.

He answered right away.

"Reese? It's Zoe."

Dead silence, then a very confused, "Zoe *Bellini?*"

His reaction put her conviction that he wasn't involved at about eighty-five percent.

"Yes. It's...uh...someone said they saw you here the other day."

"In Lost Harbor? Not me. I'm in Hawaii working on some rich guy's boat."

That sounded sketchy. "Some rich guy? You don't even know his name?"

"I know his name. But *you* don't need to know it. What are you calling about, Zoe? We're dead as a skunk."

"The phrase is 'drunk as a skunk.'"

"We're dead as a dead skunk," he clarified.

Sweet Jesus, what had she ever seen in him, beyond those strong mechanic hands and arm muscles? Had she really been that shallow?

"You're right. I shouldn't have called. I was just...if you come to Lost Harbor, it'd be nice to get a heads up, that's all. No hard feelings. I'll even give you a slice of Surf 'n' Turf pizza. I'd just like to be prepared."

"You can keep your freaking pizza. I'm not going near Lost Harbor. No need. I got a new life in Dillingham, a hot new lady, and we're thinking of moving to Hawaii permanently."

"Wow, that's good, Reese. Congratulations."

"Whatever," he muttered. "Don't call again, my girlfriend wouldn't like it."

"I won't. Bye, Reese."

Well, that settled it. At least one of her exes had nothing to do with sending white powder to Padric. Should she test the other two?

She was just gearing up for another excruciating phone call when Padric finally came back. He carried a pile of folded laundry in his arms.

"The chambermaid finished the laundry while Maya interrogated the life out of me," he told her. "Sorry it took so long." He set her clothes on the armchair and opened his arms to her.

She flew across the room and launched herself against him. "I missed you," she murmured against his chest.

"Longest half hour of my life," he agreed, laughing.

"Not that. The fifteen years before that."

They held each other so close that she felt his heartbeat vibrating through her own chest cavity. Desire hummed between them. Would it always be like this, instant lust as soon as they touched? Or were they making up for those lost fifteen years?

And it struck her then—why she'd gotten involved with Reese and the others.

She'd known in her heart that no one would ever compare to Padric. So she'd grasped at whatever other possibilities came her way.

Being with him now—the joy was over the top. But so was her

fear.

They drew apart and their eyes met. In his, she saw the same worries she'd been grappling with. "I don't want to put you in danger," he said soberly.

"I don't want to put *you* in danger."

He frowned briefly. "What are you talking about? That powder was meant for me. I told her about another incident, too. Someone threw a bottle at me outside the Olde Salt. This is about me, not you."

"Maya said they're looking at all possibilities. But anyway, that's not the point."

He took both her hands in his. "What do you mean?"

"Have you noticed the pattern? It's a little hard to miss."

"Spell it out for me."

She pulled away from him and crossed to the pile of her clean clothes. "The first time we went across the bay and kissed, it was a total disaster. The Scandal and everything that came after."

She stripped off the crop top and put on her bra. As she was fumbling to fasten it, Padric came to her aid, his fingers light and clever with the hooks.

"Then we went across the bay again. We kissed again. And what happened? A plane crashed. Then we came back here and you got a death threat. What if..."

"What? What's your point?"

She pulled on her clean thermal top and turned to face him. His eyes had darkened to a stormy deep blue. "Everyone knows I have bad luck. But maybe the combination of the two of us is even worse. What if we're...I don't know, cursed? Or just very, very unlucky? What if we're *bad* for each other?"

"Do you know how ridiculous that sounds?"

"Well, I got my superstitious side from my mother. She always believed the 'strange things in Lost Souls' stuff. But she's not always wrong."

He snagged her arm so she faced him. "What are you saying, Zoe? That we should stay away from each other because occasionally bad things happen? Don't bad things happen anyway?"

Under the intense focus of his blue gaze, her worries vaporized and all that mattered was being here with him. "Of course they do. I don't know what I'm saying. I just don't want you to get hurt."

"You know what would hurt me more? If you ended this before it's ready to end."

Ready to end. That phrase sank through Zoe's soul like a lead weight. Of course things *would* end between them. They had to, since their lives were so very different.

But being *ready* to end it...what would that mean? Who would decide? Was another enormous rejection headed her way —bigger and more devastating than any of the others?

"And what about this, Zoe—what if we're *never* ready to end it? What if this is it for us? Do you really want to walk away already?"

Her lips parted as she absorbed his words. Was Padric saying he wanted a future?

Maybe a future together wasn't out of the question. Maybe a rock star and a pizza maker could find a way.

"No," she whispered. "I don't want to walk away. I don't even know if I can."

He hauled her against him. Heat instantly ignited deep in her belly. Her inner thighs trembled and her nipples tingled.

"I know I can't," he said firmly. "But I can't decide for you. All I can do is try to make the risk worth it."

And in his arms, everything else faded away and lost all meaning. The only thing that existed was this feeling, right here. The feeling of being with Padric, her heart beating so close to his. Nothing else would ever compare.

CHAPTER TWENTY-ONE

Once Padric had told Maya about the PJ parties and the incident at the Olde Salt, she had agreed there was very likely a connection. They'd scheduled a more thorough interview for later in the week.

By the time his meeting with the detective rolled around, Padric knew what he had to do. To keep Zoe out of danger, he had two choices. Not see her anymore, or find out who was behind the attacks.

Clearly, option one was off the table. He wanted to be with her all the time. He wanted more Zoe, not less.

That made option two all the more urgent. He needed to draw the guy out. Lure him into a trap. Stop him before he caused real harm. He came up with a plan, which he ran by Zoe first during a quick phone call.

"If I do this, your mom might find out that I'm in town."

"I guess it was inevitable." She whooshed out a breath. He could picture her balancing the phone between her ear and her shoulder. "I can't decide if it's better coming from me or from the grapevine."

"Do you want me to wait?"

"No, do what you have to do. I'll find the right moment to tell Mama. I should have told her by now anyway."

When he arrived at Maya's office, he found Nate lounging in the single chair facing her desk. Maya looked ruffled, of all things.

He knocked lightly on the doorjamb. "Should I come back later?"

Nate didn't look happy about the interruption, but Maya beckoned him in. "No, no. Come in. Nate was just leaving."

"Actually, it might help to have Nate here."

"No," Maya said firmly. "It rarely helps to have Nate here." She made a shooing gesture at the lanky guy in the chair. Nate narrowed his gray eyes at her, but did her bidding and loped out of the room.

Padric settled into the chair Nate had just vacated. "I came up with a plan."

"A plan? This is supposed to be a follow-up interview."

"We don't need all that. I want to catch this idiot, and I think the best way is to set a trap for him."

Maya sat back and pinched the skin between her eyebrows. "Lord help me."

"It's a good plan. Just...listen. I think I should do an interview on KLHW." Most people in town listened to the local segments on Lost Souls radio. "I'll talk about how welcoming the town has been. I won't mention the powder. It'll be like it never happened. Guaranteed to drive him crazy. Then I'll talk about the auction for the volunteer fire department, and how I'm going to be there, and I'm offering up a private serenade. I'll bet you anything the dude will be there."

"That's a big leap."

"Think about it. He's gotta know that he can't try anything at the hotel again. I'm not exactly predictable in my schedule, except for the training shifts at the fire station. There's no way he'd try anything in a place full of first responders."

"All those same first responders will be at the Olde Salt for the auction."

"Yes, but so will lots of other people. It'll be easier for him to do something without being noticed. He won't know that we're watching for him."

Maya fiddled with a pen. "You also buy a lot of pizza."

"I see your investigation is well underway," he said dryly.

"Some things don't need a lot of investigating. I worry about the Last Chance. I need you to stay away from there. Too many people in the line of fire, if you know what I mean."

He nodded slowly. That made sense. "So what about the auction?"

"It makes me nervous. It's always a good crowd, especially if you're giving away a performance. I gotta think about this, Padric. My first priority is public safety."

"Like you said, it'll be packed with first responders."

She cocked her head, considering. "True. We can all be there monitoring the crowd, and it will look like we're just helping at the auction."

Was she actually leaning towards his plan? "Exactly. That's why it's such a good idea."

"My sense is that he's focused on you and isn't trying to hurt anyone else. But things can always change with these crazies, and we need to be prepared."

"Okay, well, let me know your decision. I'm willing to do anything and everything."

"Well, there's one thing you won't do. Leave," she said wryly.

His jaw tightened. "You think I should leave?"

"Didn't say that. Just making an observation. How long are you planning to stick around here?"

"At least until the beach festival. I'm considering performing a song there." He hadn't actually given another thought to that, but it popped into his mind as a good reason to stay.

Maya gave a heavy sigh. "You just live to make my life difficult, don't you? That festival is already giving me a stomachache."

He raised another idea that had been percolating in his mind. "How about I bring in private security? I know you guys are spread pretty thin."

She gave a reluctant nod. "That might be helpful for the auction and the festival. We have very limited man and woman power."

"Done. I know just the guy. He'll stay low-key, I promise."

"Gavin Strike?" she asked dryly.

He laughed. "No, not him. Someone else I've worked with."

"Okay, then let's move forward with this plan. The auction's this weekend. Pretty good timing. Our perp will be paying close attention."

"Thanks." He stood up and reached over the desk to shake her hand. "Sorry for causing so much trouble. It's not what I wanted."

"Don't blame yourself too much."

He took those words with him as he left her office and headed one block over to the volunteer fire station. *Don't blame yourself too much.* That was easier to do when the issue was baking soda instead of kids hurting themselves.

But it seemed like something he should take to heart. Maya was one smart cookie, after all.

THE LOCAL RADIO station jumped at the chance to interview the hometown boy made good. He played his part perfectly, raving about how much love he'd been getting from the town. He talked about wanting to give back to Lost Harbor by contributing to the annual volunteer fire department auction. He made no reference at all to mysterious white powders or envelopes.

Hopefully the suspect was gritting his teeth in frustration.

He kept up the act at the Olde Salt—which rivaled the radio station in terms of spreading news. He enlisted Lucas Holt in the effort, after filling him in on the situation.

Lucas had recently sold his family's boat, the *Jack Hammer*, and assumed the position of head of the harbor commission. More importantly, he was head over heels for his new fiancée, Zoe's friend Megan.

"You should start saving your pennies for the auction, Lucas. I bet Megan would love a romantic love song. Or maybe Ruby needs a lullaby. I'm versatile."

"I might do that." As always, Lucas' dark eyes warmed at the mention of his new fiancée. He signaled to Toni for another beer. "Toni, did you hear that? Celebrity drop-in at the volunteer auction."

Good thinking, to rope the bartender into the conversation. That was how news got spread the fastest.

"Heard about it on the radio. Any chance we'll get a sample during the auction?" She handed each of them another bottle of IPA.

"Maybe, maybe. Spread the word."

Eyes alight with that juicy tidbit, she slung a bar towel over her shoulder and moved on to another customer.

"That ought to do it," Lucas said under his breath. "Nice one."

"Don't tell my manager. I'm supposed to be resting my voice."

"No problem. Listen, you're being careful, right? If anything happens to Zoe this town will never recover."

Padric pretended to be offended. "Just Zoe? Not your old friend Padric?"

"Zoe has the pizza. And besides, she's Zoe. Mistress of the helping hand, queen of the withering stare. She's always there for people around here. She gets a lot of sympathy for all the bad luck she's had."

"You're saying I'm more bad luck for her?"

"Fuck no. I hope you're the opposite. Sometimes I think she's been waiting for you to get back. I'm just saying, take that seriously. No matter what happens, this town will take her side."

"Hey, you can back off now," Padric warned. "I'm not trying to hurt Zoe. I'm trying *not* to hurt her. That's why I'm doing this."

"I'm not referring to her physical safety, hotshot."

He got it. Of course he did. But why did everyone assume that things weren't going to work out between them?

"What if Zoe decides she wants to leave Lost Harbor and come with me?" He hadn't even dared to voice that thought until now—with a few beers in him. "Is everyone going to hate me for stealing her away?"

Lucas looked at him strangely. "Is that your plan? Good luck."

"What do you mean?"

"You don't know? Zoe can't leave. She made a deal with her mom."

"What deal?" Padric's heart sank. Zoe had never mentioned anything about this. She'd hinted at her intention to stay in Lost Harbor, but hadn't explained why.

"After her husband died, Mrs. Bellini signed the house and the Last Chance over to Zoe on the condition that Zoe take care of her until she died. Mrs. Bellini gets to approve the 'care.' For instance, she can't be forced to go into a nursing home if she doesn't want to. So as long as she insists she needs Zoe, she's got her."

Jesus. No wonder Zoe hadn't mentioned that. She was bound up with her family just as much as when she was a kid.

"So Zoe's stuck here until her mother...what, dies? That seems insane."

"Or until her mother lets her go. But that's not likely. You know how she is. Anyway, Zoe loves it here. Her business is doing great and she's riding herd on the twins. She was happy until you showed up. Now..." Lucas shrugged. "Just watch your step. Anyone who messes with our Zoe might have to move to Dillingham, like Reese the Greaseball."

"Don't worry, your pizza queen can make her own decisions," Padric grumbled. "What do you think I'm going to do, kidnap her?"

Lucas laughed and drained his beer. "I dare you to try. Lost Harbor is not about to let that happen. Have you tried the Surf 'n' Turf pizza? Enough said."

CHAPTER TWENTY-TWO

Padric's favorite security specialist arrived at the tiny one-runway Lost Harbor airport the next day. He'd first hired Ethan James for a show at the Hollywood Bowl in Los Angeles. At the time, Ethan had been working with his sister, Olivia, as part of James Investigations. Now he ran the firm on his own, which meant he had even less available time than usual.

"The only reason I'm doing this is because your last song fucking ripped my heart out," grumbled Ethan after the two of them had exchanged hugs. Ethan already knew how Padric liked to deliver his hugs, and didn't object. "And because it's Alaska. Bucket list, baby. Check it off."

"Fun fact: this little town is the most beautiful place in the entire state." Padric grinned at him as he showed him to Zoe's car, which he'd borrowed for the pickup. "Not that I'm at all biased."

"So you grew up here? And now someone wants to kill you?"

They slid into the little red Subaru.

"I wouldn't go that far. Scare me, probably." As he started the Subaru, he noticed Ethan's gaze straying to the objects scattered on the dashboard. Zoe had a habit of collecting beach debris, like some kind of magpie, and leaving it on the dashboard to bake in the sun. A sea urchin shell, an iridescent raven's feather, a dried wild rose. She'd explained that these things would all end up in a clay figure at some point. In the meantime, her car was a mess and always smelled like low tide at the beach.

"Rental car?" Ethan asked mildly.

"No, it's Zoe's. She's…" He hesitated. What was Zoe, exactly? "An old friend. My best friend growing up. We're seeing each other. You'll meet her."

"I feel like I know her already." Ethan touched a decapitated doll's head that had been bleached by the sun and mottled with algae. "Bit of a morbid streak?"

"Not at all. You like pizza?"

Even though Maya had asked him to avoid the Last Chance, he couldn't resist taking Ethan there at least once.

"I like it in LA. What the fuck does Alaska know about pizza?"

"You're going to eat those words, my friend. With extra cheese."

NOT ONLY DID Ethan acknowledge that Lost Harbor might have the best pizza this side of Little Italy, he also fell instantly for the entire staff of the Last Chance—or at least the Bellini part of it. Monica and Alexis had him laughing within two minutes of his arrival.

"Please stay for our festival!" they begged as soon as they found out he did security. "It's the world premiere, and we can't pay you but you can have all the pizza you want. We'll be your own personal pizza carriers. We'll follow you around with a pizza plate wherever you go."

"Damn, that's tempting. Not quite as much as a salary, though."

"Celery? We can give you celery. The biggest celery you've ever had."

Ethan's booming, infectious laugh captivated the girls and everyone within earshot.

He hit it off with Zoe, too. Her charm had him eating out of her hand—literally, when she dropped a locally brined anchovy into his open mouth, after teasing him about mutant fish in LA.

"Well? Best anchovy you ever tasted?"

Ethan smacked his lips and grinned widely at them all. "Not that it's saying much, but yes. Best weird little fish I ever had."

Zoe high-fived Ethan, her eyes glowing. Everything about her was so radiant and breathtaking that Padric wanted to whisk her to the back pantry and feel her up right then and there.

Why not? Their time together was running out. Soon he'd have to leave, and she would never come with him. They had to grab every opportunity they had.

"Zoe, can I speak to you in private for a second?"

"Sure. Girls, you're in charge. Ethan, keep an eye on them." Zoe finished giving orders and led him to a quiet corner of the glassed-in deck.

Not exactly what he'd had in mind.

"What's going on? Did you find something out about the evil baking soda perp? I like that word, perp. It sounds so authentic."

"Nothing's going on. I just want you so bad I can't fucking see straight."

Her pupils dilated and a flush came across her cheeks. The chemistry between them was so hot and fluid and easily ignited. It ought to have a periodic table all its own.

"I'm right there with you," she whispered. "You're making my nipples tingle, just talking like that."

"I want to lick them right now. Fuck all these customers. Tell them to get out so I can spread you across this table and taste every inch of you."

He watched her throat move as she swallowed, and imagined her mouth around his cock. Under the table, he moved her hand to his crotch.

"Feel this? Happened as soon as I saw you in your damn apron."

Maybe he really should avoid the Last Chance, because he couldn't handle himself around Zoe.

He tightened his jaw as she stroked him under the table. Good thing Mrs. Bellini had always insisted on tablecloths. His gaze dropped to her chest, and he imagined her nipples swelling behind her dress.

"You busy later?" His rough voice could have scraped the scales off a fish.

"Very busy, apparently." With a wink, she drew her finger-nails across the fabric stretched over his bulge. "How long is your friend hanging around?"

"I'll get him his own damn room. He's extra security for the public, not for me. Are you coming to the auction?"

"As if I would miss that. I heard you might sing a little bit at the auction."

He grinned at the speed with which the news had made the rounds.

"I'll give you a private show anytime, babe. No bid required."

He'd pictured it already—her naked in the Jacuzzi, him singing to her as the moon rose over the bay.

"Don't you want me to bid on you and save you from some crusty old fisherman? Or Boris Clancy? What if you end up sere-nading his chicken?"

He chuckled at that. "I have thought about the risks here. I might end up twenty miles out of town on some homestead, singing to an old Russian trapper in his outhouse. I may need to add some fine print before this thing kicks off."

Smiling, she gave him one last lingering caress, then drew her hand away. "I have to get back before the twins set another fire. See you later?"

"Unless some crazy disaster happens, yes."

"No, those only happen when we're together," she pointed out.

"Aren't you thinking of orgasms?"

"Haha." And by the flush on her cheeks, he knew that she *was* thinking of orgasms. The wild and wonderful ones they gave each other, over and over, every single time they found each other together in his bed.

His bed. Always his bed. In his hotel room.

"Hey." He snagged her wrist as she got up to leave. "How about I sneak through your window tonight?"

"Are you getting tired of those thousand-thread-count sheets already?"

"No, it's just—it's a hotel room. It's impersonal and temporary. Your bed, on the other hand, is drenched in you. Your scent, your presence, your dreams." He made it sound like a song lyric.

"You make it sound like I need to wash my sheets," she said dryly, refastening the string of her apron.

Only Zoe felt free enough with him to mock his off-the-cuff songwriting. "I'm being poetic. People pay me for that, you know."

"I know. And it's a lovely image. Nice thought. But I just can't take a chance on my mother seeing you."

"I thought you told her I was here."

"I haven't had a chance."

"She probably heard me on the radio."

"I don't think she did. If you were anyone else..." She hesitated, biting her lip. "But you're a Jeffers. And I really worry what would happen if she caught sight of you. Her health is so precarious. Actually, it's more that her mental state is precarious."

"But Zoe...you can't let her hold you hostage like that."

She stiffened. "Hostage? What are you talking about?"

"I remember how your mom was. Seems like she hasn't changed much. She's got you right where she wants you."

Zoe's expression shifted. "You're talking about...who told you all that?"

"Seems like it's common knowledge for everyone except me. Why didn't you mention it?"

"It never came up. But I told you I'm a Lost Harbor lifer, and I'm not going anywhere."

That wasn't exactly what he remembered her saying. "Is that your choice or your mother's choice?"

"Stop that. It's both, and obviously you don't understand." With as icy an expression as someone with Zoe's natural warmth could manage, she stalked back toward the counter, where Ethan was still laughing it up with the twins.

Not understand? That was a load of crap. No one understood better than he did, since he'd witnessed the Bellini family in action.

As soon as she was back behind the counter, he sent her a text. *Sorry. I just want to see you, that's all. All of you. Bed included.*

She glanced up, her expression already softening. *I'll send you a photo of it.*

Will you be naked in it?

Absolutely. Oh, I nearly forgot. I have something for you.

A blank envelope with baking soda? Are you that mad?

Close.

He laughed out loud, drawing glances from a few customers.

I'm actually serious. I'm going to put it in the backseat of my car. I'll walk to the hotel after work and pick up my car.

Wild with curiosity about what could be "close" to an envelope with baking soda, he texted, *Any more hints?*

Just 1. If you don't want to see me after you get it, leave my car here, so I don't have to come to the hotel to get it.

I guarantee I'll still want to see you. Ethan and I will walk to the hotel so you can have your car back now.

She picked something up and disappeared through a back door that led to the garbage enclosure where he'd talked to the eagle. As the door swung open, he caught a glimpse of that same eagle perched on the railing. Probably waiting for a pizza snack. He probably hung out here a lot.

But Zoe wasn't carrying a bag of garbage. Craning his neck, he saw that she held a shoebox. The eagle didn't seem too disappointed. He settled down to clean his wings with his beak.

The door swung closed. Now Padric was beyond curious about that shoebox.

CHAPTER TWENTY-THREE

Padric shoved his phone back into his pocket and rejoined Ethan. "You okay here for a minute? I have to do something outside."

"I'm ready to go. See you later, kids." Ethan slapped some money on the counter and stood up. Damn, now Padric was stuck with Ethan when all he wanted to do was see what the hell Zoe was leaving in her car for him.

"How about an ice cream cone before we head back to the hotel?" he asked his friend.

"I feel like you're throwing me a kid's party. Pizza, ice cream, what's next? A bouncy house?" Ethan ambled out of the pizza shop, his limp barely noticeable. Padric knew that he fought an ongoing battle against the effects of childhood osteosarcoma. When they'd first met, Ethan had been wearing a cast.

"Just showing off the wonders of Lost Harbor." He gestured toward a deck built into the boardwalk, with benches and a set of industrial binoculars set onto a concrete post. "You can get a closeup view of the glaciers over there. Lost Souls Wilderness has at least four of them visible from the harbor. They're shrinking fast, so better look while you can."

Ethan zipped up his jacket against a gust of wind—all too common on the ocean side of the boardwalk. "As an investigator, I know perfectly well you're trying to get rid of me so you can flirt with the gorgeous pizza goddess. As your friend, I will obediently stare at the glaciers while you do your thing. And then I need to get to the hotel and do some work."

He should have known he couldn't fool Ethan. That was the whole point of hiring an investigator; they noticed things. While Ethan strolled toward the overlook, Padric hurried back to Zoe's Subaru.

An open shoebox sat on the backseat. It was filled with envelopes and sheets of notepaper. He picked up the envelope on top—blank, just like his joking guess. Smiling at that, he slid out the piece of notepaper inside.

Dear stupid Padric,

I hate you for not being here. I should probably be over it by now but I'M NOT. I'm still mad. I'm stuck here with these looney-tunes parents losing their shit and there's nowhere I can go for a break. THIS SUCKS. Where are you? Nate said he thinks you moved to Texas, but then Mrs. Donovan said she got a postcard from your mom from Nevada. No one even knows where you really are! You could at least tell me, your supposed best friend. I really hate my life right now. And I know you'll never see this letter so I can just say whatever I want. So here it is.

I wouldn't hate you so much if I didn't love you.

There. I said it.

Bye now. I'll write again soon because it's the only thing that keeps me sane while my parents rage at each other.

His pulse racing, Padric dropped the letter back into the shoebox. *Holy shit.* All that fresh teenage anger poured into his veins like an injection. And that line—she loved him, yet she hated him, and somehow the two were intertwined. The more she loved him, the more his absence made her hate him.

He got that. And it broke his heart a little.

He picked up another letter.

Dear Idiot.

Very bad despicable humiliating day. I overheard two boys on the hockey team talking about me. One said I was trying to "get with him" and that "girls with big boobs always want it bad." It felt so slimy and horrible and I couldn't even look at them afterwards. I think they knew I heard, because they snickered when I walked past. But they just didn't care.

I want my best friend. I want my *boy* best friend who doesn't look at me like a piece of meat. Those boys make me want to become a lesbian. I might try it because it can't be worse than those hockey boys. But Nanette says it doesn't work that way, you either are or you aren't, and she should know because she just came out as bi.

The thing is...I can't stop thinking about you. And you're a boy. My brothers keep saying you're gay but I think they're trying to make me feel better because you're gone. I should tell them that we kissed, then maybe they'd stop. But then also my parents would kick my ass and they have enough to worry about already. Where are you now? Someone said you were in Florida and that your dad is going to sell real estate there. Are there manatees there? I've been reading about the manatees. All I do is read now. Everything else sucks.

PADRIC GROUND his teeth at the thought of those boys and their demeaning comments. He knew how it went down. One boy said something and then the others felt they had to keep up. It was a bonding, competitive kind of thing, each trying to out-asshole the others. But for Zoe to overhear it? How crushing, especially at that age.

He remembered how nervous she sometimes got about her curves when they started to develop. One day she'd dress to show off her body, the next she'd pull on a baggy hoodie and hide herself away.

Excitement used to course through him when she wore her tight clothes, but he'd do everything in his power to hide it. He didn't want to freak her out with his constant half-chubbies. Her hoodies had helped a little, except then he'd fantasized about what she looked like *under* them. Especially because every day her boobs seemed bigger.

The memory of all those lustful teenage thoughts made him wince. Was he just as bad as those hockey asshats?

No, because he never would have talked about Zoe like that.

A memory came back to him from the end of a fishing trip, when he was offloading the catch onto a fishing tender. He knew the tender deckhands from school; they were seniors and he was a freshman. The entire time he and his father were transferring the silvery salmon to the tender for processing, the deckhands teased him about Zoe.

"That girl you hang out with, she's hot. What do you guys do, homework? Anatomy? She let you touch those melons?"

He'd refused to even respond, figuring anything he said would make it worse.

"Seems like any guy who can keep his hands off that piece of ass gotta be gay. You gay, kid?"

Eventually he'd lost it and launched himself across the tender like some kind of teenage pirate. Since it was two against one, he'd wound up on the deck rolling in fish slime while the two deckhands whaled away at him. His father had rescued him before things got out of hand, but he'd wound up with a cut lip and a black eye and very sore ribs.

The only thing his father had said was, "Not bad for two against one."

Even though he'd been in pain for a week after that, the satisfaction of landing at least a couple of blows made up for it.

Back to the letters. None of them had any dates, but he could vaguely place them according to their maturity level and the level of Zoe's anger and pain. The last time-related reference she made was to the death of her father, which he knew had happened three years after the Scandal.

Either she'd moved on by then or been too busy to fill up a notebook with her emotions. Or maybe that was when she'd gotten a boyfriend and didn't want to "betray" him by continuing to write to a phantom.

The letters were so raw and personal that he knew she never would have actually sent them. If she'd intended to, they would have been very different. They would have been less "ripped from her diary." The fact that he was far away, in another world, meant that she could express herself with no limits.

He loved the letters, even though most of them included some kind of insult in the greeting. *Dear Stupid-head. Dear Fish-for-Brains. Dear Dweeb.* They all started out that way, but they ended on a tender note. A wistful question about where he was at that moment, or a familiar joke, or a "miss you so much," or a "I don't really hate you, you know."

He looked out at the boardwalk. Ethan had struck up a conversation with Trixie Tran, who was walking her dog along the boardwalk. Most people around here had Huskies or retrievers or other rugged dogs who could handle the winters. Trixie always liked to stand out, so she had the world's biggest unkempt Newfie. She herself was tiny, so the contrast between the two of them always made people laugh.

Padric kept leafing through the letters, keeping a wary eye on Ethan and Trixie's conversation. When they waved goodbye—had they exchanged numbers?—and Ethan headed his way, he quickly closed up the box.

"Making friends already?" he asked Ethan as his friend reached the car.

"It's all part of the job. Gotta know the locals." He winked at Padric. "Trixie filled me in on some of the local legends. Is it true that strange things happen around Lost Souls Wilderness?"

Padric thought of his and Zoe's doomed hiking trips. "Completely true. Visitors aren't immune, so be warned." He closed the door of the Subaru and tucked the shoebox under one arm. Come on, we're going to walk from here."

Ethan snorted as they strode down the boardwalk. "I'm a hard-boiled detective. Ain't nothing strange to me. I've seen it all. I've solved most of it."

"Yeah? Then maybe you can figure out what happened to the tribe that wandered into the Zertuche Glacier and was never seen again."

"Of course I can. What happened was that it didn't happen. They died of smallpox or got lost at sea or moved to Springfield, Illinois. They didn't wander into a glacier. What does that even mean?"

"Okay. What about the fact that the storms blow up out of nowhere? The forecast will call for a calm day, or a light squall, and before you know it, you're fighting gale-force winds and hoping you don't get swept out to sea. As so many have been." He pointed out the mournful statue of a mariner gazing out to sea, which they happened to be passing at that moment.

"Is that why they call it Lost Harbor?"

"Legend has it that the first explorers drew the map wrong, so when people came back trying to find the beautiful harbor they'd described, it was nowhere to be found. They thought the original explorers had either lost their minds or deliberately thrown them off course to keep the discovery to themselves."

"Kind of a Brigadoon type thing? Or a Shangri-La?"

"Sort of. Without the tropical paradise part. Or the fountain of youth part."

Ethan hauled in a long breath of air. "This air is so pure, maybe it *is* a fountain of youth. Especially compared to *my* native land. West Covina," he explained with a grin.

They reached the end of the boardwalk, where the Eagle's Nest perched in all its out-of-place elegance.

Ethan whistled. "These are my digs?"

"Yup. Might as well live it up while you guard me from baking-soda-wielding villains. The auction is in two days, so until then you're off the clock. You could do a fishing charter, take a trip across the bay for a hike, or just hang out in the Jacuzzi." He smoothly segued to the Jacuzzi when he realized he'd put his foot in it with the hiking reference. Ethan James probably wouldn't want to tax his leg with a rugged trip into the alpine.

"You're a good guy, Padric. No matter what they say online." Ethan headed for the entrance, which was adorned by a carving of a bald eagle landing on a nest. "Need some more time to read all those love letters from Zoe?"

"How did—"

"It's my job. But don't worry. It's also my job to keep your secrets. So where can I find the police station? I need to talk to this adorably named Officer Badger."

"If you call her adorable, she might shoot you."

"Noted."

CHAPTER TWENTY-FOUR

Zoe felt as restless as a cat while she waited for some word from Padric about her letters. She kept dropping things, like a tin of sardines and an entire package of unbleached flour. The twins were laughing too hard at the sight of her entire body covered in flour to be any help with the cleanup.

When she finally finished, she realized she'd gotten several messages from Padric.

A broken heart emoji. A teardrop emoji. And then—*I'm dying for you to get here. You're taking forever. I keep reading your letters and now I feel trapped in yesterday. Time should be moving faster.*

Trapped in yesterday. Trust Padric to put that feeling into words. It described how she'd felt when he left. Her heart had never quite moved on at the pace of life. A piece of it had stayed behind, as if preserved in honey.

Honey made her think of Padric's kiss, of course, and she raced through the remainder of her day. Then she drove home to check on her mother, very aware of the absence of the shoebox she'd left in the backseat. She found Mama at the stove, of all places, stirring a pot of red bean soup. Her mother looked more alert and healthy than she had in some time.

"How are you feeling, Mama? You look good." Zoe kissed her on the cheek. Was this the right time to deliver the news about Padric?

"I feel marvelous. Just marvelous. I could dance a jig."

Zoe answered her own question with a 'no.' She didn't want to ruin her mother's rare happy day with a mention of the name Jeffers.

"Wow, what sparked all this joy?"

"I really couldn't say. A friend brought me some wild strawberries. Maybe that did it."

"Who brought you strawberries?"

"Oh, I can't remember." Her mother poked at the soup vaguely. "She comes by now and then."

Zoe frowned, trying to imagine which of her mother's friends visited that frequently. As far as she knew, visits were few and far between in the summer. Everyone got so busy.

"Layla," her mother said abruptly. "She brought the strawberries."

"Well, that was nice of her. How's her summer going?"

"She has a new neighbor."

Zoe waited, but her mother had nothing more to add to that topic, and instead launched into a rant about her TV not working right. It took over two hours for Zoe to eat some soup with her mom, fix the TV (the channel had gotten switched, launching her mother into a no-man's land of strange networks), and get her to take her medicine.

Finally she was able to free herself and run down the driveway to her car. With her heart revving faster than her engine, she raced all the way across town and down the boardwalk to Padric's hotel.

It was nearly dark by now, and a quarter moon left a path of glitter across the waves, a carpet of gold stretching toward the mountains. Even though the night would be brief at this time in late summer, it would be gloriously clear.

Padric greeted her with a deep kiss, then told her he had a surprise for her. Then he led her to the balcony. Enclosed in glass, with upper vents to let out the steam, it held a round cedar hot tub, filled with bubbling water deep enough to stand in.

Next to it sat a bowl of wild strawberries and the bottle of champagne they kept forgetting about.

"Did you pick these at—"

"Yup. The lake where the swans nest. Best strawberries in Lost Harbor…"

"…because of all that swan poop." They said that last line together and laughed.

"I wonder if that's actually true, or just something your mom used to say," Zoe mused as she popped one into her mouth. The burst of tart, juicy flavor nearly brought tears to her eyes. She thought of her mother's strawberries, and the mystery friend who'd brought them.

"No idea. My mother knew a lot about the local plants and wildlife, though." He ripped off his shirt and tossed it aside. "Last one in pops the champagne."

Once naked and immersed in the deep hot tub, with a flute of champagne in hand, Zoe felt as if she was floating over the ocean in a bubble. The low lights didn't interfere with the view of Lost Souls Wilderness, lit by the remains of the sunset and the valiant quarter moon.

Best of all, right across from her, his feet tangled with hers, sat Padric. The underwater light created a play of shadows and shine across his muscled chest. His eyes glowed a mysterious blue.

"Thanks for letting me read your letters," he said gravely. "I got the impression you never intended that to happen."

"I didn't," she confessed. "I never would have called you so many names if I'd actually planned to send them."

He laughed. "I didn't mind the names. But I hate that I missed so much of your life. Lots of shit went down that I had no clue about. And then you stopped writing. Why?"

"Because I got engaged. The funny thing is," she hesitated, then shrugged, figuring she might as well spill everything, "I'd already started seeing Bjorn when I wrote the last letters. But I never mentioned him because it felt like cheating. How ridiculous is that? It wasn't cheating and you were never going to read it anyway." She laughed, but Padric didn't.

"When you wrote them, you felt as if you were communicating with me. You didn't want to talk about him. I get it. Anyway, it really means a lot to me that you decided to share them. You could have burned them years ago."

"I thought about it. I also thought about making an art project out of them. Decoupage made from old-school love-hate letters. I even came up with a title. 'Yours Since Yesterday.' But I couldn't bear to cut them up."

She moved her hands through the water and watched the ripples lap against his chest. "Okay, your turn. What's the surprise you mentioned? I mean, besides the champagne and wild strawberries."

He reached behind him for an iPod, which he set onto a speaker deck. "It's time for the musical miseducation of Zoe Bellini. I finally got that playlist together."

He pressed play and his voice sang out from the iPod. "*When the lion falls, when the porpoise drowns, that's the time when you'll come around.*" Even *she* had heard this song. It was probably his most famous.

"I actually know this one," she told him, flicking water at his chest. "So maybe I'm already educated."

"No, you don't. Not really. This song," he pressed pause, "is about you."

"When the lion falls? How is that about me?"

"Because you're a lionheart. Until it all fell apart. The porpoise refers to me. Remember how I always loved watching the porpoises when I was supposed to be fishing?"

"Of course. But what does it mean?"

"It means that I always thought I'd see you again, but I knew it would be a long time. Maybe not until we were both dead."

"Well, that's a little bleak. The tune isn't sad, though. It's kind of...jaunty."

"Yes. Intentionally. I had hope, so why not? Also, the contrast appealed to me, this tragic scenario with an upbeat melody."

"Twisted. But I like it. I like it even more now that I understand it." She listened for a while, letting the melody wind its way around her heart. Padric had written this beautiful song with her in mind. The thought was nearly overwhelming.

The song came to an end, but it seemed to still echo in the steam hovering over the hot tub.

He scrolled ahead to another song and hummed along. *"We'll go to the forest and bear their sins. Brighter than blood, deeper than skin.* That's about you, too."

"It is?" Her eyes widened as she listened to the words. "I get the forest part. What sins?"

"Their sins. That we paid for."

The haunting melody paired with his husky singing voice brought tears to her eyes.

Her throat tightened and she struggled for words. "That's... really beautiful."

"Thanks, but that's not why I'm walking you through these. It's so you can see how important you were to me, even after I left. All my first songs were about you, or missing you, or trying to come to terms with our situation. I never stopped feeling things for you."

His eyes burned into hers through the shimmering steam.

"Back then, I didn't have the words for what I felt. I couldn't label it. But now that I'm with you again, I know what it is."

Her heart stopped. She couldn't have said another word if her life depended on it.

"It's love. I love you, Zoe. I've always loved you. I did when we were kids, and I did when we were apart. And I do now."

Her throat closed up entirely and goose bumps ran wild across her skin. It felt like an out-of-body experience, as if her soul had taken flight and hovered overhead.

"I do too," she whispered. "I love you, too."

They gazes held for a moment that could have lasted a few seconds, or hours, she didn't know. Before she entirely grasped how it happened, they were floating together in the middle of the Jacuzzi. pool. Every bit of their bodies twined together—her leg curled around his, his hand spread between her shoulder blades, supporting her in the swirling water. The steam murmured in their ears, telling tales of wild hopes and impossible dreams.

Could it really be this easy? Just two people loving each other? No disaster striking them apart?

His hands wandered down past her hips to cup her ass. Holding her steady, he nudged his hips between her thighs. She followed his lead and brought her legs around him, her skin sliding smoothly against his. She hooked her ankles around his rear and felt his erection nestle against the soft triangle between her legs.

The warm water made her so languid that everything felt effortless. Her body opened for his like a night-blooming flower. He slid inside with a deep sigh that seemed to come right from his core. She pressed her breasts against his front, seeking closeness and friction, the abrasion of his chest hair against her nipples.

He caught onto her need and lowered his head to tongue the swiftly swelling peaks. She arched her back to give him all the access he needed. That move also tilted her hips and brought the thick head of his penis even deeper inside.

He groaned against her nipples. Ah God. To see his thick brown hair against her chest, his broad shoulders straining, tendons taut, gave her such fierce satisfaction. At a basic, primal level he was hers and she was his.

A slow surge of arousal rose like the tide inside her. It felt like a genuine force of nature, like something governed by the moon instead of her desire for him. As if somehow, on that trail in Lost Souls Wilderness, they'd become part of something bigger than themselves. Destiny? Fate? The strange miracle of timing?

Whatever it was, she didn't care. Maybe it was nothing but her imagination. The only thing that mattered now was the pleasure he was sparking in her core with each thrust.

"Zoe," he murmured, hands on her ass, in complete command of her body. He moved inside her, filling her with his rock-hard shaft, surrounding her with heat. "Beautiful Zoe. My heart and soul. It's all you. Always was."

She tilted her head back and looked up at the first shine of stars overhead. She didn't have any more words, just a joyful moan of completion as the two of them lit up the sky.

CHAPTER TWENTY-FIVE

"We should make plans," Padric said after they'd torn themselves away from the Jacuzzi and dried each other off. He'd taken his time patting every droplet of moisture from Zoe's lush body while she stood on the balcony naked, arms and legs askew.

Of course that process got him turned on again, and he'd dragged her over to the bed and spread her out like a starfish. He'd pushed her legs open and fastened his mouth to her sex., lapping at her pulsing clit and slick folds until she'd screamed his name.

And that was better than any concert with thousands shouting out his name.

Or at least just as good, but in a sexier way.

"Plans?" she said vaguely, still dazed from the way he'd fucked her senseless. She'd tucked a blanket around herself as the warmth from the Jacuzzi faded away. Her dark hair spilled against the pillow and her eyes glowed with hazy contentment. She looked like a pictorial illustration of the word "afterglow."

"We're together now. We know that much. I love you, you love me. That equals 'together,' right?"

Her striking dark eyebrows drew together. Those eyebrows always gave her away, always had. "For now. Yes."

"For now? We love each other. That's not a 'for now' kind of situation. This isn't some kind of hit-and-run, one-and-done thing."

"Obviously not. We're way past 'one.'" Smiling wryly, she rolled onto her side and stroked a finger down his arm. "We can *talk* about plans, but this is all so fast."

"You call fifteen years fast?"

"You know what I mean. You just got back and here we are." She swept a hand to indicate the two of them twined together. "I have no complaint about that, by the way."

"Good to know," he said dryly.

She dropped a kiss on his shoulder, her hair tickling his skin.

He tried again. "Maybe it happened fast because it started a long time ago. We just hit pause for a while."

"Maybe. I don't know. I get nervous when things fall into place too quickly. I start bracing for disaster."

"Maybe you should brace for bliss, instead."

She laughed at that. "Sounds like a line from a song."

"Think about it, Zoe. With me, you'd have complete freedom. You could travel the world. Remember how we used to make lists of the top ten places we wanted to visit, and we'd change the order all the time? You could go to all of them. For as long as you want. As many times as you want. We can go anywhere and do anything. I'm a star, baby. That's what it's like when you're a star."

She shot him a look. "I think I just threw up a little."

He laughed. "See? I need you around to keep me honest."

"I'm glad to see I'll have something to do," she said wryly. "I thought I would be keeping you well-fucked."

"That too. See? It's a win-win." He brushed her hair away

from her face. "It's not all about me, in case that's what you're thinking. You can do your art anywhere, right?"

She didn't answer. Why wasn't she jumping all over this idea? The freedom to travel, time to work on her art projects, *lots* of time in bed with him. Surely they could work something out with her mother.

Why was she hesitating? Didn't she understand what he was offering?

"I will need to get back to my tour pretty soon," he told her softly. "I was able to reschedule the Scandinavian leg, but I'm due in Stockholm soon. And I don't want to go back without you."

"Padric, you know I can't just leave. I've got the pizza shop, I've got my mother. The twins would run wild without me."

"Can't you take a break? You deserve a break."

"Maybe. But I can't promise anything. The summer season isn't over yet—"

"It's almost over. Just a few more weeks. You could join me then. Just for a break," he repeated. "Will you think about it?"

Looking troubled, she tugged her lower lip between her teeth. Whatever she wanted to say, she must have decided not to, because instead she slid her hand to his deflated cock. "Sure. I'll think about it. Right now, let's just be happy that we're together."

With her fingers stroking him, stirring the embers of arousal back to life, he had to admit she made a good point. Why worry about details when they agreed on the most important thing—they were together.

The hell if he was going to leave this alone, though. He didn't want to be separated from Zoe again. They were two grownups who loved each other and ought to be together. They deserved this. Period.

He held his tongue and let her play with him until his cock

was fully engorged and ready to explode into—ah, sweet Lord—her mouth. His orgasm held the wistful taste of honey and spruce.

THE ANNUAL "DEFINITELY-NOT-SILENT Auction to Benefit the Lost Harbor Volunteer Fire Department" always took place at the Olde Salt. No other venue in town would do for the kind of raucous atmosphere the auction encouraged. For fifteen years now, so many locals had crammed into the bar that the floors sagged and the walls bulged, as if the entire building might break apart.

And yet somehow it survived the event every year, and every August, locals and tourists gathered to bid on the mix of random, bizarre and occasionally stellar items offered up by their fellow community members.

The list was posted on two giant whiteboards mounted in the middle of the floor. All the tables had been cleared away so everyone could peruse the offerings.

A ride on Mrs. Holt's Tibetan Yak.

A pair of angora rabbits, complete with their own hutch.

A tour of Old Crow's collection of narwhal bones.

A bottle of whisky that had been sitting in Russell Banks' basement since pioneer days.

Mrs. Yates' record collection from the '70s—which she clearly just wanted someone to take off her hands.

All the wool from one alpaca for a year, offered by Aurora Alpaca Farms.

Twenty raspberry canes from Cindy Baker, famous throughout the Misty Bay peninsula for producing the sweetest berries.

A kayak trip from Wild North Kayaks.

Dog-walking from Ruby, Megan Miller's daughter.

A two-night stay at Aurora Lodge, nestled deep in Lost Souls Wilderness and accessible only by helicopter.

Ten pounds of seaweed harvested from the most pristine cove across the bay and carefully dried in Otto Shine's shed.

Smoked salmon from Mark and Yaritza Minsk, famous for their secret brine recipe.

The list went on and on, and there, tucked between a free tattoo at Octopus Ink and a basket of treats from Sweet Harbor Bakery, was a handwritten note with Padric's offering: A private serenade from recording artist Padric Jeffers.

"Interesting approach," Ethan murmured in his ear. "I'm surprised they don't highlight the fact that an internationally known rock star is part of this hoedown."

"I was a last-minute addition. Besides, that's not how things work here," he told Ethan. "It's a down-to-earth kind of place. I wouldn't be surprised if that smoked salmon goes for more than me. That shit is out of this world."

"Okay then. I'll have to save my pennies for that. I was thinking of bidding on Trixie's Ultimate Hot Fudge Sundae for twenty. I could invite my entire extended family of Rockwells up here to share it."

"Good choice," Padric said absently, scanning the crowd for Zoe. She'd warned him that she was going to be late. The Last Chance traditionally provided pizza for the event—that was their contribution to the cause.

Ethan continued in a casual voice. "So I noticed a homemade bomb on the bar."

"Cool. Good job."

Ethan whacked him on the shoulder, and Padric turned to glare at him. "What?"

"You aren't paying attention. You're looking for Zoe, aren't you, all lovesick and shit. I can't monitor this entire crowd by myself. You need to keep your eyes open for danger."

"Okay. I'm sorry. I just—I find it hard to believe that anyone here would try to hurt me. Except you. I think you just bruised my biceps."

Ethan looked at him sternly. "Don't be naive. I know this is your hometown and it's at the ends of the fricking Earth, but people are people. If someone's jealous of you, or angry with you, or just crazy, you don't know what they're going to do. Be smart, my friend. I don't know the cast of characters here like you do. Maybe something will jump out at you."

"Message received. Got it." Rubbing his arm, he shifted his focus to the crowd. "Cast of characters is a good way to put it."

"I'll say."

Just the vast diversity of beards alone would qualify the crowd for that description. Full and shaggy ranging all the way to close-cropped goatees, with a detour at hipster shapes and even a few beards adorned with little braids. Fishermen in their rubber boots and pocket-laden vests mingled with native Alaskan carvers and hunters and storytellers. Farmers from the hills around Lost Harbor chatted with local artists in their hand-woven skirts and abundant tattoos. He spotted the owner of the bakery, who had a tattoo of a raven pecking at a cinnamon roll on her neck. A few members of the Russian Old Believer community scanned the whiteboards. The women wore floor-length dresses and the men wore tunics belted over trousers.

On a normal day, these different groups might not get along with each other. But for tonight, for the purpose of raising money for the fire department, all conflict got banished to the back burner.

Darius Boone, the fire chief whom he'd met briefly at the first volunteer training, was leaning one elbow on the bar, chatting with Toni the bartender. He had to lean; he barely fit in this low-ceilinged place. The guy was huge, especially in his off-duty cowboy hat.

A small crowd gathered around Art Dinty, the pilot he and Zoe had helped to rescue. He wore crutches and a neck brace, but grinned widely as he tipped his head toward Padric.

"Saw your name up there on the board." One of the guys he'd been training with at the station—Willie, the retired long-shoreman—appeared next to him. "Wish I could bid on you for my granddaughter, but I don't have that kind of cash."

"Oh yeah? Is she a fan?"

"I guess." Willie's attention wandered to the crowd, but he didn't move away from Padric's side.

"I could sign something for her if you want."

"Like what?"

Didn't the man understand how autographs worked? "A CD, or a photo, or a napkin. Whatever."

"Right. She'd probably like that. You coming back to training soon?"

"I'd like to but I've had a couple of crazy things go down, and I'll be leaving town soon. I'll try to get back a few more times."

"Yeah, I heard about the envelope."

"You did?"

"Paramedics were talking about it. First biohazard incident in Lost Harbor. Hope they catch the asshole."

"Yeah, me too." Padric finally spotted Zoe. "Catch you later, Willie."

Everyone else, including the grizzled longshoreman, faded away as if they'd never existed. All he saw was Zoe's bright smile as she propped her chin on the stack of pizza boxes she was carrying.

"Make way for pizza!" Monica trumpeted as she followed behind Zoe. She and Alexis each carried another towering pile of boxes. The crowd parted to allow them to make their way to the bar.

After they'd unloaded their booty, Zoe hooked her foot on the lower rung of a stool and hoisted herself above the crowd. Under her apron, she wore a snug garnet dress that set off her dark hair and creamy skin. "Courtesy of Last Chance Pizza, help yourself, everyone! We've got pepperoni, veggie, and of course, Greek pizza, because that's how we roll."

Cheers and applause swept through the crowd.

"Zoe, Zoe, Zoe," they chanted.

"Hey, no fair," Monica piped up as she waved both hands over her head. "What about me and Alexis?"

A new chant took hold. "Zoe's sisters, Zoe's sisters..."

Monica stuck her tongue out to the sound of laughter.

The hungry crowd milled around the bar. Zoe stepped down and made her way toward Padric, like a salmon swimming upstream.

"Phew," she said as soon as she reached his side. "I always forget how mobbed this event is. Was that Willie Marsh you were talking to? He's an old friend of my mom's. I hope--"

But he didn't want to talk about Willie. He took her hand and pulled her against him. "Hi."

"Hi." A soft flush warmed her cheeks. "Hey, did you hear how they chanted my name, like I'm some kind of rock star?"

"Yeah, I did. Guess I can retire now. One rock star in the family is more than enough."

Her blush intensified. "Speaking of family, it seems Theo might be moving back to Lost Harbor. Remember my oldest brother?"

"Yeah, of course."

"He's getting divorced, and his wife is taking the business. So he might be needing a new full-time occupation."

He finally realized what she was getting at. "The Last Chance." A grin spread across his face. "Holy shit! That timing is perfect."

"I thought so, too. Maybe my luck is changing. About damn time." Light danced in her eyes. He wanted to sweep her up and spin her around in a circle. Were things finally starting to go their way?

Glancing around the crowd, he saw that no one was looking their direction. "Are you thinking what I'm thinking?"

"That we're trying to keep this under wraps but no one's paying attention and it's hard to keep our hands off each other?"

"Exactly. It's like you can read my mind."

"Or your body," she murmured. Sheltered from any prying eyes, she brushed her hand across the front of his jeans. What had been only a slight erection hardened under her caress.

"Okay, enough of that." Circling his fingers around her wrist, he moved her hand firmly away from his crotch. Her pupils dilated.

"You know it turns me on when you take charge like that."

Of course he knew. He'd been studying her responses more closely than a chemistry final.

"Had no idea." Playing innocent, he hauled her against him. "Oops, what just happened?"

Quickly, he bent down to steal a kiss before anyone noticed.

But as soon as their lips touched, he couldn't drag himself away. The plush feel of her mouth, the lingering taste of honey, the click of her teeth against his, the warm puff of her breath—it all went straight to his head.

In a second, they were in so deep it would have taken a team of oxen to drag him away from her kiss. He lost all sense of where they were or why they shouldn't be kissing in public like this.

What did it matter, anyway? They were together now, and the roadblocks were melting away like butter in the sun.

"I love you, Zoe Bellini," he whispered against her mouth.

He felt more than heard her response in the movement of her lips.

Because just at that moment, a hair-raising shriek ripped through the bar.

CHAPTER TWENTY-SIX

He tore himself away from the kiss and automatically shoved Zoe behind him. Had the baking soda attacker struck again, with something more lethal?

Still light-headed, he looked around the room. Ethan was pushing his way through the crowd, shouting something he couldn't hear because the screaming continued. Words were being yelled at the top of someone's voice. A woman's voice.

He relaxed. This was probably a personal drama. Someone's wife or girlfriend had just discovered they were being cheated on. Or maybe someone had missed out on the last slice of pepperoni. His attacker was a man, most likely...or *maybe* a woman, but at any rate, it was someone who wanted to be anonymous. He or she wouldn't be screaming at the top of his lungs in a crowded bar.

Ethan sprang free of the crowd and threw himself in front of Padric.

"Dude. Relax. This isn't about me."

"You sure about that?" Ethan jerked his head toward a figure trundling across the worn planks of the Olde Salt toward him. He gaped at the sight of an elderly woman rolling her walker at him, her shouts mixed with heartbroken sobs.

"Mrs. Bellini?"

Behind him, Zoe startled and peered over his arm. "Mama?"

"How dare you! With that devil! I saw him kissing you! Get out, you!" She stopped right in front of Ethan and brandished a pizza cutter in the air.

Ethan made a calming gesture with both hands, but she jabbed at him with the cutter. He managed to snatch his hand away just in time.

Jesus, she really meant business.

"Mama, stop that!" Zoe stepped from around him, but Mrs. Bellini slashed at her, too.

"Not with him. Why *him*? You break my heart!"

Ethan used his body to shield both Padric and Zoe from her mother's rage.

"Mama, I swear if you hurt Ethan, I won't forgive you. He's not even involved in this. He's a bodyguard."

"Security specialist," Ethan said under his breath. "For the record."

"Hurt him?" Mrs. Bellini ranted. "*I'm* the one who is hurt. This boy's family destroyed my life! Stole my husband. Broke his heart and killed him. No one has paid for that crime. And now he's here with his mouth on my daughter? I won't stand for it!"

Padric spoke up in a soothing tone. "Mrs. Bellini, I'm really sorry about what happened—"

"Sorry? Sorry will never be enough. It cannot be enough! Your sorry isn't worth my spit." She spat toward the floor, but it hit Ethan's shoe instead.

Keeping his voice calm and even, Ethan spoke to the trembling woman still gripping her pizza cutter. "Ma'am, it sounds like you have some real grievances. Maybe you'd like to talk about it somewhere more private. Everyone in here is listening right now."

They all glanced at the throng of bidders gathered around, watching with various expressions of glee and disbelief. Padric caught sight of a few smartphones recording the action.

Great, if this went viral, he was going to look like a jackass.

"Ethan, step aside. If Mrs. Bellini wants to yell at me, I'm okay with that."

"But Padric—"

"It's okay. Please."

Ethan reluctantly stepped to the side, but every alert line in his body said he wasn't going to let anyone get hurt.

"Mrs. Bellini, I know you have things to say. But I hate to interrupt the auction. Can we go talk somewhere else?"

Mrs. Bellini finally seemed to realize where she was. She lowered the pizza cutter a few inches. He put out his hand to take it from her but she pointed it at him again.

"Okay, okay." He held up his hands in a "you win" gesture. "If you want to get into it here in front of the entire town of Lost Harbor, that's up to you."

"I was humiliated once already." Her cheeks quivered as if she were holding back too much emotion to handle. "Thanks to your bitch of a mother."

Padric hissed in a breath. It hurt more than he'd imagined to hear Mrs. Bellini's fury toward his family.

"Mama!" Zoe darted forward. "This is wrong. Padric didn't do *anything* to you. You're blaming him for something he didn't do. Let's just go home."

Mrs. Bellini fixed her with a tragic look. "You're a bad daughter. You're dead to me."

"Oh, I'm dead to you, am I? Not the first time I've heard that. Come on." Giving the pizza cutter a wide berth, Zoe came around her other side and took hold of the walker. "Let's get you home. You shouldn't even be here. Why didn't you tell me you were coming? How did you get here?"

Mrs. Bellini didn't answer, but she dropped the pizza cutter on the floor. Ethan bent to snatch it up before something else could happen to it.

Zoe continued. "And I have every right to kiss whoever I want, including Padric. You can't control me with your histrionics. I'm not fifteen anymore."

Padric kept his gaze on Mrs. Bellini's face. She didn't seem to be listening to Zoe. Her gaze wandered and face looked strange, almost distorted. She'd always been a queenly, bustling figure, ruling her household with a mixture of strict rules, fiery love and stormy outbursts. Now she was more hunched, more wrinkled, but still forceful.

Except that the fight seemed to have gone out of her. She slumped, gripping the handles of the walker as Zoe talked on.

"Wait," said Padric. Zoe didn't hear him, so he took a step forward. "Mrs. Bellini, are you okay? Can you breathe?"

Even though he hadn't gotten far with the volunteer firefighter training, he knew something was wrong. She swayed back and forth, as if she was having trouble keeping her balance.

"Can you say your name, Mrs. Bellini?"

She made a garbled, unrecognizable sound.

"I think she's having a stroke," he called to Ethan. "Someone get help!"

About ten people leaped forward. Of all places to have a stroke, the auction for the volunteer fire department was a pretty good spot.

Nate shoved Padric aside and took charge. He yelled, "Call dispatch. We're going to need an ambulance."

They lowered her to the floor and loosened her clothing.

"Mrs. Bellini," Nate said in a calm voice. "Please listen carefully. Do you know who I am?"

"N..." She couldn't complete the word, which could have been "Nate" or "No."

"Can you try a smile? I know this isn't exactly a good time to laugh it up, but try."

She produced a grimace, one side of her mouth rising, the other drooping.

"Oh my God," cried Zoe. "Oh my God!" Padric stepped to her side and wrapped his arm around her, but she seemed completely unaware of him, her attention on her mother.

Nate continued. "We think you're having a stroke, Mrs. Bellini. But we're taking care of you. The ambulance is on its way. Are you cold? Uncomfortable?"

She nodded, her eyes frightened and desperate. It was surreal that just a few minutes ago she'd been brandishing a makeshift weapon at him.

He ripped off his jacket and handed it over. Nate tried to lay it over Mrs. Bellini but she flinched away from it.

Okay then. Clearly she wanted him gone.

"I'll tell the ambulance crew where to go," he told Nate tightly.

"Good man."

And so that was how he wound up outside the Olde Salt, holding the door for the paramedics, while Zoe dealt with the crisis without him. As she'd dealt with everything else the past fifteen years.

ZOE SPENT the rest of the night at the hospital with her mother while the twins took care of business at the auction. The CT scan revealed that this wasn't the first stroke her mother had experienced.

The doctor who explained the situation was new to Lost Harbor. She introduced herself as Dr. Bethany Morrison. Her kind eyes and calm manner helped the news go down a little better. She put the brain scan against a lightbox and pointed out areas that all looked the same to Zoe.

"She's had a series of small strokes—you can see here and here—but she probably didn't even notice them. This one is different. It caused a fair amount of damage to her right side. She'll have some trouble talking, and she'll need assistance to eat and walk."

"She already uses a walker. But she's never had trouble talking before. Like ever, in her whole life. Talking is one of her favorite things to do."

"Then this will be a difficult adjustment for her. Does she live with you?"

"She does."

"Try to keep stress to a minimum for a while. She'll need lots of rest at first, then we'll need to start on some physical therapy."

A feeling of despair wrapped around Zoe's heart. Her mother was going to need more care than ever before. How was she going to take care of the pizza shop, the twins *and* her mother?

If Theo came back—it still wasn't definite—he would be a big help with the shop, but not with Mama. He was coming back for the business, not to be a caregiver. She couldn't imagine her big, macho brother helping to feed Mama.

As for Padric...that might be the worst part of all. She needed to stay very far away from him. She couldn't risk giving her mother another shock like that.

Her mother's friend Layla had explained the whole thing. Apparently, Mama had begged Layla to take her to the auction so she could bid on the angora rabbits. She'd wanted it to be a surprise so she could gift the rabbits to the twins.

Monica and Alexis would have loved that.

She also wanted to bid on the dried seaweed for Zoe, because she thought it would add an extra little something to her clay figurine project.

Instead, she'd walked into the Olde Salt and gotten slammed by the sight of Padric Jeffers kissing her oldest daughter.

Zoe sighed and pushed her hair behind her ears. "Whatever Mama needs, we'll make it happen. When can I take her home?"

"She's asleep right now. Once she wakes up, we'll do another assessment. Dr. Finnegan—he's the neurologist—will weigh in on that. Here he is now."

Right on cue, another doctor walked in. An attractive one, about her age, and someone definitely flirt-worthy under normal circumstances. But apparently Padric had ruined her for any other man, because she was numb to his good looks.

She zoned out as he talked about the long-term effects of stroke and what to expect next. It was all so overwhelming. Finally, she threw up a hand. "Can I just get back to my mother? I don't want her to wake up alone."

"Of course. Come find me whenever you're ready."

"Thank you, Doctor..." She blanked on his name.

"Doctor Finnegan. Ian Finnegan."

"Can you get any more Irish?"

She caught the glimmer of interest in his gaze and quickly took a step back. He might be cute, but he was no Padric, and anyway, she was going to be a nun from now on.

She curled up on the armchair in her mother's room and slept —badly—until she heard her mother stir. Leaping to her feet, she went to her mother's bedside.

The droop in her weathered face made her heart clench.

"Hello, Mama," she said softly. "How are you feeling?"

"Aw...ful," she managed.

Zoe gave her a tender smile. "That's certainly understandable. You had a stroke and you're in the hospital. But the good news is that you're going to be fine."

Tears leaked from the corners of her mother's eyes. "Not...fine."

"I know you don't feel at all fine. But you're alive. I was so terrified, I thought we'd lost you." Feeling tears skim her own eyes, she lifted her mother's hand to her lips and kissed it. "Thank God you're okay."

"P...p..." She couldn't quite manage to form the word she was looking for. Zoe tried to help.

"Private? Pizza? Pizza party? Pour some water?"

A ghost of a smile lifted the unaffected side of her face, but she shook her head.

"Pa..."

"Pet? Are you thinking of Athena? She's fine, the twins will feed her."

A more impatient shake of her mom's head told her she'd missed the mark. "Pad..."

And then it clicked. "Are you trying to say Padric?"

She nodded, pain flashing across her face.

"You don't have to worry about Padric." Saying those words felt like ripping her own heart out and dumping it in the sharps container mounted on the wall. "I won't be seeing him again. I'm sorry you saw that. If I'd known you were going to come to the auction... Anyway, I'm so sorry, Mama. I don't want you to think about him again. That's all done with. Now we have to focus on getting you better. There's going to be physical therapy and all sorts of fun stuff, so why don't you rest now, okay, *carina*?"

None of her words seemed to reassure her mother, who struggled to say something else. Finally she fell back, exhausted, and her eyes fell shut. Zoe held on to her hand until it went limp.

Then she sat in the armchair and let her own tears fall freely down her face like rain. And picked up her phone.

First she texted the twins. *Mama's awake. She's okay but she had a stroke. We're in Room 152 at the hospital. Xoxo.*

Then she texted Padric. Text message had to be the worst way to end something, but she didn't want to leave him hanging and she couldn't handle a phone call right now.

Sorry. She texted. *I can't. I know you understand.*

CHAPTER TWENTY-SEVEN

Back home, there was more bad news. Or not exactly "bad" news, but "haha, so close and yet so far" news. An email had arrived with the news that she and her project, *At Sea (Lost/Found)*, had been accepted into the Far North Arts Fellowship program. It started in one month, a week after the Last Chance switched to part-time winter hours. Perfect timing.

And there was no possible way she could accept it.

She'd deal with that later. First she had to make the house wheelchair accessible, since Dr. Irish had warned her that Mama would be chair-bound for at least a couple of weeks. She had to hire a carpenter to make a ramp for the front steps. She also had to order adaptive silverware and other items that would help Mama function.

It all felt completely overwhelming, especially when all she wanted to do was cry.

Athena was curled up on her mom's favorite recliner, purring in blissful ignorance. Would Mama still be able to pet her? Would the white fluffy ball of love bring her the same joy as before?

Someone knocked at the door, and a chill swept through her. Just from the sound of the knock, she knew it was Padric.

She shouldn't even open the door. What good would it do? She'd just be torturing herself, and probably him, too.

But she couldn't resist.

Sure enough, Padric stood outside the front door, arms folded across his chest, face tight.

"Your sisters said your mother's still at the hospital, so I figured it was safe to stop by."

The bite in his voice made her wince. She stepped outside and closed the door. Even allowing Padric inside felt wrong. "Let's go over to my place."

She led the way to the barn and ushered him into her space. A quick glance showed her that she'd left it a big mess. She hadn't been home much lately, since she'd been spending so much time with Padric. Mostly she'd been rushing in and out for showers and changes of clothing. A stray bra was draped over her sculpture of a mermaid. A pile of clean laundry that she'd left on a chair had toppled over. The remains of a burrito lay molding on her kitchenette counter.

Padric didn't seem to notice any of that. He took in the display of clay figurines, the shelves of art books and bins of art supplies. He noticed the ladder leading to her loft, and the shafts of morning sun coming through the octagonal window up there.

"How's your mom?" he finally asked.

"She'll be okay. There's some permanent damage to her right side, but with enough therapy she should be able to manage. I have no idea how we're going to afford it all, but at least there's hope." Her voice sounded hollow and exhausted. Pretty much how she felt.

"I'm so—"

She threw up a hand before he could finish. "Don't. It's not your fault. I handled this all wrong. I should have known Mama would find out you were here. I should have told her myself, instead of letting her be surprised."

"Did the doctor say that's what—" She heard the same guilt in his voice that she felt in her heart.

"No, she didn't say that. Neither did the neurologist. But then again, I didn't ask. They did say that she's had other mini-strokes, which explains why she's been struggling lately."

"But you think it's our fault?" The blunt, direct question made her flinch.

"I don't know."

He gave her a somber look. "But just in case, you want to end things between us?"

"Padric..." Why did he have to make this harder than it already was? "How can we have any kind of future when my mother has a stroke at the very sight of you?"

"So you *do* think it's our fault."

"Not ours. *My* fault." She fisted her hands, wishing she could beat something up. "I let her be surprised. Don't you know that's how she found out about my dad and your mom? She spotted them kissing in the grocery store, then followed them to a motel."

Practically vibrating with tension, he scrubbed a hand across the back of his neck. "That was *them*. They were cheating. We aren't. We're grown adults who happen to be single and consenting and we're *not doing anything wrong*."

"But it hurts my mother, and she's already been through so much. You didn't see her after the affair, or after my dad died. Maybe I could have changed her mind if I had enough time, but now I'm afraid to even say your name. So there's no point in you being here right now. I can't do this. What chance was there anyway? You have a rock star life to get back to! Don't put this all on me!"

His voice lowered to a dangerous level. "We were working that out. Remember how you were going to take a break—"

"Considering."

"Were you actually considering it?"

She didn't answer.

"Theo was going to take over the pizza shop, remember that? You'd be free to do what you want, to be with me, do your art."

Somehow the way he said that—"do your art"—came across as patronizing.

"Does all this look portable?" She swept her hand around her studio space. "Your idea is that I'll sit in some hotel room in Bucharest and 'do art' while you perform before five thousand screaming fans?"

"More like ten thousand," he muttered.

"Oh, in that case, if it's ten thousand, that changes everything." Her Bellini battle skills were in full fiery form now. "Give me a call when it's fifteen thousand and I'll abandon my family and come running."

"I'm not asking you to abandon your family. I'm asking you to stand up for yourself."

"Then this is me, standing up for myself. Take a good look. *I can't be with you, Padric.* Our lives will never work together. The sooner you see that, the easier it will be."

His expression shifted, as if a shutter was being closed, and she could no longer see inside.

"Jesus, Zoe. Is that really what you want?"

She held his gaze, letting her expression do the job her words couldn't.

"Then do yourself a favor and stop blaming other people or bad luck. *You're* choosing this, Zoe. No one else. Not me."

But that was the thing. He had choices. So many choices. How could he possibly understand?

Now that she'd made her point and gotten what she wanted, she couldn't summon her voice anymore. She couldn't order her mouth to open and say the word "goodbye."

She nodded, her mouth twisting against the urge to burst into tears right then and there.

"I love you, Zoe," he said softly. "No matter what, I want you to know that."

Frozen, she didn't—couldn't—react. *Me too,* she wanted to scream. *I love you, too. I always will.*

But she didn't.

He turned away, his broad shoulders slumped, his head bent.

Even though it shattered her heart to watch him go, she refused to tear her eyes away until he disappeared from sight. This might be the last time she ever saw him, and she wanted to store away every second of it.

CHAPTER TWENTY-EIGHT

At least one person was happy about this turn of events. His manager, Mikey, practically danced a jig when Padric called to tell him the news. "So I can take the tabloids off node-watch?"

"No more nodes. Thanks for making this happen. I needed the break."

"I'm just glad that's all it was. A break. I was starting to worry."

"You worried for nothing." His voice sounded just as empty as his broken heart. "But I guess that's your job."

"Yeppers. I worry so you don't have to. Alrighty then, checking the calendar now." Padric smiled at the way Mikey always narrated his actions. "When should we book your flight to Stockholm?"

"I just need a day or so to wrap things up here. You book it, I'll be on it."

"You just made me the happiest man in London."

And he was the most miserable man in Alaska, so that probably balanced out. He put the phone on speaker while Mikey rattled off his ideas for Padric's big return to the tour. A media blitz to prove nothing was wrong with him despite the wild rumors. A *Rolling Stone* reporter wanted to follow him around for a week. Several morning shows were interested in live performances.

Mikey didn't mention the PJ parties. He probably didn't want to put anything in the way of Padric going back on tour.

But Padric didn't want to ignore it. He couldn't do that. "I need you to do something for me, Mikey. In regards to the PJ kids. I've been watching the kids here—a couple of teenage girls with real leadership talent. I want you to figure out which kid is the one people follow. Or maybe there's more than one. I want to talk to those kids in person. Face to face. Can you make that happen?"

"I can try. I'll put my best social media expert on it. Good plan."

"Thanks."

Stopping the PJ parties would be one good thing in the wreckage of his day. "Send me the flight information when you have it and I'll see you in Stockholm."

"Glad to have you back."

After that call was over, Padric dialed the Misty Bay Regional Hospital. He asked to speak to the billing department and arranged to cover all of Mrs. Bellini's treatments.

Ethan stopped by as he was packing up his things. He handed his friend a check, which Ethan looked at, askance. "I defended you from an old lady with a walker. I really don't think I've earned this."

"You came all the way to Alaska to help me out. You earned it." He shoved the check into Ethan's hand.

"Not exactly a hardship. Nice town you got here."

"It's not mine. But I'll pass it along to the locals."

"Pass what along?" Nate sauntered through the door Ethan had left open. "I'm a local."

"I was just complimenting Lost Harbor."

"You're taking off?" Nate stuck out his hand. "It was good to have you around. You're welcome back anytime."

"Thanks. I may take you up on that." They shook hands, which irked Padric to no end, since he doubted he'd be back anytime soon. Not while he could still cause harm to Mrs. Bellini's precarious health.

"Can you guys go bond somewhere else? I have to pack."

"Pack? You can't leave yet." Nate whipped out a notebook from his back pocket. "You have a prize to deliver."

Padric was already shaking his head. "I can't. I need to hit the road. Actually, I need to hit the bay, get my rented boat back to Aurora Bay and catch a plane to Anchorage. I have a show in Stockholm."

"I'm sorry, but the Swedish blonds will have to wait. You committed to this serenade, and I'm holding you to it."

Nate's level gray gaze made it clear he'd accept nothing less.

"What about something of comparable value?"

"What's the value of a private song from an international star? How would you even calculate that? Fuck that, my friend. You can do this. Just squeeze it in before you go. Or come back in between Sweden and Finland or wherever."

"I can't come back here." He said it through clenched teeth as he stuffed a t-shirt into his travel bag. "And you both know why, so don't fuck with me."

"Are you talking about Mrs. Bellini?" Nate followed him across the room as he searched for more stuff to pack. "Sure, she's a little high-strung. But you can't let her scare you off."

"I can't let her scare me off? She had a stroke! I'm not afraid of her. I'm afraid of *hurting* her. Do you see the difference there?"

"I do," Ethan volunteered from across the room. "Bad guys are one thing. Injured moms are a whole other thing."

Padric pointed his index finger at Ethan. "Exactly. What he said."

"So let me try to understand here. You love Zoe. Zoe loves you. But she freaked out because her mom is in the hospital, and so you're just going to leave."

"Yes," Padric said firmly, using his shoulders to shove Nate to the side on his way to the bedroom.

"As a first responder, I've seen a lot of people in hospitals, in emergencies and so forth. They all have one thing in common. They're not thinking clearly."

Padric hesitated over the drawer into which he'd very optimistically unpacked his clothes. "She seemed pretty clear to me."

"You're not going to fight for Zoe, then?" Nate planted his hands on his hips.

"I can't fight *her mother*." Why wasn't Nate getting this? "Zoe is thirty years old. She's made her decision. And the thing is, I get it. What kind of life would she have trailing around after me?"

"What kind of life are you going to have without each other?"

"We'll manage. We did before. I'll write sad songs, she'll take care of everyone except—" The prospect was so bleak after the joy of being with Zoe that he cut himself off. He wheeled around and held out his hand to Nate. "Who's the winner? I'll take care of it before I leave town."

Nate ripped out a page from the notebook and passed it to him.

Padric read it quickly and let out a bitter laugh. "No. Not happening. You have *got* to be kidding."

"Come on. The twins pooled all their money, and Zoe matched everything they made. They also spent the entire auction begging and pleading with everyone else not to outbid them. It was shameless."

"Fine. I'll give them a call. Maybe they can record it for their festival, since I won't be here by then."

"That's between you and them. I did my part." Nate flung up his hands and backed away as Padric passed him on the way to the living room. Ethan stood near the balcony taking photos of the view. A brisk wind was whipping up whitecaps on the surface of the bay. Seas were at least six feet, with a strong northeast swell.

So much for leaving today. He certainly couldn't take the boat out in those conditions. He'd have to wait at least until tomorrow.

With a little salute, Nate headed out the door. "I'm not saying goodbye because I'm in denial."

"Goodbye," Padric called after him.

Ethan pocketed his phone. "I found a ride to Anchorage, but are you sure you don't need me to stick around? We never caught the baking soda villain."

"I'm not worried about that. I'll be gone soon enough. The dude got what he wanted—I'm leaving. I brought you in because I didn't want anyone else to get hurt, that's all."

"Okay, tough guy. You got my number if you need me again."

They hugged briefly, then Ethan left, too.

Padric stood alone in his hotel room. He could practically hear Nate teasing him about his missing "entourage."

He'd take Nate and Ethan over an entourage any day. They cared about him as a person, not just as a product. Soon he'd be back in that other world in which the only piece of him that mattered was his ability to please crowds and make money for people.

He looked down at the piece of paper that held the names Monica and Alexis Bellini, and the amount they'd bid—five thousand three hundred and seventy dollars. If Zoe had kicked in half, they'd still contributed over twenty-five hundred dollars. That was a lot of tips, and scrimping and saving.

He dug out his phone and dialed Monica's number. "Can we meet? We need to talk about your auction prize. Are you at the Last Chance?"

She was. He told her he was on his way, and ended the call.

The Bellini women were nothing but trouble.

God, he was going to miss them.

<hr>

HE HAD a plan for dealing with the serenade worked out by the time he reached the Last Chance. The only reason he was okay with dropping by was that he knew Zoe was either at home or at the hospital. He had no desire for another painful encounter with Zoe right now.

Even walking into the Last Chance made his heart ache. The warm interior, with its tiled brick oven and colorful touches—a ceramic rooster, a mirror in the shape of a golden sun, even the purple chalk on the menu blackboard—it all radiated with the spirit of Zoe. The fragrance of baking pizza crust and oregano-spiked tomato sauce nearly brought tears to his eyes.

He steeled himself and leaned over the work counter, where the twins were bickering over how many olives was too many.

"Your five-thousand-dollar man, reporting for duty," he said.

They looked up with identical eager expressions. Alexis told her sister, "You talk to him, Monica, I'll finish the pizzas."

"Done. No more than ten olives, though."

"Monica!"

Ignoring her sister's annoyed protest, Monica skipped around the counter and took Padric's hand. She dragged him to a relatively empty corner of the glassed-in terrace and sat him down at a table. "First of all, you're worth a lot more than five-thousand dollars, but we were on a budget."

"I heard. Nate said you tried to keep the bids down. Kind of defeats the purpose of *raising money* for the fire department."

"I know." A fleeting expression of guilt crossed the girl's face. "We didn't really think about that."

Her resemblance to Zoe made it hard for him to look at her, and he glanced out at the foam-flecked bay.

"Never mind. I'll write the department a check. That's what I do these days. Write checks. So how are we going to work this? I need to get back to my tour, so I won't be here for the festival. I know that's when you want me to perform. I have a couple ideas. We can prerecord, or I can try to set up a live video—"

He broke off because Monica was shaking her head to all those suggestions.

"I'm sorry, but I can't break away from the tour to come back here. It's a very tightly packed schedule and—"

"No, that's not it. You've got it all wrong. We don't want you to sing at the festival. I mean, we do. Of course. But that's not why we bid on you."

He frowned at her, utterly confused. "So who do you want me to sing to?" A horrifying thought occurred to him. "Not Zoe. No. Bad idea."

"Not Zoe. Duh, you probably already sang to her."

A memory hit him—her eyes shining through the steam rising from the hot tub as he hummed along with "*Forest*."

"Before we tell you, you have to understand this is *for* you and Zoe, because you're obviously perfect for each other, and she's a lot nicer when you're around," Monica explained.

"I'm confused. Who do you want me to sing to?"

Try as he might, he couldn't imagine who else they would want him to sing to. A boy one of them liked? A teacher they were trying to bribe? A friend they wanted to impress?

The answer, when it came, couldn't have shocked him more.

"Mama. We want you to serenade Mama."

CHAPTER TWENTY-NINE

"We've decided to keep your mom here a few more days so we can monitor her more closely." Dr. Morrison wrote something on her clipboard and handed it to Zoe.

"A prescription?" She squinted at the piece of paper. The doctor had caught her fast asleep, head resting on her forearms, splayed across her mother's hospital bed. Hair stuck to her sweaty cheek.

"You look like you could use some rest. This might help. Don't worry, it's a simple sleep aid, over the counter. I'm not breaking any rules."

She handed it back to her. "I'm good. I probably look like crap, but really, I'm fine." What ailed her couldn't be fixed by a prescription, anyway. A deep sadness had settled into her heart, as if etching it with permanent ink. Padric was probably gone by now. But even if he was still in town, she'd never see him again.

"You should listen to the nice doctor."

Her head shot up at the sound of her oldest brother's voice.

"Theo!" She jumped to her feet and rushed to give him a hug. "You came early!"

"Well yeah. Mama had a stroke. Why wouldn't I come early?" He set her back on her feet and scanned her, head to toe. "Yeah, you need a break, girlie."

She gave him a weary smile. He was so tall and broad and grinning, energy vibrating from every dark curl and corded muscle. But she detected the sadness lurking in his eyes, too. Word had it that he hadn't wanted the divorce, but she didn't know all the details yet. "I'm fine. This is what the end of the season looks like."

He ruffled her hair in that way that she'd always secretly liked but loudly protested, then walked to Mama's bedside. "How is she doing?"

Bethany Morrison, who looked slightly stunned by the mountain of masculinity that was Theo, cleared her throat. "She's still very tired. She's been sleeping a lot and her vitals aren't quite where we like to see them. But overall, she's doing well."

Theo picked up her wrinkled hand and stroked it. "Oh, Mama. Looking good, beautiful."

Zoe smiled at the phrase he always used with her, the one that made her giggle like a kid and shoo him away. "Suck-up," she teased.

"Come on now, you don't want to get on my bad side. I'm here to rescue you."

"What are you talking about?" She pried a lock of hair off her cheek. She must really look like shit if everyone was talking prescriptions and rescue ops.

"Mama's going to be here a few more days, right?" Theo turned to the doctor for confirmation. She nodded. "So this is the time for you to take a break. After she goes home, she'll need you. But here, she's got this fine doctor and the rest of the hospital staff."

"But I have to get the house ready—"

"Do you see these muscles?" Theo flexed his biceps, bodybuilder style, dropping a kiss on each one. "You were probably going to hire a carpenter. I can take care of that."

"But the pizza shop—"

"We'll cut back the hours. I'll supervise the twins. We'll make it work. Come on, Zoe. You've been slamming all summer, like always. And now you're going to have your hands full with Mama. Take the offer."

Dr. Morrison finally found her voice and chimed in. "I recommend it. Caretaker burnout is real."

Caretaker burnout. Zoe skimmed her fingers through her hair to untangle it. That was what she was going to be from now on. A caretaker. A pizza maker. A surrogate parent. A wannabe artist. A lonelyheart.

Ugh, stop feeling sorry for yourself. She rolled her shoulders to get the kinks out. "I suppose I could do with a break, even if all I do is go home and sleep."

"No." Theo shook his head firmly. "You need to get out of town. If you're here, everyone will want something. The twins, the shop. Me. Think, Zoe. Isn't there somewhere outside of Lost Harbor where you want to go?"

She stared at him for a long moment. The email from the Far North Arts Foundation flashed through her mind. She still couldn't accept, but maybe she could do the next best thing.

"I gotta go," she said abruptly. "Thank you, Theo." On her way past him, she stood on tiptoe to drop a kiss on his stubbled jaw. "You're a good brother. I'll try to be back before Mama gets discharged."

"Wow, I thought I was going to work a lot harder to talk you into this," he teased her as she practically flew out the door.

"Sorry to disappoint. Give Mama a hug from me when she wakes up. And tell the twins what's going on!"

"Don't worry about a thing. I got this."

Back home, she carefully packed up a bin of her favorite

figurines, wrapping each one in several layers of bubble wrap. She threw a few outfits into a bag, grabbed her purse, and headed for the airport. She thought about notifying the twins, but didn't want anything to get in the way of her trajectory. Achieving escape velocity out of Lost Harbor could be a real challenge.

At the tiny Lost Harbor airport, she bought a ticket for the next flight out and spent the wait time booking the rest of the trip. Anchorage to Banff didn't come cheap, but she had lots of miles accrued on the credit card she used to order for the Last Chance.

The Last Chance. This was it. *Her* last chance to do something that wasn't pizza. Her last chance to take a brief, glorious flight outside of Lost Harbor. Her last chance at a taste of freedom before the realities of her life closed in around her.

PADRIC HAD to wait until the next day's visiting hours at the hospital to fulfill his debt to the twins. They picked him up in their car—a beat-up gold Toyota—in the morning. The hospital was built snug up against a hillside on the other side of town, which gave him plenty of time to try to talk the girls out of this insane idea.

"Explain to me again why this is a good idea. The last time your mother saw me, we had to call 911."

"Technically, there was no need to call 911 because all the paramedics were already there," Alexis corrected him.

"Literal, much?" he muttered.

"This time, she's already in the hospital with plenty of medical people around," Monica added.

He nearly screeched the car to a halt. "That is not exactly what I want to hear."

"I was joking. Geez. You're so sensitive."

Yeah, he was sensitive about this situation. Right now, he'd much rather be heading to the Lost Harbor airport and getting the hell out of town. He could always ask Lucas Holt to deal with his rental boat. Hell, he could buy it. What difference did it make? "Can you blame me?"

"Okay, here's the thing. Your music is amazing. It's like…that first sip of hot chocolate on a winter day. Or when the sun comes out after a week of rain and you feel like everything's going to be okay."

Wow. That might be the best review of his music he'd ever received. "Thank you. But your mother is a different generation."

"But she loves music, and yours is timeless. It's about the lyrics, the melody. All you need is your voice and a guitar." Which sat on the backseat next to Alexis, because they'd badgered him into stopping at the hotel for it.

"This is all very flattering, but come on. Your mother hates me. She hates my mother, and she's transferred that hatred onto me."

"She *thinks* she hates you. But really she misses Dad."

That observation struck him as very astute. Whether it was true or not, he couldn't say.

"This time, you won't be kissing Zoe. Zoe won't even be there. Theo is with Mama right now." Alexis rested her chin on Monica's seat back, but Monica pushed her away, muttering something about breathing in her ear.

Padric couldn't help asking, "Where's Zoe?"

"We're actually not sure. But Theo texted us that she left this morning. You don't have to worry about running into her. She probably went home to catch up on sleep."

That was a relief—and yet also a massive disappointment. He wanted to see Zoe again because he *always* wanted to see her. It was a primal thing, as if his eyeballs craved the sight of her. But he also didn't want to upset her.

"So your theory here is that if I sing to your mother, she might soften toward me?"

"Yes. In her mind, you're part of the demon family that wrecked her marriage. She doesn't *know* you."

"She used to know me. I used to hang out at your house all the time."

"Exactly. She's forgotten that. Once she hears your music, she'll see everything differently. She won't hate you anymore." Certainty rang in Monica's voice. Too bad he didn't feel the same. This whole thing felt terribly risky, and the only reason he was going along with it was the effort they'd put into their five-thousand-dollar bid.

"And what if it backfires?"

"Honestly, things are already as bad as they can be," Alexis said frankly.

"That's not true. Her condition could get worse. I can't be responsible for that."

Alexis and Monica both answered at once. "We'll talk to her first. It won't be a surprise. She'll have a choice. She can say 'no' if she really wants to. But she won't. Here's the secret about Mama."

Padric cocked his head to hear the big revelation as Monica lowered her voice.

"She *loves* being the center of attention."

Now *that* statement had the ring of truth.

There was no sign of Zoe's red Subaru in the hospital parking lot. Padric shoved aside his disappointment and hauled his guitar out of the backseat. The twins went first, dashing through the front doors on their way to prepare their mother for a private serenade from the son of the woman who had stolen her husband.

Except that she'd kept her husband.

Mom had surrendered to Dad's demand that they move away

immediately. They'd gone into counseling. They'd repaired their marriage—and presumably the Bellinis had done the same.

Although it was probably a louder process.

Nicola Bellini had held on to her husband and her grudge. Would she be able to let the grudge go, long after the husband was gone?

The charge nurse directed him to a room on the second floor of the A wing. Outside the room, he propped himself against the wall and softly tuned his guitar while the twins disappeared inside.

Theo stepped out and greeted him with a short hug. "Good to see you again, man. You got thoughts about this?"

"First thought, terrible idea. Second thought, the twins know their mother better than I do."

"True that. Same holds for me. Do you mind if I keep an eye on her while you play?"

"I want you to. Maybe a couple of doctors, too."

"Good thinking. Okay, stand by."

Fifteen minutes later, Monica poked her head out and beckoned for Padric to come in. "She's ready."

"You didn't browbeat her into this, did you?"

"I don't know that word," she said innocently.

"Funny, because there's probably a picture of you next to it in the dictionary. Any song in particular you want me to play?"

"Yes. 'Lost Chance.'"

"Are you *sure*?"

She nodded firmly, her dark ponytail bouncing behind her. "That song got me through my first crush. It's like an angel wrote it."

He was definitely no angel, and he'd been filled with both rage and sadness when he wrote it. "I hope you know what you're doing here."

"Me too."

On that not-so-encouraging note, he stepped into the hospital room. Mrs. Bellini lay under a pink woven blanket, her gray-streaked dark hair nicely combed, her eyes more clear than he'd expected. The flesh around her right eye sagged.

He imagined her insisting on getting her hair combed before anyone outside the family saw her.

Monica pushed him toward a stool set up next to the bed.

"Hello, Mrs. Bellini," he said softly. "I'm here to sing you a song."

She blinked once but didn't say anything. Maybe talking was still hard for her.

He didn't have anything to say, either—what topic could possibly be safe? The fact that he loved Zoe? That she had turned him away? That he would be heading to Sweden soon? That his mother had written an apology letter and never sent it?

No. Sometimes music was the only language possible.

He strummed a few chords on his guitar, the soft intro to his song about heartbreak. When he performed this song in concert, he used a backup band that created a lush soundscape, like a rainforest. Like Lost Souls Wilderness.

But before he'd gotten successful enough to afford backup musicians, he'd performed just like this. Alone on a stool with a guitar, his voice, and his bared heart.

His voice, a little rough from disuse and the remains of the nodes, wafted through the air. Very male and yet tender. That was the contrast that drew people. He closed his eyes and let the music pour out.

A fork in the trail, one step to the edge
Happened so quick, burned by a touch
Don't know where we went, don't know why.
Did I know we would break?

Did I know you would cry?

One chance, all we had. All we had is goodbye.

Nothing so cruel as a chance lost with you.

HIS VOICE BROKE at the end, because all he could think about was Zoe, and yet another chance lost with her.

He opened his eyes and saw that he wasn't the only one moved by the song. Tears made their way down the wrinkled valleys in Mrs. Bellini's face. Theo wiped the heel of his hand across his eyes. Monica had an arm slung around her sister, who held their mother's hand.

Even the medical personnel who had assembled for the performance gave a sniffle or two.

He looked only at Mrs. Bellini. He met her eyes, holding back none of his pain and regret. She saw it and understood. He saw it in her silent communication.

She lifted her hand to indicate his guitar.

"More?" he asked.

She nodded. "Mo."

"Okay. How about a new song I've been working on? Just since I came here. It's still rough, so no recording devices, please." He looked sternly around the room as Monica tucked away the phone she'd started to hold up.

Was that a smile lurking in the corner of Mrs. Bellini's mouth?

The song was nothing more than few lines that he had yet to flesh into lyrics. But the melody was perfectly clear. It had been running through his mind ever since that crazy trip to the Larkspur Trail. The lyrics had been inspired by Zoe's letters. He hadn't even jotted any of it down yet. It was all in his head.

He established the chords—a wistful mix of D major and C minor. Combining major and minor keys was another of his trademarks. Hopeful and mournful, just like life.

> I got yesterday in my pocket
> I got tomorrow in my dreams
> Standing here with you
> Today I got my queen.
> Yesterday lives in my bones
> And tomorrow comes like a hunter
> But today I get to say,
> I'm yours since yesterday.
> Yours since yesterday.

HIS LOVE for Zoe echoed in every line of the song, and he knew that Mrs. Bellini understood that. Every member of the Bellini family would, since they knew the history between him and Zoe. To the rest of the world, it was a catchy song. Here in this hospital room, it was a declaration.

As he wrapped up the final strum, Monica and Alexis burst into applause as well as a million questions. "When are you going to record it? Are we really the first ever in the world to hear it? Does that mean this is the world premiere?"

Theo shushed them, but Padric kept his gaze on Mrs. Bellini. Was she beckoning to him? He stepped off the stool and came closer to her bedside. She offered her hand in a trembling gesture. He enclosed it in his two hands. Inside his grasp, it shook like a butterfly.

Her eyelids drifted shut. Neither of them said anything.

A moment later, she was asleep.

He glanced around at the rest of the Bellini family. "Do you think she no longer hates me?"

"That's my interpretation," said Theo. "Nice song."

"Thanks."

This was huge. Monumental. If Mrs. Bellini no longer

hated him, and could actually tolerate being in the same room with him, what stood in the way of him and Zoe being together?

They all filed out of the room so they didn't bother Mrs. Bellini while she was sleeping. The twins launched into a flurry of thank yous, but Padric kept his attention on Theo.

"Where's Zoe?" he asked Theo. "Is she at home?"

"To be honest, I have no idea. I told her to take a few days' break before the real work started. She ran out of here with some kind of mission on her mind. But I don't know what."

"Do you know when she's coming back?"

"All she said was that she'd try to be back before Mama gets discharged."

"Girls, do you know?" he asked them.

"No, and we texted her a couple of times. No answer." Monica was staring at Theo with a fascinated expression. "You actually gave her time off? What about us?"

"You'll survive, if it's meant to be."

Monica and Alexis burst into giggles, shushed by Theo as he closed the door to their mother's room.

"So..." Padric tried to wrap his head around the situation. "Zoe left, no one knows where she is or when she's coming back, and I have to be in Sweden in two days."

"You can always come back," said Monica hopefully. "You know what's a good date? Labor Day. September fifth."

"I already told you, I can't make it to that festival. But you know what I'll do? I'll finalize that song I just sang and premiere it for real via video."

"Fine," said Alexis dejectedly. "I guess that's pretty good too."

Padric shook his head at the ungratefulness of teenagers. "I'd better get going. Can someone give me a ride back to the harbor?"

"Are you leaving already?" Theo asked.

"No, it's still too choppy today. Aiming for tomorrow."

Theo tossed his car keys in the air and grabbed them. "I'll run you out there. Girls, stay here in case Mama wakes up."

"Oh, so that's how it's going to be with Zoe gone? You just order us around?"

Theo just grinned, then muttered, "Yeah, like that's going to work," as he and Padric strode down the hallway.

CHAPTER THIRTY

Zoe barely had the wherewithal to appreciate the majestic setting of the Banff Institute of Contemporary Northern Art, home of the Far North Arts Fellowship. She was so nervous her teeth were practically chattering. It had taken her nearly twenty-four hours to reach Banff, find a hotel, get some sleep, then make her way to the institute. At some point, she realized that she'd left her phone at home. She knew exactly where it was, right on her worktable next to an unfinished figure of a selkie.

She gave her name to the receptionist outside the director's office. The director, Rose O'Rourke, had sent the acceptance email, so there really was no reason for Zoe to be so nervous.

And yet she was. This here, what she was about to do, she'd never done before in her life.

The receptionist beckoned her into the director's office. Clean and expansive, the decor an elegant mix of blond wood and touches of stainless steel, like an architect's studio, the space gave Zoe a sense of infinite horizons.

"Ms. Bellini." A woman wearing a sapphire velvet jumpsuit rose from behind the desk to shake her hand. She had a nose piercing and a tattoo of a rose next to her eye. "We don't usually get our acceptances in person."

"I'm not actually here for that. I can't accept the fellowship. I wish I could." She heard the yearning in her own voice. "But I'm hoping I can do something else."

Rose O'Rourke cocked her head, then gestured for her to sit down. "You've got me even more curious now."

Zoe awkwardly took a seat. She'd never felt like such a country bumpkin before. If only she'd noticed the clay stains on the black pants she'd brought, or the way the cuffs of her gray sweater were unraveling. At least she'd remembered her suede boots instead of traveling to Canada in her XTRATUFS.

She tucked her hands together in her lap, hoping the ultra-chic woman across from her wouldn't notice her cuffs, not to mention her stubby fingernails and burn scars.

Clearing her throat, she launched into her pitch. "I was truly honored when I got your email. I'm so grateful to the entire board."

"The vote was unanimous. We all loved your work. Can you explain why you can't accept the spot?"

"Family reasons. My mother just had a stroke, and I can't leave right now."

"I'm so sorry. That's very understandable. We might be open to postponing your participation. Perhaps next semester or next year?"

Zoe closed her eyes briefly, almost overcome by the kindness in the director's voice. "No. That sounds...wonderful, but realistically, I just don't know when I'll be able to take part. My life just isn't cut out for this sort of thing. When I applied, I...I guess I wasn't thinking clearly. It just sounded so tempting."

The director nodded a few times, somehow both sympathetic and cool. "It's a life-changing program for many. It's not easy to get accepted."

Dig the knife a little deeper. "I'm incredibly honored to be accepted. I wish things were different. I've always done my art in the spare moments that pop up in my life. I finally got to the point where I wanted to try putting it first—and then my mother had her stroke, so..." She broke off. "I know what they say, that you have to protect your creative time, that no one else is going to take you seriously if you don't take yourself seriously, and I agree with all of it. I just can't seem to make my life fit into that. I'm sorry."

Her frustration burst out of her, causing the director to pull back in surprise.

"You certainly don't have to apologize to me. I love your work and hope you keep at it, even in the nooks and crannies of your life."

"Oh God, you're just making this harder because you're so perfect." Zoe groaned at her own impossible gaucheness. "I feel like I'm just making excuses for myself. I'm not even married! I don't have kids taking up time, just my sisters and my mother. But somehow they take up *so much time*. But maybe it's not even that. Maybe it's me and my fear of rejection, and I know I'm not the only one who experiences that, not by a long shot, probably everyone does, so that's no excuse either and oh my God, why am I still talking?"

She clapped her hand over her mouth because that seemed like the only way to stem the flow of her words.

The director laughed kindly. "Look, I completely understand. Everyone here does. We're your tribe, whether you accept the fellowship or not. You're an artist, and it's painful to think about people not appreciating your work. But let me tell you, people do. I do. You have talent and originality, as well as a kind of...wilderness ingenuity. I hope you know that."

Zoe dropped her hand and allowed herself to take a deep

breath. She let it out, then breathed in again. In and out. *Breathe. Don't die.*

"Thank you," she finally said. "That means more to me than I can ever describe."

Rose O'Rourke smiled at her—probably wondering how much she could charge for this impromptu therapy session. "Is that what you came here to say?"

"No. I came here to make a request. Even though I can't accept the fellowship, would I be allowed to include a few pieces from my project in the gallery show? I've never had a show before, and the pieces are the same ones I submitted, so I guess you all liked them and—"

"Absolutely." The director didn't even hesitate. "We'd love to display your work."

"You...what?" Zoe had lined up so many arguments that the director's easy agreement threw her off.

"We can't include your work in the exhibit at the end of the fellowship, but we can add it to our current show on cutting-edge eco-Art. It would fit perfectly."

"Oh. Wow. Thank you so much."

The director shook it off, smiling. "No need for thanks. I think your work will be a great addition." She stood up and offered her hand again. "I hope you can find your way to a fellow-ship sometime in the future. My assistant will take things from here."

With the sense of sending her precious children off to school for the first time, Zoe handed over her tote bins of clay figurines to the assistant. Not all of them would make it into the exhibit, since there wasn't enough space. Zoe promised to come back and pick everything up when the show ended—unless a gallery or private buyer expressed interest.

Zoe found that idea nearly overwhelming. Not only were strangers going to see her work, but someone might want to pay for it? That would have seemed like fantasyland just a short time ago.

If only she could tell the one person who would really appreciate this incredible breakthrough. Her family would be proud, of course, and so would her friends. But only Padric knew how much her art meant to her, and how hard it was for her to push it into the world.

However, not only had she forgotten her phone, but it wouldn't be fair to muddy things between her and Padric. Maybe someday they could go back to being friends—like in their eighties, say.

At the B&B, she celebrated with a goofy solo dance around the room. Should she stay in Banff for a couple more days and enjoy her break? The thought held no appeal. She'd done what she came here to do. She missed Lost Harbor and it drove her crazy that she couldn't call to check on Mama. With the twins and Theo handling everything, who knew what crazy misadventures were going on?

Besides, if she left now, she'd be back in Lost Harbor by tomorrow morning and could possibly catch Padric before he took off.

Catch Padric? Yes. Hell yes.

He would want to know about this amazing thing that had just happened, even if it "muddied the waters." Padric cared about her on every level, as a person, as an artist, not just as a lover. To think otherwise would be to sell him short. She'd done that as a teenager, after his family had left, but she knew better now.

Padric would always be part of her and she would always be part of him, even if they never even kissed again.

She checked out of the B&B, packed up her rental car and headed to the airport. Lost Harbor awaited, a beloved shimmer on a distant horizon.

CHAPTER THIRTY-ONE

In his touring life, Padric was constantly saying goodbye, and he'd grown to loathe it. So instead of letting everyone gather to see him off, he took the time to say his goodbyes individually. He stopped by the volunteer fire department and shook hands with his training group. He'd brought signed photos for Willie's granddaughter and Carrie and whoever else wanted one.

"I'm leaving early tomorrow, so this is goodbye," he told them. "Keep crushing it, you guys."

Nate wasn't around, but Padric knew he'd be seeing his old friend somewhere, at some point. He left a check for the department that doubled the twins' bid.

"If you can find a way to give their money back, I'd appreciate it. This covers it and more."

"We can do that," Chief Boone assured him. "Appreciate your help. Great fundraiser, aside from poor Mrs. Bellini."

"Yeah. Thanks again for the chance to learn some skills."

"Come back any time. I know it's not likely, but I'm saying it anyway."

After more goodbyes around town—he dropped in at the

Olde Salt, and then caught Trixie Tran between rushes at Soul Satisfaction Ice Cream—Padric spent one more lonely night at the Eagle's Nest. Zoe still wasn't answering her phone and his time was running out. He had to get to Stockholm or there would be hell to pay.

He woke up early the next day and headed for the harbor. Wearing a watchman's cap and sunglasses, he hoped none of the early-bird tourists would recognize him.

But Lucas and Megan did. They were doing some maintenance work on the *Forget Me Not*. Whatever it was, it seemed to include frequent kissing.

Lucas hailed him as he passed. "Heading out?"

"Yeah, it's time. I was hoping I'd run into you guys before I left. How's it looking out there?"

"Seas are down to two feet, light northeast breeze about five knots. You should have an easy ride."

In his new position as head of the harbor commission, Lucas always seemed to know the conditions out on the water.

"Thanks. This is goodbye, then." He reached over the railing to shake Lucas' hand, but Megan jumped onto the float to give him a real hug.

"We're going to miss you around here." From the meaningful look in her eyes, he knew she was referring to Zoe.

"Keep an eye on her, would you? She's going to need a lot of help." Damn, he couldn't even say her name at the moment.

"Of course. We're already setting up a schedule to give her regular breaks. Harbor rats to the rescue."

"That's great, she'll need some time to herself now, and—" He broke off. Zoe wasn't his business anymore. Her life didn't involve him. She couldn't possibly have made that more clear. "It was good to meet you, Megan."

Finally he reached his absurdly high-end little cabin cruiser.

He slung his bag onboard and did a quick check of the fuel level and instruments.

Ruby, Megan's daughter, came running down the float just as he was turning on the engines to warm up.

"Bye, Padric!" she called, waving. Lucas' old dog Fidget trotted at her heels.

He waved back with a big smile. She was such a bright little spirit, but right now she was shooting him a stern glare.

"Don't you know you're supposed to wear a PFD?"

"Technically, only children have to actually *wear* them," he told her. "Adults can simply keep one within grabbing distance." He picked up an orange life jacket he'd left on the hatch door to dry out. "See? Grabbing distance."

She rolled her eyes. "Why do kids have to do it if adults don't? It's so unfair."

Catching Megan's pleading glance, he switched gears.

"You know what? You're right. Everyone should follow the same rules." He put on the life jacket, but didn't bother to zip it. He'd be ripping it off as soon as he was out of her sight. The damn things got in the way. "Happy?"

"I wish my mom didn't make me wear one."

"Moms are like that for a reason. Hey, want to cast off for me?"

Of course she did. All kids liked to unfasten the lines from the cleats and toss them onboard. It made them feel like grownups. Ironic, since he felt like a kid in his goofy orange PFD.

"Goodbye!" He waved to Ruby, Lucas and Megan as he maneuvered the boat out of the slip.

"Bye!" Ruby jumped up and down as she watched from the float.

So he'd gotten a sendoff after all, and it turned out that he didn't mind. The saddest part was the reminder of the moment when he'd arrived, and had seen Zoe watching him from this very float.

As he glided across the glassy water of the harbor, he soaked in the sights and sounds and smells one last time. Tar mingled with seaweed. The moist gaze of a sea otter surfacing to check him out. The chatter of fishermen loading groceries onto their trawler.

It wasn't all idyllic. He also noticed iridescent floating patches of diesel. Fumes from an idling engine. The cacophony of gulls fighting over a halibut carcass. This was a working harbor as well as a tourist destination.

As he reached the breakwater that marked the entrance of the harbor, his gaze was drawn to the Eagle's Nest. Its windows reflected the bright afternoon sun, forcing him to look away. Just as well. He didn't need the reminder of what he was losing. All of the steamy memories he and Zoe had created were burned into his mind forever.

He opened up the throttle to bring the boat on step so it hydroplaned across the surface of the waves. Lost Harbor quickly receded as he steered towards Far Point. No more looking back at Lost Harbor. He'd come here to make sure Zoe was okay, and he'd found something even more important. He'd gotten her back —the Zoe of yesterday, anyway. The Zoe of his past, the friendship that had meant so much to him.

Now she meant even more. He loved her. He loved her too much to cause trouble in her life. At least this time she *knew* he loved her and wouldn't spend years believing that she wasn't worthy, or that he'd rejected her.

The *Jaunty* tilted to one side as it skimmed over a wave. He heard sloshing somewhere in the inboard engine compartment. He throttled down to a calmer pace and stepped onto the deck to listen more closely to the engine—

And then he was flying through air as a sound like a thunder-clap slammed his ears.

Some implacable force was expelling him from the boat. Heat licked at his heels.

Fire? Explosion?

No time to think. The ocean was coming at him. He closed his eyes as his body smacked against the surface and plunged underwater.

An automatic gasp reflex filled his mouth with seawater. The cold felt like a full-body electric shock. It stopped his breath. Was his heart even beating anymore?

Get to the surface. Air. He needed air. He'd learned about this in training. If he could keep his head above water for a few minutes he'd be able to breathe normally.

He still had his life jacket on, but one arm was coming off and getting in the way of his arm movements. He used his legs to kick up toward the surface. Gasping for breath, he managed to pull the two parts of the life jacket together and zip it up.

At least he was floating now. He felt like a cork bobbing on a vast sea of ice water. He smelled the acrid stench of burning plastic and turned himself around to look at *the Jaunty*. The entire back half of it was blackened and torn apart from the explosion. A fire still burned above the engine compartment, but it wouldn't for long because it was rapidly sinking below the surface.

Should he try to hang on to any part of the boat? Could he use it to paddle toward shore? How far was he from the harbor? Why had a brand-new boat fucking exploded? Had someone witnessed it? Could he call for help? Where was his phone? Why wasn't his brain working properly?

Shock.

He remembered this in the volunteer training program. Boat

accidents were one of the things the fire department helped with because there wasn't always a Coast Guard boat handy.

Best way to survive an unexpected immersion. Information swam to the surface of his brain. Under the ice assault of the Alaskan water, his shivering would turn violent in about fifteen minutes. In thirty minutes his muscles would cramp. In an hour, he'd be unconscious, and in two hours he'd be dead from hypothermia.

But that wouldn't happen because someone must have seen the explosion. He wasn't in the middle of the ocean, he was about fifteen minutes outside of Lost Harbor. Too far to swim, but surely he could stay alive until a rescuer arrived.

To conserve energy, he kicked up his feet and lay on his back, letting the PFD do all the work. *Okay, personal flotation device, let's get personal. My life depends on you right now, so it doesn't get more personal than that.*

He tucked his hands under the armpits of the jacket. Extremities would go first as the body fought to protect vital organs. His feet were insulated by socks and boots, but his hands were completely exposed. If he got frostbite on his hands, he'd have trouble playing the guitar ever again.

Did that matter right now? He laughed at his own foolishness. He could die out here, floating on his back like a piece of driftwood, or an otter enjoying a mussel. And he was worried about his music career? Try worrying about the possibility that no one had noticed the explosion.

Keeping his movements minimal, he turned his head this way and that to look for any signs of a nearby fishing boat or a charter or a water taxi. Misty Bay was so remote that it was generally fairly empty. He'd seen other waterfronts with dozens if not hundreds of sailboats and a constant flow of pleasure boats and trawlers. Not here. That didn't bode well for his prospects.

To the sound of the hiss and crackle of the *Jaunty*'s last

moments, his mind drifted as he gazed at the sky. Such a pretty day, with cotton ball clouds flitting across a tender blue sky. A bird circled overhead, its long wingspan creating a shadow on the water.

A vulture, eager to pick his bones?

He laughed at that, since vultures were rare in Alaska. This must be a heron or a sandhill crane or even a very large eagle. He squinted at it, trying to make out its color.

Dark wings, white head. Bald Eagle. *His* Bald Eagle? The one he'd talked to behind the pizza shop?

"Hey you," he said softly to the bird. "Do you remember me? We didn't get off on the best foot the last time. In fact you pooped on me."

The eagle caught a wind current and rose higher into the air.

"Come back! Don't go yet. Stay and talk to me."

The eagle tilted its wings and cocked its head. But it didn't leave.

"Here I go, talking to birds again. Any chance you could spread the word that I need help? Hey, how about a song? I told you I was going to put you in a song. I thought of one the other day. About eagles returning to their nests. You'd like it."

He half-closed his eyes, trying to summon his song about the eagle.

It was gone.

Maybe it was too new. He hadn't worked out all the lyrics yet. He tried to think of another song, but again he came up blank. Were all his songs gone? Had the ocean frozen them all out of his brain?

Heart racing, he thought of sitting in the hospital room with Mrs. Bellini, strumming his guitar and singing his newest creation. Something about yesterday? What the fuck? Why couldn't he remember?

Truly panicked for the first time, he splashed himself into an upright position. *His songs were gone.* His mind was completely empty of all his music.

A deep grief twisted his insides, and he lay back again and uttered a sound somewhere between a sob and a croak. Where was his voice? Same place his songs had gone?

The eagle flapped its magnificent wings and he knew it wasn't a bird after all, it was an angel. An angel of death come to collect him.

He closed his eyes, regret dragging at him like a current reaching from the deep. All this time he'd been beating himself up about his music and the kids misinterpreting it. But now that it was all gone, images flashed across his vision like a movie in fast forward.

His first performance at a coffee shop. The girl who'd cried at the table in the front and thanked him afterwards. The boy who'd called the radio station during an interview and revealed that he'd listened to "Lost Chance" a hundred and eighty-three times to pull himself out of a depression. The feeling of expressing something true. Something from the heart. The feeling of adding his voice to the river of magic that was music.

God, he loved that.

As his vision grew dark around the edges and numbness crept over his body, a new feeling took hold. *Gratitude.* More memories came at him, a whole flock of them. Even if he was about to die, he couldn't complain. He'd spent his life singing and making music and he was thankful for every second.

And he'd gotten to see Zoe again, to tell her he loved her, to take away that shadow of doubt that clung to her.

"Thank you," he whispered as a roar of sound reached his ears. The angel must be getting close. Another second or two and it would all be gone. Zoe's face came to mind, that tender, curious expression as she came in close for their very first kiss.

Right there. That was what he'd hold on to as the angel of

death lifted him up to whatever came next. "Thank you," he repeated, still in a whisper.

"Dude, we haven't even rescued you yet." A familiar voice came from the direction of the angel-eagle. "Don't thank us until we get you onboard."

Padric opened his eyes to see a boat floating a few yards away. It was roaring like the angel had been. He looked upwards. Where was the Bald Eagle? It was gone. Maybe the rescue boat had scared it away.

What did that matter?

He shook his head to clear away the fog. Had he gone unconscious? He wasn't even sure what had just happened. "I'm freezing," he managed.

"We're coming to get you." The boat eased closer to him. He couldn't see who was at the wheel, but Nate and two other first responders leaned over the side with a float attached to a line. "We're going to toss this to you and all you have to do is grab it. We'll do the rest."

He untucked his hands from the life jacket and gave them a thumbs-up. A woman tossed the neon orange float toward him. Nice shot—it landed just a few inches from his face. He used the last of his energy to wrap his numb arms around it and hang on for dear life as they towed him toward the side. He spotted the red stripe that identified the boat as a Coast Guard vessel.

From there, Nate and another crew member reached down and grabbed onto his arms. They hauled him up the side of the boat, which must have taken a lot of strength, because not only was he dead weight, but all his clothes were soaking wet.

Nate helped him take off his life jacket and bundled him into the cabin of the boat. Since he could barely move his hands, he needed more help getting his clothes off. Nate wrapped a dry blanket around him.

"You sure know how to make an exit."

Padric laughed, or tried to. His throat was sore from swallowing so much saltwater. "Guess I wasn't ready to leave."

And even better—that wasn't a whisper, that was a full-on statement in an almost normal, if rough, voice.

"Hey, you stay as long as you want. No need to blow up a boat."

Padric frowned. "I didn't...brand-new boat."

Nate's gaze sharpened. "Someone sabotaged it?"

Padric nodded slowly as his sluggish brain pieced together what must have happened. "I think so. Maybe someone at the station. I went to say goodbye. They knew."

"You mean one of the volunteers?" Horror crossed his good friend's face. "No. Who would do that?"

Padric shrugged his shoulders, since he was in no shape to argue. The truth would come out. A more important question had flashed through his mind. If his voice was back, what about—

"*I got yesterday in my pocket...*" he sang. Then pumped his fists in the air. "Yes! They're back!"

Nate peered at him curiously, then called to the rest of the crew. "Make sure an ambulance meets us at the harbor. Possible concussion." He paused, then cocked his head. "Pretty good song, though."

CHAPTER THIRTY-TWO

Zoe went straight from the airport to the hospital. Outside her mother's room, a nurse filled her in. In the two days Zoe had been gone, Mama had made excellent progress. She could form words better, and her vitals had improved. She slept only eighteen hours a day instead of twenty, and had even been seen to smile.

Zoe received one of Mama's tremulous post-stroke smiles when she walked into the room, straight from the airport. She hugged her so tightly that her mother squawked in protest.

"It's so good to see you looking better, Mama. You really scared us."

"Zoe. *Carina.*"

Zoe teared up at the familiar endearment. "Do you want to hear about my trip to Canada?"

Her mother listened eagerly, not saying much but clearly soaking in every word. When her eyelids started to droop, Zoe said, "Listen, Mama, I came straight from the airport and really could use a cup of coffee. You rest for a little bit. I'll be right back."

In the cafeteria, she went right to the coffee machine. Yawning, she pressed the button for "black coffee" and watched the liquid fill her cup.

Snippets of conversation drifted her way.

"Some fishermen in the lagoon saw it…"

"A tourist called it in from a Jacuzzi at the Eagle's Nest…"

"An explosion in Misty Bay. That's got to be a first…"

"Lucky there was a Coast Guard cutter in port."

Even though Zoe's coffee cup was full, she lingered by the machine to hear more.

"They didn't know if they were going to find any survivors." A nurse was talking to a lab tech at a table nearby. "The boat was so damaged, they couldn't tell anything about it. Name, class, size, anything. When they got closer, they saw someone in the water. Non-responsive at first."

"Alive though?"

"That's what I hear. He's on his way here in an ambulance right now. I guess he's conscious but I wonder how much damage has been done. My cousin went overboard once and he had to get his toes amputated. But guess what else?"

The nurse lowered her voice so no one else could hear this apparently confidential information. Zoe knew she ought to walk away so she didn't overhear anything private. But her curiosity was piqued. An explosion in Misty Bay. That didn't happen every day.

"They're saying it's that rock star who grew up here. The one all the teenagers like."

Zoe's coffee cup slipped through her fingers and dropped to the floor.

Everything crystallized into hard, clear truth.

She needed to be with Padric the second he got here.

But she needed to do something else first.

She launched herself into a sprint across the cafeteria. Across the hall, down to the A wing, into her mother's room.

"Mama!"

Her mother turned her head in surprise. Her sisters had just arrived, but she barely paid attention to them.

"I have to say this, and you have to listen." Not that her mother had any choice, but Zoe skipped past that part. "I love Padric. I'm going to him right now, because he's on his way here because his boat blew up, and I have no idea how he is and," sobs threatened to choke her off, but she blew past them, "and nothing is going to stop me from being with him. It doesn't mean I won't still take care of you. I always will. I promise you that. But I love him with every particle of my heart and soul, and he loves me, and you're just going to have to get used to it!"

Her mother's dark eyes went wide as she listened. She didn't say or do anything at first. It felt as if the entire room was holding its breath.

Then the twins burst into chatter. "Is he okay? What happened?"

"Where is he? What room?"

"Don't worry, Zoe, Mama likes Padric now. He came here and sang to her and everything's all right now."

Zoe waved her hands around her head as if trying to bat away mosquitoes. "*Excuse* me?"

"Well, not *everything*, because what if he's in a coma or something?"

"*Monica!*"

"Oops, sorry, that was tactless. But the rest is true. Padric came here and sang so beautifully to Mama, and she held his hand. She likes him now."

Zoe looked at her mother in utter confusion. Why hadn't anyone told her about this? Maybe because her mother couldn't really talk much yet, and she hadn't seen the twins or Theo until this very moment? "Is that true, Mama?"

"True." She managed to form that word perfectly. She

pointed at herself. "Wrong." Then jabbed that same finger in Zoe's direction. "You. H-happy."

<hr>

ZOE RACED down the hallway to the emergency room. "The man they're bringing in, from the boat explosion. Padric Jeffers. Where will he be?"

"Are you family?" the charge nurse asked.

"No, but I'm the closest thing. I'm his best friend. His family doesn't live here anymore."

The nurse squinted at her. "Wait, you're from the pizza shop."

"Yes." She tried some puppy-dog eyes. "Free pizza on me? For a month?"

The nurse lowered her voice. "You're trying to bribe me with pizza?"

"I'm sorry, that was completely inappropriate. The thing is, he doesn't have anyone here, and I don't want him to be alone. Please?"

"Okay, I'll make an exception because of *that*. Not the pizza. Mushroom-pepperoni," she added in an even lower voice, before writing the room number on a piece of paper. "But if the surgeons or doctors need you to step out, you do it."

Surgeons?

Oh my God. How badly was he hurt? Visions of blown-up limbs and bloody wounds chased her down the hallway. She caught sight of Nate and some other paramedics pushing a gurney through the ER and ran after them.

"Nate! Nate!"

He looked up and beckoned to her.

"How is he?" Breathless, she raced to the gurney and looked

down at the exhausted face of the man she'd always loved, and always would.

"Ask him yourself," Nate answered.

Padric gave her a tired version of his magical smile. "Zoe. Look at you. Running."

A sob masquerading as a laugh burst out of her. "I guess I can run fast if it's important enough. Are you okay?"

"Better now. I can't hold your hand because I have to stay in this warming blanket. Hypothermia, frostbite, blah blah."

Tears stood in her eyes. "But you're in one piece?"

"Far as I know."

"Yes," Nate confirmed. "Pending full evaluation, all his parts seem to still be attached. Fucking amazing, considering the engine exploded."

They reached the exam room and on a count of three, heaved Padric onto a hospital bed. Zoe had to back away while the medical professionals checked his vitals and asked him some questions.

Nate pulled her aside. "Listen, I have to go look into something. Are you going to stick around?"

"You couldn't pry me away."

"Okay, I'll check in later and see how he's doing. Are you okay?"

"No." Her tears did the inevitable and ran down her face. "I almost let him go. I *did* let him go. And then I almost lost him."

"Bet you'll never let that happen again, huh?"

"Never." It sounded like a vow, which was exactly what it was.

"Then you didn't lose him, you found him."

As soon as everyone else had cleared out, she came to Padric's side. His exhaustion showed in his face, but his eyes were clear. "I love you, Zoe," he said in his ocean-roughened voice. "I—"

She held up a hand to stop him from straining his voice any more. "Let me. I have loved you forever. I tried to love other men, but I could never quite manage it. It was always you, even when I thought you were lost to me. Let's never let that happen again. Even if we just see each other between your tours, or if I come visit you on tour, or however we decide, we'll make it work. I love you. With all my heart and soul. I should never have sent you away. I should have—"

He shook his head fiercely, then extracted his hand from under the blanket. She took it in hers, shocked by how cold it still was.

"Don't. I understand. I spent some time with your mom and—"

"I know. The twins told me. I wish I'd been there to see that."

"You left. No one knew where you were. I wasn't sure I was going to see you again."

"I wasn't either," she admitted. "I went to Banff, thinking it was my last gasp of freedom. When I came back, I thought you were already gone. I was planning..." She squeezed his hand, thinking again of him on his boat, the explosion.

"What?"

"I was going to write you a letter." She shrugged at how lame that sounded. "A really, really good one, with some ideas about how we could still see each other. And then I heard about..."

"The boat?

She lifted his hand to her cheek. How cold it felt, and yet how wonderful. Instead of answering, she nodded. The thought of the explosion made her words dry up in her mouth.

"I was going to come back," he told her. "That wasn't going be the end of it. I sweet-talked your mother. You were next."

"You don't have to sweet-talk me. I'm yours. Yours forever."

His eyelids fell shut as a smile drifted across his face. "I love you so much. I hope I'm not dreaming all this. Good thing Ruby made me put on that jacket. You aren't an eagle, are you?"

"Excuse me?" Now he was just rambling, it seemed.

A soft snore was her only answer.

She tucked his hand back under the blanket. Then, since no nurse was around to tell her otherwise, she eased onto the bed next to him, careful not to disturb the warming blanket. It couldn't hurt to add more body heat.

This way, he wouldn't wake up alone and possibly confused. And she could revel in the pure joy of feeling his body against hers. The relief of hearing each raspy breath, which right now sounded better to her than any song could.

Padric was alive. They were together. They loved each other. Everything else would work itself out.

CHAPTER THIRTY-THREE

After a solid twenty hours of sleep, Padric felt a lot better. So much better that he used his newfound strength to get on the phone with his manager and thrash out an agreement. Zoe brought him his phone and curled up next to him as he talked.

"I'll be in Stockholm on schedule," he promised. "Can't let a little thing like an explosion get in the way. The show must go on."

"Thank you, Jesus," said the man. "This'll be huge. PR wet dream."

Padric cringed. "No publicity about the explosion. Promise me. Otherwise I'm retiring."

"Fine. Radio silence on your near-death experience. What else?"

"I want to cut back on touring. I want to build a studio in Lost Harbor and shift my focus to songwriting and producing. I want to offer studio time and help to younger artists."

"No more tours?"

"I'll still tour on occasion. But less. You can't have a life while touring. I want a damn life, since I almost lost mine."

Zoe spread her hand across his chest, as if checking to make sure his heart was still beating.

"One more thing. I need to be back in Alaska on September fifth."

"That's impossible. You have press scheduled for that—"

"Make it happen. I need to repay a debt."

After some more grumbling from his manager, he ended the call. Zoe lifted her head and gazed at him curiously. "What debt?"

"The twins. They used their hard-earned money to help us. They knew if I sang to your mother, she'd soften. I owe them. They're good sisters to you."

"I suppose they have their moments. I'm not complaining at all, I'll love having you back even just for one day."

"But after this tour, it's for good," he told her sternly, brushing a wild lock of hair away from her face. "And I want you to be able to go away, too. Art fellowships, for instance. And occasionally you might want to come on tour with me. This studio that I plan to build, I want it to be inside a house that we live in. Together. I know you're worried about your mom, but she's welcome to live with us, too. We can bring in caregivers to fill in as needed. We can afford it."

"We?" She wrinkled her forehead at him. "Speak for yourself, superstar."

"We," he said firmly. "What's mine is yours. I want to make it official. But not here. Somewhere less—"

Nate strolled in just then, along with Officer Maya Badger.

"Crowded," Padric finished. But he knew from Zoe's expression that she understood, and that her answer would be yes.

Good, because he wasn't messing around anymore. Clarity. That was what he'd gotten from nearly getting blown up. Clarity.

"We caught him," said Nate grimly. "We caught the fucking bastard."

Maya put her hand on his arm to check him. "Cool it, Nate. He wants answers, not all your cursing and ranting."

Nate flopped into the armchair and stretched out his legs. "You tell them, Maya. I don't have the heart."

Officer Badger gave Padric a steady look. "How are you doing, first of all?"

"A lot better. Thank you."

"You ready for this?"

He interlaced his fingers with Zoe's. With her in his life, he was ready for anything. "Shoot."

"It was Willie Marsh, who was doing the training with you."

Damn. He'd suspected someone from the program, but *him?*

"The retired longshoreman? The one whose granddaughter is a fan?" Padric sorted through all his encounters with Willie. At the fire station. At the auction. What did that guy have against him?

Maya was still talking.

"He tampered with the intake valve, so air was getting into the engine compartment. It took a while to build up, then went boom halfway across the bay. Says he didn't want it to happen in a crowded harbor."

"Boom? Ever heard of tactful phrasing?" Nate complained.

"Sorry. Padric's fine, so I didn't think—"

"It's okay," Padric reassured her. "Do you know *why* he did it?" He braced himself for the inevitable. "Was it because of the PJ brands?"

"Nothing to do with that. It was because of the Scandal, believe it or not."

Zoe and Padric exchanged a look. "How? Why?" Zoe demanded.

"He was in love with your mother back then. He worked for a while at the Last Chance."

"I remember." Zoe looked mystified. "They were friends, I thought."

"She confided in Willie, so he got a front row seat to all of her anger at Annie Jeffers. His own marriage had ended because of an affair, so it affected him deeply. After Zoe's dad died, Willie made his move but Nicola told him she was done with men forever."

"That's true," said Zoe. "She never considered a new relationship, as far as I know."

Maya continued. "Later, his son got hooked on heroin and had some rough years. So he watched his son go in and out of rehab while the Jeffers kid got famous. His words. It all festered into a stew of hatred and resentment. When you showed up again, Padric, he went a little bonkers."

Padric put his arm around Zoe, who was listening with wide, appalled eyes. "Did he send the baking soda, too?"

"It was all him. He's Layla Drummond's neighbor. He convinced Layla to bring Mrs. Bellini to the auction. He was hoping that would chase you away."

"It nearly did. So why'd he go to the trouble of blowing up my boat?"

"Final nail in the coffin—so to speak," she added quickly, after Zoe clutched at Padric in horror. "He claims he wanted to scare you so much you'd never come back."

"Then he'll be especially happy to know that I intend to move here and set up a studio."

"Right on." Officer Badger tucked her thumbs in her pockets. "Any questions about the investigation or what happens from here? We'll need you to testify at the trial. We're charging him with attempted murder."

"Is there any chance he's, you know, not all there?"

Nate piped up from the armchair. "That's what I keep asking myself. Why didn't I notice something was wrong with him?

Why did I let him into the training? He shouldn't have been able to come near you, the mother—"

"Okay, okay." Maya stopped him with one sharp gesture. "I can think of a lot of things to blame you for, Nate, but not this. As for his mental state, that's not up to me to determine. Padric, I suggest you focus on your recovery and your future and your," she gestured toward Zoe, "second chance. Leave Willie Marsh to us."

"Deal." Padric leaned forward to shake her hand. "Thanks for the quick resolution."

Maya shook his hand, then jerked her head toward Nate. "He actually had a lot to do with that."

"Finally I'm getting some credit." Grumbling, Nate rose to his feet. "Come on, let's leave these two in peace. I want to know about these other things you're blaming me for."

"You really want to go there?"

Bickering, the two of them left the room.

Zoe nestled her head back onto Padric's shoulder. "Interesting relationship they have."

"That's one word for it." He gave a huge yawn. "Getting sleepy again. Will you make sure I'm up by five? They're sending a charter plane to get me to Stockholm in time. There's supposed to be a new guitar onboard and hopefully some clothes."

"Of course. But wait, I almost forgot!" She jumped out of the bed and reached under it. "You know I have arrangements with a few fishermen and wilderness guides that they'll bring me odd items they find washed up on the beach. Look at what Boris Clancy found!"

With a gesture of triumph, she heaved an object onto his bed.

His guitar case. Waterlogged, with a scorch mark on one end, and a sprig of seaweed stuck in one buckle.

"Have you opened it? Do you think it's okay?" He touched it

reverently. This seemed like almost too much of a miracle. "Where did they find it?"

"Just bobbing away in Driscoll Cove."

"I know strange things happen around Lost Souls Wilderness, but this has to be one of the strangest."

He flipped open the two buckles and peered inside. His poor guitar was definitely going to need some drying-out time. "I think I'll stick with the one they're sending me from home. I'm really glad to have it back, though. This guitar has seen me through a lot. Good and bad."

He handed it back to Zoe, who stashed it against the wall. "How about I hang on to it while you're gone? I'll look online and find out how to fix it. I have stuff in my studio I can try. Desiccants for seaweed, that sort of thing."

"Sure. Just promise me you won't stick it in the pizza oven."

"Darn it, you guessed my first trick." Laughing, she bent down to give him a kiss. Their lips clung together for a long, achingly tender kiss. When they drew apart, they were both breathing fast.

"I'm pretty sure there's a steam room in this hospital," he told her. "Rehabilitation wing. I remember it from high school hockey. Should we sneak in before I have to leave?"

"Are you sure? You just went through a major trauma."

"Yeah, the part where I thought we were through. That was the trauma. Nearly getting blown up? That was just practice."

"Practice?" She frowned, looking a bit worried.

"Yeah. Practice for when I blow your mind in that steam room. And when I get back from Sweden. And when you're mine every single night."

Her face flushed in that way he loved. "I'll just go make sure the coast is clear."

"I'll be waiting."

And he always would be.

CHAPTER THIRTY-FOUR

"So are we all agreed that next year, this festival will happen in midsummer instead of early September?"

Zoe stamped her feet to keep warm. Not that it was cold, exactly—freeze-up was still at least a month away. But the wind off the bay had a cutting edge to it and the sun kept whisking behind the clouds.

None of that bothered the twins. They were about as ecstatic as two over-caffeinated and under-slept teenagers could be. A healthy portion of Lost Harbor had turned out for this event. More people had come from elsewhere on the peninsula, and even some late-season tourists had joined the fun. The bands all rocked, people were dancing on the beach, bonfires were burning under the supervision of the fire department, and the boardwalk businesses were all thrilled. Normally at this time of year, things were slowing down drastically. A special event to draw one last burst of business would mean an extra cushion going into winter.

"They did good," Padric agreed. He'd just flown in from Sweden that morning and was about to go onstage as the surprise headliner. His one condition in exchange for performing was that no one have advance notice, just in case he couldn't pull it off. But his manager had come through, and Zoe had picked him up at the airport and they'd spent the rest of the day in bed.

Until now, of course, when he was about to step onstage.

He bent over the wheelchair in which her mother was sitting. "Are you keeping warm, Mrs. Bellini?"

She snorted. "This? I used to s-start the coal f-f-fire in our house before the kids got up."

Zoe smiled proudly. In just a couple of weeks, Mama had made amazing progress. She still couldn't walk more than few steps, but to be honest, she liked talking more than walking anyway. Being wheeled around like a queen suited her just fine.

Nate left the bonfire he was monitoring and ambled over to them. He gave Padric a "welcome back" hug, then dropped a kiss on her mother's cheek. "Look at you, up and about, looking more gorgeous than ever."

"Oh silly." Even though Mama waved him off, Zoe knew exactly how flattered she was. Mama loved nothing more than a handsome man flirting with her.

Maybe that was why she'd finally accepted Padric. Having Padric sing to you was an intensely amazing experience. She could vouch for that.

"I found you a g-girlfriend," Mama told Nate.

"Oh no. No. You're very nice to think of me, but I like to take care of that sort of thing on my own."

"Not v-very well," Mama said firmly. "I m-made a date for you."

"You...what?" Nate glanced at Zoe and Padric for help, but they were too busy smirking to offer any.

"I insist. You d-don't want another ss-sss-stroke on your hands, do you?"

"Oh now...wow. When you put it that way, Mrs. Bellini."

Nate straightened up and shot Padric and Zoe a death glare. "I await the details."

Joseph Kenai took the stage and tapped the microphone.

"Oops, there's my cue." Padric kissed Zoe on the cheek and strode toward the makeshift stage, which was shielded by a white tent to protect the performers. Behind it paraded the panorama of Misty Bay and the jagged mountainous outline of Lost Souls Wilderness.

Zoe watched him go, unwilling to miss a single second of feasting her eyes on him, now that he was back. The last two weeks had been tough, even though they'd spoken every day and she'd watched every YouTube or news clip she could get her hands on.

Her twin sisters chose that moment to check on Mama, so Nate tugged her away from the wheelchair. "What do you know about this woman your mom's setting me up with?"

"Me? Nothing. I think you should just see what happens. Take a chance. You've been pining after Maya long enough. She's not interested."

"How—" He gave a double take. "Not fair. I've been over that for years. She's a friend. A real friend, not a 'we really want to bone' friend, like you and Padric."

"Have it your way. All I know is that she's a doctor at the hospital, she's new in town, and Mama adores her."

Nate straightened up abruptly. "Wait. Are you talking about Bethany Morrison?"

"You already know her?"

He tilted his head back and laughed long and loud. "I wouldn't say that I know her. But we've met."

"And? Isn't she great?"

She found the expression on his face impossible to read. "If you say so."

"So...will you go on a date with her? Even if it's just to make my mom happy?"

"Sure." His gray eyes gleamed with something she couldn't pin down. Mischief? Schemes? Gleeful anticipation? "Looking forward to it."

But Zoe didn't have time to figure it out, because Padric was taking the stage to absolutely thunderous applause. She joined in with the rest, clapping and whooping.

"First off, let's give a big hand to Monica and Alexis Bellini and Joseph Kenai, who pulled together an amazing show on a shoestring budget. Nice job, kids!"

The grinning Joseph, standing at the edge of the stage, took a bow. Monica and Alexis dropped into sweeping curtsies next to Mama's wheelchair.

An eagle landed on the corner post of the stage, and peered down at the scene. No one paid much attention except for Padric. Zoe was pretty sure she saw him wink up at the eagle.

Then he turned back to his human audience.

"Before I play my first song, let me just say it's really good to be back in Lost Harbor. I'm really, uh, *blown away* by the welcome."

Laughter swept through the crowd. Everyone here knew what had happened, but the national press was still in the dark. Hopefully it would stay that way. On top of being charged with attempted murder, Willie Marsh was on everyone's shit list.

"I was away for many years, but I never forgot about Lost Harbor. How could I, when the love of my life still lived here?" He looked across the crowd at Zoe. As their eyes met, a deep thrill went through her from head to toe. "I promised her that I'd propose somewhere that wasn't a hospital room. So what do you think, Zoe? Will this do?"

The smile he sent her was so intimate and sweet that she nearly melted right there on the beach.

"Yes!" she called over the hushed crowd.

"Yes, it will do, or yes to the proposal?"

"Both!" she said through the laughter of the crowd. "But that doesn't let you off the hook. You still have to ask."

He shook his head, as if chiding her. "I wouldn't skip that part. Kind of important."

She was amazed at his ability to capture the crowd and hold them in the palm of his hand.

"To help me with this very important proposal to Zoe Bellini, our own pizza queen and artist extraordinaire, I'd like to play a new song I've been working on. It's a world premiere. In fact, I've only played it once before, except for in the shower."

Zoe's mother preened and said loudly, "He played it for me."

Padric took a seat on the single stool at center stage and bent over his guitar. He began softly strumming as he sang,

> I got yesterday in my pocket
> I got tomorrow in my dreams
> Standing here with you
> Today I got my queen.
> Yesterday lives in my bones
> And tomorrow comes like a hunter
> But today I get to say,
> I'm yours since yesterday.
> Yours since yesterday.

The crowd absorbed the music as if it was ambrosia pouring from the heavens. The melody was so romantic and yet whimsical at the same time, and his resonant voice gave it a deep tenderness and longing.

She knew the feeling well. It had started with a friendship, been tested by fifteen years apart, and then bloomed into an all-encompassing love.

A sigh swept through the crowd. Judging by all the iPhones lifted to catch every second, this song would be going viral in no time.

How had Padric known that being proposed to in front of all of Lost Harbor would feel so good after all of her failures and rejections?

He'd just known, that was all. Because he knew her. And he loved her. Maybe even as much as she loved him. Her "terrible luck" was really just the fact that no one else could ever take Padric's place in her heart.

"So, Zoe Bellini, queen of my heart? Will you marry me?"

As if anyone could say no to that. She nodded through the giant lump in her throat.

He cupped his hand around his ear. "Sorry, I didn't catch that."

"She s—s—says yes," her mother called.

The crowd laughed again.

"Thank you, Mama, but I got this."

She cupped her hands around her mouth, then paused, holding her breath. Waiting.

Nothing happened.

Clear as a bell, she called out, "Yes! I will marry you!"

Padric grinned widely, blew her a kiss, and launched into his next song.

Later, snuggled in her loft bed, they relived the proposal, sharing the thoughts and emotions they'd experienced at each moment. Padric asked her why she'd paused before answering.

"I was waiting for disaster to strike, like with other big moments in our relationship. You know, a scandal, a plane crash, a boat explosion. A stroke. But nothing did."

"So do you think we're in the clear now?"

"I don't know. But I'm willing to chance it if you are."

"Then we'll jump off the cliff together. Not literally," he

added quickly when she glared at him. "No cliffs. No jumping. It was a metaphor…" He lost himself in helpless laughter as she pounced on him.

"Save it for the songwriting." She stopped tickling him and straddled his hips. "Are you ready to consummate this engagement?"

"Ready as a match next to a lighter. Ready as a fish chasing a hook. Ready as a—" He groaned as she settled onto him. "Never mind."

That was one good thing about losing fifteen years, she thought as they surrendered to the constant passion between them. It might have taken her a long time and a lot of disasters, but she'd learned her lesson.

From now on, she intended to appreciate every single second they were together. After all, how many last chances was a girl going to get?

THANK you so much for reading! SEDUCED BY SNOWFALL, the next Lost Harbor, Alaska novel, will be coming in January 2020. Want to be the first to hear about new books, sales, and exclusive giveaways? Join Jennifer's mailing list and receive a free story as a welcome gift.

ABOUT THE AUTHOR

Jennifer Bernard is a *USA Today* bestselling author of contemporary romance. Her books have been called "an irresistible reading experience" full of "quick wit and sizzling love scenes." A graduate of Harvard and former news promo producer, she left big city life in Los Angeles for true love in Alaska, where she now lives with her husband and stepdaughters. She still hasn't adjusted to the cold, so most often she can be found cuddling with her laptop and a cup of tea. No stranger to book success, she also writes erotic novellas under a naughty secret name that she's happy to share with the curious. You can learn more about Jennifer and her books at JenniferBernard.net. Make sure to sign up for her newsletter for new releases, fresh exclusive content, sales alerts and giveaways.

Connect with Jennifer online:
JenniferBernard.net
Jen@JenniferBernard.net

Lost Harbor, Alaska

Mine Until Moonrise ~ Book 1

The Rockwell Legacy

The Rebel ~ Book 1

The Rogue ~ Book 2

THE ROCKWELL LEGACY
THE
RENEGADE
USA TODAY BESTSELLING AUTHOR
JENNIFER BERNARD

The Rock ~ Book 5

Jupiter Point ~ The Hotshots

Set the Night on Fire ~ Book 1

Burn So Bright ~ Book 2

Into the Flames ~ Book 3

Setting Off Sparks ~ Book 4

Jupiter Point ~ The Knight Brothers

Hot Pursuit ~ Book 5

Coming In Hot ~ Book 6

Hot and Bothered ~ Book 7

Too Hot to Handle ~ Book 8

One Hot Night ~ Book 9

Seeing Stars ~ Series Prequel

The Bachelor Firemen of San Gabriel Series

**Love Between the Bases Series

Made in the USA
Middletown, DE
22 November 2019

79202955R00184